A WITCH'S LEGACY

A WITCH'S LEGACY

DRAKETHORN LEGAL™
BOOK ONE

ISABEL CAMPBELL
MICHAEL ANDERLE

This book is a work of fiction. All of the characters, organizations, and events portrayed in this novel are either products of the author's imagination or are used fictitiously. Sometimes both.

Copyright © 2024 LMBPN Publishing
Cover by Mihaela Voicu http://www.mihaelavoicu.com/
Cover copyright © LMBPN Publishing
A Michael Anderle Production

LMBPN Publishing supports the right to free expression and the value of copyright. The purpose of copyright is to encourage writers and artists to produce the creative works that enrich our culture.

The distribution of this book without permission is a theft of the author's intellectual property. If you would like permission to use material from the book (other than for review purposes), please contact support@lmbpn.com. Thank you for your support of the author's rights.

LMBPN® Publishing
2375 E. Tropicana Avenue, Suite 8-305
Las Vegas, Nevada 89119 USA

Version 1.00, April 2024
ebook ISBN: 979-8-88878-922-3
Print ISBN: 979-8-88878-923-0

THE A WITCH'S LEGACY TEAM

Thanks to the Beta Readers
John Ashmore, Rachel Beckford, Kelly O'Donnell, Mary Morris

Thanks to the JIT Readers
Dave Hicks
Christopher Gilliard
Dorothy Lloyd
Zacc Pelter
Veronica Stephan-Miller
Diane L. Smith
Jackey Hankard-Brodie
Daryl McDaniel
Jan Hunnicutt
Paul Westman

If I've missed anyone, please let me know!

Editor
The SkyFyre Editing Team

CHAPTER ONE

"The Seven Dragons were named for the seven elements that built the world: Fire, water, earth, air, space, consciousness, and spirit. From these beings came the tumult of the world. While some saved and preserved, others plagued and destroyed. The Cataclysmic event of the Seven Wars drove the Dragons away. Some are hiding. Some are far gone, never to return."
—*Unknown*, The Dragon Codex History, Vol. IV

Anastasia was tempted to knock out the other attorney's teeth every time she saw him, but never more than she was now. Her hands itched with restraint, and she couldn't have bitten her tongue harder if she tried to.

The only thing holding her back? The judge's keen stare flashed between her and the opposing lawyer as the pretrial motions unfolded. Anastasia barely had it in her to listen to what Leonard Dolos was saying and to jot it down on a notepad so she could come back at him later.

"We will take a brief lunch recess," the judge announced at the end of Leonard's current argument. Anastasia had barely jotted it down before the judge spoke up. "Come back in half an hour."

Thank God, Anastasia thought. A headache had been building behind her eyes for the past few hours, and the cup of black coffee she'd gulped down before the hearing began that morning had done barely anything to keep her awake and alert. She needed more coffee and sustenance if she was to defeat Lenny today. Leonard was his first name, but no one in New York City ever called him that. He was Lenny, or Shark Lenny among the law firm people.

Anastasia Drakethorn would have preferred to contend with the Devil himself over Leonard Dolos, who was renowned for his legal shrewdness and general assholery. She felt his burning, predatory interest pinned at the back of her head and turned, eyeing him with an equal amount of ire. He collected his papers, shuffling them neatly into a folder before moving from his seat.

A cunning smile split his lips apart. "Careful, Drake. This isn't a game for amateurs." Ever confident in his arsenal of legal tactics, Lenny smirked. In the legal world, Anastasia went by Stacy Drake.

Lenny was of average height with a slight paunch that suggested a comfortable lifestyle. His thinning hair was meticulously combed over, and he carried a constant punchable look of, "I'm better than everyone." His cold gray eyes appraised everyone as potential assets or liabilities. If he considered you an asset, he'd use you. If he considered you a liability, better stand out of the way before he barreled through. Stacy wasn't sure which was worse.

He preferred his suits flashy enough to hint at his wealth without drawing too much attention. It was a trick, really. He wanted everyone's attention but didn't want to look desperate for it. His ties were always silk, and he had a penchant for shiny, ostentatious cufflinks that served as his trademark.

Stacy knew these things well from all the times meeting him in the courthouse.

She liked to think she had a trademark appearance, too,

though hers was less showy than Lenny's. She usually kept her long, dark auburn hair in a sleek bun or ponytail while working, and she wore high-collared shirts to hide an irritating birthmark on the back of her neck. Her striking green eyes were her favorite asset. The staredown with those green eyes had become one of her favorite methods. Most opposing attorneys and witnesses couldn't deal with them.

She was athletic and tall. Taller than Lenny, which was a bonus. While he preferred silk ties and flashy cufflinks, she dressed in an array of dark colors with subtle touches of reds or metallic accessories. Not enough people considered the power in being well-dressed while in the courtroom.

"Cat got your tongue, Drake?" Lenny quipped, grinning like the Cheshire Cat.

Stacy stared him down with fire building in her belly. She felt like a dragon about to burst. If only spewing flames and smoke could bring Lenny down. She doubted it could. Her striking green eyes did little to affect him. That, or he didn't let her see.

She offered him a thin smile. "Injustice has no place to hide, Mr. Dolos, not even behind procedural smokescreens." The judge had left the room, and the two attorneys were free to snipe at one another with no consequence.

Lenny shook his head, grinning as if a child had stated something they knew nothing about. She was hardly a child. Twenty-six, though she probably seemed young since he was in his early forties. He turned on his heel and was out of the courtroom in seconds, leaving Anastasia behind to grind her teeth.

She turned to her client, a pale-faced woman who looked like she needed as much coffee and food as her lawyer. "Ready, Mrs. Denninson?" Stacy asked.

Lora Denninson, a weary but determined single mother, nodded and barely showed a smile. "Can we stay in here, Ms. Drake? I prefer the quiet to collect myself."

Stacy offered a genuine smile to her client. "Of course, and don't call me that. I'm Stacy to you and anyone else with a sense of decency." In other words, people who were not Lenny Dolos.

They sat at the table and unpacked their lunches. Whenever Stacy went against other lawyers, she could count on getting out on time. Not with Lenny. They'd be here for a few more hours if the past had taught her anything. She was glad to have packed two sandwiches today.

Ever the multi-tasker, Stacy set about examining her notes while she chugged a coffee and gobbled down her sandwiches. Lora sat opposite her, keeping quiet as she nibbled on her lunch.

The deposition sitting in front of Stacy was pivotal. The testimony revealed the inconsistencies in the property boundary descriptions used by the plaintiff, Lenny's client, suggesting a deliberate attempt to misrepresent the lines in order to encroach on Lora and her family. If Lora didn't get the house, she'd be stuck on the streets. It was a house! Why couldn't the greedy businessman who'd bought the surrounding lots let it go?

Stacy had heard one sentence of Lora's story—that she was a single mother of four children whose husband had died several years ago—and knew she had to take the case, no matter who she faced in the process.

She glanced across the table to find Lora's drawn face focused on her phone. Lines of worry appeared between her eyes. "Don't worry, Mrs. Denninson. I'm going to figure this out."

"It's not that." Lora shook her head. "Bills are streaming in. I'm overdue." She pressed a thin smile to her lips despite herself. "But we have to get through today first."

The drab and worn appearance of Lora's nicest clothes told Stacy enough about her financial situation. They had figured out a way for Lora to pay off the attorney fees over time, releasing the pressure to come up with the funds all at once. If Stacy couldn't help people like Lora, what the hell was she a lawyer for? She wasn't like Lenny, wanting the job for the pure satisfaction of seeing people's lives ruined, for money, or whatever the hell else he was doing.

Sometimes, Stacy understood the appeal of fame. But fame by being an asshole of a lawyer? That she did not understand.

I have Lora's future in my hands, Stacy thought. *I should get back to this damn deposition.*

Seconds after this crossed her mind, the doors to the room opened, and the judge shuffled in. The sight of him told Stacy that Lenny and his client were not far behind. *Was that break thirty minutes or thirty seconds?*

Lora returned to her seat beside her, and the pretrial continued.

While the judge, Stacy, Lora, and Lenny's client sat, Lenny decided it was better to stand. "I urge you, Your Honor, not to admit Attorney Drake's deposition evidence. It violates the hearsay rule and lacks the proper foundation for admissibility. I further contend that the witness, a surveyor, of all people, isn't qualified to interpret the historical property records."

Stacy maintained her cool, leaning forward with fingers intertwined. She kept her attention on the judge, ignoring Lenny despite his shark-like eyes in her peripheral. "Objection to Attorney Dolos' dismissal. The exception to the hearsay rule under Federal Rule of Evidence 803(6)—Records of Regularly Conducted Activity should be enough." She fixed her stare on Lenny. "As Attorney Dolos is quite aware, I am sure."

He had better be, anyway. He had gone to law school, too, and was part of one of New York City's best firms.

"Besides, the surveyor's credentials show exactly how qualified he is," Stacy continued. "His insight into the land records is essential to establishing true property boundaries."

Lenny finally sat, sighing. "My client and I file for a continuance, then. We need more time to analyze this new evidence Attorney Drake has thrown at us today. Where was this before?"

Stacy's reply was quicker than the judge's. "I oppose your

motion, Attorney Dolos, on the grounds of Rule 403, Unfair Prejudice."

"Prejudice?" he exclaimed.

"Yes. These continued delays, of which you have made many, are prejudicial to my client, who is at risk of losing her home."

Lenny looked like he was about to burst. Maybe he finally would. Stacy had seen his face turn red before and hoped he would throw up his hands and storm out in a rage, leaving her to clean up the mess. A mess it may be, but she'd take it if it meant good favor for her client.

It wasn't the first time they had faced one another. They were nothing short of workplace rivals. While in law school, Stacy had expected to come up against other tough lawyers and even to want to strangle one or two. She had never dreamed of a nightmare like Lenny or that she would have to face him time and time again.

He had gone up against many lawyers at her particular law firm, but no one had done as good of a job against him as her. As a result, she was often assigned to go against him.

If not for the needs of her clients, she would have quit a long time ago.

I can't do that, she reminded herself. *Without a shark like me in the water, he'll take up the whole fucking ocean.* The ocean being New York City, and the other wildlife being the poor, victimized people on the streets. People like Lora.

On the inside, Stacy boiled with fury. Outwardly, she remained calm, going so far as to give Lenny a light smile. "In addition to the deposition, we have recently uncovered the property's historical deed, which I am sure can clear up this whole mess today before we have to bother going to trial."

The judge always liked to hear that. This was the goal, anyway. If Stacy could avoid entering an actual courtroom with Lenny, she'd consider her life a good one. She slid the deed toward the judge and gave a copy to Lenny, saying, "You will see here the deed clearly delineates the property boundaries in favor of my client."

Silence fell over the room, the impact of her revelation palpable. Stacy refrained from wearing a winning smile. She hadn't gained victory yet. *Almost, but not quite there.*

The judge noted the deed with reserved intrigue. "This would help your client, that is true," he amended. "However, the legal implications of this deed are yet to be fully explored."

Stacy could have sworn a higher voltage of electricity thrummed through the room. She didn't bother looking at Lenny. She knew exactly how purple with fury his face was turning, and it wasn't much different than the expression his client wore.

"No other deed has been produced up to this time," she added. "Unless Attorney Dolos can present one, this is what we have to go by. You will also find my witness' testimony lines up with what is in the deed. My witness has never seen the deed, so he can't know that it confirms what he's said."

With each word, she felt like she was tightening the noose around Lenny's neck. *A little more now...*

Though Lenny was momentarily taken aback, he quickly regained his composure. He scrutinized his copy of the deed, then met the judge's eye with a calculated smile. "Your Honor, while intriguing, this document's authenticity is highly questionable. We request a forensic examination to verify its age and legitimacy."

"No need, Your Honor," Stacy inserted lightly. She had anticipated this move. "We have already conducted a preliminary forensic analysis consistent with the standards outlined in Federal Rule of Evidence 901(b)(3), confirming the deed's authenticity. I have the report right here." She presented the third document.

Each one felt like a new bomb dropped on Lenny's head. Sure, she could have presented all three to the judge at once, but it was far more satisfying to watch Lenny work his jaw back and forth as he contained his rage with each new hit. She had to have fun at work every now and then.

He had taken her down plenty of times before and would no doubt succeed in doing so in the future. This time, however, the win was for Stacy.

Undeterred, Lenny shifted his strategy. "Furthermore, Your Honor, we move to exclude the deed under Rule 403." Of course he was using Unfair Prejudice against her! "Its probative value is substantially outweighed by the risk of confusing issues and misleading the jury should this come to trial." Was he really using Unfair Prejudice to spare a jury that wasn't put together yet?

Stacy was quick to counter. "The deed directly addresses the primary issues at hand. The true property boundaries. Its exclusion would only serve to *deprive* the jury of critical factual information."

The judge nodded at Stacy. "I will admit the deed into evidence as you have moved to do so, Attorney Drake, but its weight will depend on further expert testimony. Don't forget it."

Lenny seized the opportunity as if the judge had slapped Stacy on the wrist instead of giving her a customary word of warning that could have gone to either of them. "I have a property law expert on hand to contest the deed's interpretation. This expert will argue that the subsequent zoning changes and property divisions have rendered the historical boundaries irrelevant." Lenny's smug smile after this statement said he thought he'd gained the upper hand. Well, she still had tricks up her sleeve.

Stacy was close to seething outwardly. The satisfied look on Lenny's face, paired with his quick comebacks and the convenience of having a property law expert on hand, suggested he knew about the deed and might have already seen it. So much for "throwing it at him." She had no idea how he'd seen it already. Stacy's hands clenched on the arms of her chair. Lora had her head down. The client across from Stacy seemed pleased with having chosen Lenny as his lawyer.

"Good thing my witness isn't the only expert on hand," Stacy stepped in coolly. She had hoped not to have to bring her in, but with every countermove Lenny made, she had to keep pulling out the big guns. "She is a seasoned historian specializing in property law who will effectively discredit whatever expert analysis Attorney Dolos seems to think he has ready.

"There is rigorous and continuous recognition of the original boundaries in subsequent property transactions, and all zoning laws have fallen in line with it. You will see this recorded in historical municipal documents."

The titans' clash couldn't have been more riveting. Stacy half wished they were at the real trial already so she could feel the intensity from viewers and jurors, not only the furious attorney sitting at the next table. The tension mounted from there. They went back and forth, maneuvering through complex property law and evidentiary rules stirring enough to rival the New York City shows that would play that night.

The longer they went on, the less sure Stacy remained that she would come out on top. Her headache returned, and the coffee…

Well, it had done nothing.

Lora Denninson's fate hung in the balance.

The judge perused the evidence laid before her, and so did Stacy. Finally, Stacy caught two things in the document provided by Lenny's so-called property law expert that gave her one last motivational push. "I see here a contradiction, Your Honor. In case you have not seen it for yourself, I'd like to point it out."

"Go on," the judge allowed.

Lenny leaned in his seat as if he were watching a favorite daytime TV show, not participating in a pretrial. "The expert testimony here has certain zoning law dates in one place but not the same ones elsewhere." Stacy pointed them out. "Furthermore, the zoning laws mentioned in the testimony of my own expert historian show they have always favored the original property lines. Thus, I think we can all conclude my client has full ownership of the property determined."

A long stretch of silence followed. Finally, the judge nodded. "You are correct, Ms. Drake. Your client, Mrs. Denninson, retains full, rightful ownership of the property. The only thing left is for your client to pay some fines today to resolve everything."

Stacy blanched. "Today?"

The judge nodded. "If the fines cannot be paid, the property is not hers, and this will continue to full trial. She could still win, but I'm certain none of you would like to drag this out any further."

None of them being Stacy and her client. Lenny, on the other hand, would drag this out for eternity if he was allowed. "She'll pay them today," Stacy promised. She gave Lora a reassuring look. They had agreed on a contingency contract previously where Lora would pay her expenses as the money came along. Lora would have to pay her fines today instead of paying Stacy. *It's okay. I can wait. Lora needs help.*

The payments were arranged in short order. When the judge was satisfied, they were dismissed. Stacy stood and felt the buzz of her phone in her back pocket. She ignored the text message. Right now, she had to relieve Lora of her concerns and get out of here. What a long day it had been!

The judge left the room, and Stacy faced Lenny and his client. She gathered her final papers, her triumph overshadowed by Lenny's piercing gaze and the inevitable tongue-lashing.

He breezed past her on his way to the door. "Impressive, Drake, but be careful. You never know what might happen when you step on powerful toes." Based on his expensive attire and perfect hair, Stacy had no doubt Lenny also got weekly pedicures. It wasn't only powerful toes she'd stepped on.

His veiled threat sent a shiver down her spine, but she

straightened, determined not to let his effect on her show. After Lenny and his client were gone, Stacy turned to Lora to find her in tears. "Oh, thank you, Stacy! You have no idea what this means to me."

Lora's tearful gratitude was a heartwarming testament to her hard-fought victory. *This is why I do this,* she thought. *So fewer people in this fucked-up world have to suffer as much in it.*

"You are more than welcome, Mrs. Denninson," Stacy assured her, squeezing her hand. "I'm only happy that everything worked out. Shall I walk you out to your car?"

Lora wiped her tears with a tissue. "Yes, please. I can't wait to get home and tell the kids. I think we'll have a special dinner tonight."

"You should. You deserve it." Stacy was inclined to do the same. Decadent chocolate and a bottle of wine were on her mind. They stepped from the courthouse not long after to find a balmy afternoon breeze brushing through their hair. The courthouse was in the heart of New York City, and the thrum of a busy place surrounded them. No shortage of lights, noise, or people.

Stacy walked Lora to her car, bidding her goodbye and wishing her a lovely evening. "You too!" Lora called, waving Stacy off.

Stacy was halfway to her car when she finally slipped her phone from her back pocket to see a reminder notification on her screen. This one told her a significant withdrawal from her reserve account to cover Lora's legal expenses had been completed.

Normally, Stacy wouldn't have minded. She was more than happy to cover her client's expenses for the time being if it meant a win for Lora and a defeat for Lenny. Lora would pay her back per their contract, but Stacy tried not to think of the time in between. In addition to everyday expenses, she was also paying off a hefty college debt.

She thought she'd had more than enough in her business

accounts, but apparently not. As a result, the money had come from her reserve account, one she hadn't touched in years. Her father had set it up for her before college. Her heart sank. She hadn't spoken to her father since then and hadn't planned on doing so for as long as she could.

I'll get a call from him about this, she thought as she stepped into her car. Oh, well. She could be lucky sometimes, but luck wasn't infinite. She'd beaten Lenny today, and the price would be unwanted attention from her father.

CHAPTER TWO

> *"In the dour ages*
> *Of drafty cells and draftier castles,*
> *Of dragons breathing without the frame of fables,*
> *Saint and king unfisted obstruction's knuckles*
> *By no miracle or majestic means,*
> *But by such abuses*
> *As smack of spite and the overscrupulous*
> *Twisting of thumbscrews"*
> —*Sylvia Plath*, A Lesson in Vengeance

Stacy arrived at her apartment as the sun began setting, dreaming about a bottle of wine she'd bought last night. *First, a shower*, she thought. Those long days in the courthouse did her in. She'd been sweating bullets by the end but managed to pull off the perfect picture of cool, calm, and collected.

She did her best to push all thoughts of Lenny, Lora, and her father from her mind as she showered, then slipped into something more comfortable than slacks and a blazer. She then stood before the mirror, rubbing moisturizer into her face, then bundling her wet hair into a towel. She turned and caught sight of the edges of the birthmark on her neck.

To anyone else, it might have looked like a tattoo. It was detailed and distinct enough to be one. It was small, half an inch in diameter, resembling a tree with thorns wrapped around it. It hid beneath her hairline at the back of her neck and was only a shade darker than her warm, olive-toned skin. Despite Stacy's questions, her father had insisted it was a birthmark, and she didn't remember a point in her life when it wasn't there.

It wasn't long before she sank onto her sofa and sipped on a glass of wine while waiting for takeout. Finally, she dared to check her phone. A text she was glad to see had come through while she was in the shower.

> JENNA
>
> Call me when you're home. I want to hear how today went.

The message was from Jenna Morley, Stacy's best friend in the city, who happened to work at the same law firm. While sitting in the dim light of her living room, Stacy dialed her friend's number.

"Evening, dear," came Jenna's cheerful voice. "Please tell me you wiped the floor with Lenny's ass today."

"Wiped him clean off his feet." Stacy managed an amused tone despite the weariness in her voice. "Yes, I won. *We* won. Mrs. Denninson and I."

"You know you did all the hard work, right?"

Lora Denninson was one of those rare clients who had kept careful track of everything since moving into her home and provided Stacy with a good starting point. She told Jenna this and added, "If not for her plight, I wouldn't have cared enough to carry through."

"I thought bringing Lenny a peg down was the point." Jenna

chortled. "The whole office will be glad to hear you did it. I might buy you a cake!"

Stacy's gaze fixed on a distant point, her amusement dwindling. "I'm afraid it might have cost me something, though."

"Oh, don't worry about it. Lenny's like a dog with his tail between his legs, but he'll have another case next week to keep him occupied," Jenna assured her.

"No, it's not that," Stacy replied. She sipped more wine before continuing. "I think my dad is going to call any minute now."

Jenna gasped. "Your old man? You haven't talked to him in, what, *ages*?"

"Not since starting college. He sent Christmas cards for a few years, but that was about it. I'm fairly certain it wasn't even him who sent them but the estate butler."

"Why the hell do you think he'll get in touch now?"

Stacy explained the fees involved in Lora winning the case and how they'd come out of her reserve account. If she had gotten the notification, her father did, too. He would want to know what was up. When she started college, he had set up the fund for her in case of emergencies. Seeing the amount that had gone out today would worry him. He would think she was in trouble.

Stacy didn't blame her father for wanting to reach out with that in mind, but she also didn't want to deal with what came after his concern cleared.

"Well, whatever happens, honey, you've got it. Your father can't be worse than the asshole you dealt with today."

Stacy produced a small smile. "You're not wrong there."

"Am I ever wrong?" Jenna teased lightly.

"Never."

"I'll come over this weekend, and we can relax. Or go out. Your choice."

"I'll let you know when the time comes," Stacy promised.

"Love you, Stace. I'll call tomorrow."

"Love you too. Thanks, Jen."

They hung up, and Stacy was left with her almost empty wine glass and an intricate web of complex feelings filling her chest.

The buzz on her phone a second later sent a jolt through her body. Finally, the message had come through. She dared a peek at her screen, apprehensive at what she might find.

Her father's name flashed across the lock screen.

> **KHAN**
>
> Hello, Stacy. This is your father. I hope you still have my number. I saw money go out of the reserve account today. Is everything all right? I would love to have you out to the estate if you can spare the time. I miss you. I have all these years. Please consider it. Love,

He had never signed anything he sent her with his name. Always "love," then nothing else. She wished it was love and nothing else. No disappointment in the path she had taken in life, no rudeness about how she was "wasting all her time." Had he changed? She couldn't be certain, and she sure as hell wasn't betting on it.

She stood, downing the rest of her wine. Whatever choice she made, she'd need a good night of sleep first.

Stacy's car had been with her since college. Though it had years and many miles on it, she had taken good care of it and didn't hesitate to drive it out to the Drakethorn estate north of New York City. The long drive meant she had plenty of time to consider whether this was the right thing to do.

Her phone buzzed with another reminder to pay a bill, drawing a sigh of frustration from her. *Don't think about that now,* she told herself, clenching the wheel tighter. She was glad, at least, not to be at work. After winning Mrs. Denninson's case, the firm was more than happy to give her time off. Stacy would have preferred the firm's business to the quiet drive where her thoughts were louder than the radio, but this felt necessary.

She couldn't exactly say why, though.

She turned the radio up louder. The laughter of the two men talking annoyed her, so she switched the station. The song on the next station annoyed her, too. The others had turned to static. Huffing, she turned it off. It didn't take long to determine where the real irritation lay. The uncertainty about how tonight would go scared her. She hated feeling like she wasn't in control.

"It's a visit, Stacy. You're not surrendering, only...regrouping," she muttered, adding a hint of determination to her voice as she steeled for the encounter ahead.

It was close to evening, and her stomach rumbled. At least she had the estate cook's food to look forward to. Stacy had no doubt the cook would still be there since the last thing in the world her father wanted was change, and he would have kept her on. *Unless she quit like I did.*

Of course, Stacy had never been employed at the big house, only expected to give her whole life to the Drakethorn legacy. Whatever the hell that meant.

The sprawling expanse of the Drakethorn estate unfolded as Stacy pulled her car up the circular gravel drive. No one came to take her keys from her. Odd, since her father had always had a valet on hand. Oh, well, she didn't mind.

The wooded landscape stretched in the distance, bringing the back of the grounds to its thick vegetation. Though she had not been here in years for good reason, Stacy had to admit she missed the quiet of the country and the fresh air she breathed in. The lack of city noise had been jarring at first, but she felt at home after she grew used to it again.

The mansion always had a way of making her feel strange things. For one, it had been her home throughout her childhood. She had taken the small path leading from the gardens into the woods and played in the creeks all summer long. Her nanny often found her sprawled in the garden, toes between the soil and ladybugs crawling up her arms. When she was a small child, she and her father played countless games of hide-and-seek in the long corridors and many rooms of the mansion.

The house had been around for a long time. Over a hundred years, at least. Its imposing grandness demanded reverent silence while standing outside it. Though it felt like home inside, cozy and warm, the exterior made Stacy stare in silence as if a compulsion had come over her.

How am I supposed to be the heir to this? she thought. The idea of one day inheriting this place made her feel like life in the city as a lawyer had been a lie all these years. Like she was playing dress up in someone else's closet until she could no longer deny her true calling.

"Let's get this over with," she grumbled as she shut the car door and headed up the wide steps of the porch to the grand double front doors. Stacy hesitated, half inclined to turn back and pretend her father had never reached out. *I've made it this far,* she reminded herself. *Might as well.* Though dread curled in her stomach, the regret over doing nothing that would accompany her on the way home would be worse.

Stacy raised her hand to knock, but the door opened before she could. She expected to see her father's butler, but it was Khan Drakethorn himself standing there. She started. *He never answers his door!* Then again, he might have changed his ways in the past several years. She certainly had.

Furthermore, his opening the door before she knocked told her he'd been watching for her.

She drank her father in, and he did the same to her. His thick, mane-like black hair was touched with strands of silver and pulled back into a low ponytail to denote a sense of order. His deep green eyes had flecks of gold like hers that flashed when they caught the light. While growing up, Stacy had noticed the gold more when he was cross with her.

The olive tone of his skin had weathered with age. The skin tone and the gold in the eyes came from him, but otherwise, she resembled her mother, whom she had never met.

Khan smiled. "Stacy, it's been too long. You look good." He pulled her into an embrace.

Stacy returned it stiffly but managed to plaster a smile on her face. "I didn't expect you to answer your own door." She pulled back.

Khan's smile remained. "I'm learning new things every day. Like how to survive without an army of staff."

Stacy blanched. "You didn't fire old Mr. Blackguard, did you?"

Khan shook his head. "Of course not. The cook, the butler, a driver, and a housemaid stayed on, but I've given them a month off to travel and see whatever distant family members they wish to. The others left because I simply didn't need so many people without you living here. I thought simplifying things would do me good."

He glanced around, seeming suddenly nervous, and why wouldn't he be? His estranged daughter had finally come for a visit. Stacy noticed he had not yet invited her in. "Look, uh, you caught me ill-prepared, but I'm glad you came all the same. The house isn't quite clean, but...well, come in." He opened the door wider and ushered her through.

The sight of the front hall was like a slap in the face. Stacy had forgotten many things since leaving home, like the cherry red wood paneling and the stairs leading to the second floor. Her father hadn't changed a single thing about the entrance. A rug that appeared centuries old lined the wooden floorboards, flanked by frames of old family photos and paintings. At the end of the hall was the grandest painting of all. Bordered by a heavy gold frame was an oil portrait of Khan's late wife. Stacy's mother.

Growing up, Stacy had always seen aspects of herself in her

mother's portrait. Now that she was an adult, it felt like looking into a mirror.

Her heart twisted with an ache. She had grown up with a myriad of women playing the mother role in her life, including nannies, housekeepers, the cook, and eventually, tutors and instructors. None of them had been able to replace the hole Stacy felt at the absence of her real mother, who her father said had died in childbirth.

She remembered these things as her father scurried around to dispose of local restaurant bags. Stacy felt a hint of amusement. It was strange to find her father looking after himself, and a small amount of pity arose. "Come in, come in," he urged. "We can sit in here." He led her into the living room, which, like the hallway, was unchanged.

Shelves full of books and artifacts her father had collected throughout the years lined two walls. The third wall was full of floor-to-ceiling windows over which Khan had drawn dark curtains. A fireplace occupied the fourth wall, with a sofa and two armchairs positioned before it. Memories of her father telling stories in this room engulfed Stacy. She clutched the edge of the couch as if needing balance against the memories.

Khan sprang toward the TV on the mantle above the fireplace, quick to switch from a soap opera Stacy recognized as *The Secrets of Saturnalia* to a financial news channel. Khan's fluster made Stacy realize he was embarrassed and didn't mean for her to see him watching a soap opera. Stacy smothered a smile.

"Please, sit," Khan insisted after clearing the sofa.

Stacy dropped onto it, scanning the room with her green eyes. Not only was the room unchanged in appearance, but it also hadn't been cleaned in some time. A trash bin in the corner was overflowing. Dust lined the shelves. A pile of blankets sat in one of the armchairs.

It was quite different from the order Khan had demanded growing up. Had he changed with age, or was this simply the result of having no staff on hand? Now that Stacy thought about it, she hadn't seen her father clean a single thing until today.

He sat opposite her and smiled again. "I'm glad you came, Stacy. I'm further glad you're doing all right. I was worried out of my mind when I saw the reserve account."

"I came to apologize about that," Stacy told him, setting aside her purse and sinking back into the sofa. She had not expected to feel so relaxed here, but when she was sitting where she had always curled with a book as a teenager, she couldn't help it. "I didn't mean to dip into the reserve fund, and I hope not to have to do it again."

She explained the situation to her father but only the barest details. Her father had disapproved when Stacy announced several years ago that she wanted to go to school to become a lawyer. He had nothing against lawyers, but he had expected Stacy to devote her life to the Drakethorn legacy.

While he saw it as the beginning of their estrangement, Stacy considered it the last straw. From her perspective, the estrangement had built up for years, especially as a teenager without a mother who had sought the truth about her mother's death.

After she finished, Khan was brought up to speed on Leonard Dolos and Stacy's empathy toward Mrs. Denninson's situation. "I'm pissed that facing Lenny resulted in that," Stacy confessed. "I didn't see any other way, though. You don't know him, Dad. They call lawyers sharks, but Lenny really is one."

The second the word "dad" was out of her mouth, Stacy wished she could take it back. He was her father, sure, but using the word spoke of more closeness than existed.

Khan either didn't notice or didn't want to make it a big deal. "Don't use the word 'pissed,' Stacy. 'Displeased' is a better word. I warned you that you might face people like Mr. Dolos when you went into law school."

There it was. His annoying imperiousness. Khan didn't mean it; he wasn't trying to seem superior. It had a way of leaping out of him whenever he had the chance. Stacy bit her tongue as he went on. "You were enraged, and rightfully so."

She relaxed.

"You wanted to bury the bastard." The sharpness in his eyes told her despite his disapproval of her job choice, he was proud of her. He might as well be. She was his only child.

Stacy nodded. "I sure did."

"It's your genetics, I'm afraid. I apologize for that. You got it from me." The barest hint of a smile graced his lips as he draped his long arms over the chair. He'd always been tall and angular, sharp and distinct from every other man Stacy had ever encountered. Sometimes, she had the feeling her father was much older than he looked. He was late-fifties in appearance, but he spoke as if he'd experienced centuries of life.

And that makes him think he's better than everyone, Stacy thought.

It reminded her of Lenny, but that was as far as the comparison went. Khan could be imperious and frustrating, but he was good at heart. He had common decency and an affinity for impactful, emotional stories. Growing up, it had been ancient poetry. Somehow, that had morphed into soap operas.

Khan spoke again, his voice joined by the crackling fire. "I know I've been less than ideal as a father, Stacy, but I would like to help you." Sincerity laced his words.

Stacy shook her head. "I came to apologize, not accept charity." Her voice was firm but tinged with surprise at his offer. She had expected a lecture followed by a limp acceptance of her apology. He *had* changed. His lingering stare said he saw the changes in her, too.

Stacy was the same short-tempered, spirited, intolerant of injustice young woman she had been when she was eighteen, but she had changed in many ways. She had made friends that allowed her a broader view of the world. She was more cultured and knew how to balance a life of work and fun.

Khan seemed to expect his daughter to say this and replied, "Think of it as a loan, then."

Stacy smiled. Of course he had a comeback. She had learned that skill from him. All those years of arguing with him over stupid things had paid off in its own way.

Conflict simmered inside her. She needed the money. Lora needed the money. Being a lawyer meant she made good money. Sometimes. Right about now, Stacy was struggling. Rent in the city was no fucking joke. On the other hand, taking the money meant tying herself to him in a way she wasn't prepared for.

She still had money in her normal accounts and had not drained the reserve account, so she could use it as a loan and pay him back when she could.

Think of Lora, Stacy thought. *Think of making rent on time and paying down your other debt.*

"Fine. A loan, then." She paused, summoning as much sincerity as her father had expressed. "Thank you. I mean that."

CHAPTER THREE

"The Gold Dragon once ruled the world. Through its might, wars were won and turned in favor of the greater good. The Gold Dragon had one weakness, and for that weakness, it met its doom. The demise of the Gold Dragon has since been a great sorrow of the world, so great that most do not know it ever existed."
—*Unknown*, The Dragon Codex History, Vol. IV

Stacy did not stay long after that, stating she had to get back to the city before it was too late. Khan suggested she stay the night and leave in the morning, but Stacy would not be ready for that step for a while yet. It had taken enough out of her to come home for a few hours.

Stacy reflected on the visit during her drive back, wrestling with the conflict she had not been able to push away with self-reassuring thoughts. Her parting with her father had been bittersweet. He had asked her to come again soon, and before she thought about it, she'd heard herself say she would try. Eighteen-year-old Stacy would have been shocked by this turn of events. *Eighteen-year-old me would also be proud I won the case yesterday despite the cost,* she thought.

A mixture of disbelief and reluctant admiration for her father battled for dominance inside her. Despite his sometimes overbearing attitude and thinking he was right all the fucking time, Stacy could not help but feel a sense of respect toward him. He had built his life from the ground up and maintained it through sheer will, determination, and intelligent insight. Many of the skills she carried into her field of work were a direct result of being raised by him and having his blood in her veins.

Stacy's phone rang, and she was delighted to see it was Jenna. She answered through the car's Bluetooth.

"Sooo," her friend drawled. "How did it go?"

Stacy laughed. "How did you know it was over?"

"It's dark, and I knew you'd want to be back in the city by midnight. Tell me, did you move so far away from him, hoping you would never have to make the drive?"

"That was part of it. The other part was being stuck in a bubble all my life and needing something else." New York had certainly done the trick. "You won't believe it, but it went okay. More than okay. He's trying to be…decent."

Jenna snorted. "For once." Jenna had never met Khan and only had Stacy's stories to go by. Stacy told her friend of the deal they had come to, and Jenna voiced concern. "He won't try to hold it over your head, will he?"

"I hope not," Stacy muttered. "He'd make me feel guilty for the rest of my life."

"Don't let him. You've got this."

"Thanks, Jen, but enough about me. What's going on with you?"

Jenna explained a big new case had hit the firm and sent the office into a frenzy that day. "I'll spare you the details, but you're warned now. Next time you come in, don't be surprised when they ask you to get involved."

If anything, Stacy was ready to return to the office and be distracted from recent events.

"Today was long, but I'm home now with my feet up," Jenna added. "Derek is coming over, so that will be nice." Jenna's on-and-off boyfriend made extended appearances every few months, then disappeared for "business reasons," breaking Jenna's heart. Something about him was irresistible to Jenna, though, so each time he was back in the city, her apartment became his home.

Stacy didn't have much room to judge. She didn't have poor taste in men. She had no taste. Since finishing college, she'd kept her life too busy with work to worry about dates and preferred to fill her weekends going out with her colleagues or relaxing at home.

Stacy chuckled. "Don't get too drunk with him and text me gross things."

"I would never!" Jenna feigned.

"I can think of a few times where you, a bottle of wine, your nerdy boyfriend, and a text thread to me were involved. Don't make me remind you of the descriptions you sent."

"Oh, hush. Be happy for me, doll."

"I am happy." Stacy meant it.

They said goodbye, but before Stacy could tap the call to end it, a message pinged. She gaped at the notice of a one-hundred-thousand-dollar deposit made into the reserve account. "That's one hell of a loan." What was her father thinking?

She pulled into the parking lot of her condo shortly before midnight, having gotten past her conflicted feelings and indulged in her favorite playlist. Still humming the last song that played, she stepped out of the car. She had hardly a second to register the movement among the shadows nearby before a figure concealed in the shrubbery beyond her parking space launched at her, a knife shining in his hand.

One hand grabbed her arm, pressing hard enough that it would leave bruises. He snarled something, but Stacy couldn't make it out. Not that it mattered. She kicked outward, hitting his stomach. The attacker reeled but regained his footing quickly.

He lurched, swinging, and pure instinct took over Stacy's body. She ducked, then launched for his middle, crashing to the pavement on top of him. She hadn't learned to go for the waist for nothing. She clambered to her feet. Before the attacker could get the upper hand again, she slammed her heel into his wrist, then plucked the knife from his hand. She landed a hard kick to his face, making him groan.

He wore dark clothing and a black mask that obscured his face. Other than his height of over six feet, she couldn't determine a thing about him.

"What the hell are you doing?"

The man scrambled to his feet and ran off in the opposite direction without a word.

Stacy stood there, panting and holding the knife. She examined it. Nothing about it was out of the ordinary. It was a simple kitchen knife. Who the hell was the man who had attacked her? Had he done it simply because she was a woman, or had he been waiting for her specifically?

Years ago, her father had insisted on teaching her self-defense. Though she'd thought the lessons arduous back then, she'd been grateful for them ever since moving to a big city by herself as a young woman. Now more than ever, she was glad to have gained the skills. She was out of shape and had not needed to defend herself like this in a long time. She was panting by the time it was over.

"What's this?" she asked aloud after noticing a scrap of clean paper on the ground. She picked it up, surmising that her attacker had dropped it. The words scrawled on the paper were rough and hard.

Better learn fast. Guess Lenny doesn't like losing.

Stacy scoffed. "What the hell?" Had Lenny hired the assailant? Feeling uneasy, she headed inside. *Better call the police before that fucker comes back,* she decided.

Stacy couldn't believe she was back at the Drakethorn estate a week later, much less with a homemade lasagna in hand. She could count the number of times she'd made a homemade meal in the last month on one hand, and this was one of them. Better to make sure her father had something decent to eat than let him fend for himself, she thought. For his sake, Stacy hoped the staff's month off was almost over.

She pulled in a deep breath before leaving her car. Her father had asked her to come again, saying he wanted to talk more about the loan. She didn't know why he couldn't tell her what he had to say over the phone. They had spoken on the phone once, with Khan asking her to come when she had a spare day.

Stacy had told him it would be difficult to find since she was busy with work and wanted to spend a weekend in the city with Jenna. Then Derek surprised Jenna with a getaway to a beach house in Massachusetts, and Stacy was left alone for the weekend. She figured it wouldn't hurt to drive out to her father's estate and see how he was faring.

At the door, she knocked and waited a solid minute before he opened it, looking frazzled but pleased to see her. Stacy extended the lasagna as if it was a peace offering, not that she should have been the one offering it.

"I brought some lasagna. I figured you might be tired of takeout by now. It needs to be warmed up, is all." She forced lightness in her tone, noting the domestic disarray of the hallway behind him. It was almost comical to see him attempting to manage living in such a large house without staff.

Khan took the container from her, a hint of a smile tugging his lips. "Thank you, Stacy. I appreciate it. I might have some brandy somewhere we can drink with it."

Stacy fished a bottle of wine from her purse, grinning. "I prefer this, but thanks."

Khan's eyes twinkled as he beckoned her inside. The kitchen, dining room, and living space had some semblance of order, but Stacy noticed it had been cleaned in a hurry. Either Khan had struggled with cleaning all day or had waited until minutes before her arrival. At least this time, he didn't have to worry about her seeing a soap opera. He had the TV turned off.

In the kitchen, Khan chuckled and fished two glasses from a cupboard. It took him a moment to find them. "You have no idea how tired I am of ordering food. I attempted cooking last night. Nothing fancy, but I almost burned down the kitchen."

He took the bottle of wine from her and poured some into both glasses before handing one of them over. Khan clinked his glass against Stacy's. "To my daughter, for pitying her poor old man."

Stacy smothered a smile as she sipped. She set the glass down to shrug off her jacket.

"I apologize," her father stated hurriedly. "I should have taken it from you when you arrived." He grabbed the jacket and sprang into the hallway, searching for a hook where he could hang it. The task took longer than normal. Their butler normally hung jackets and coats, and Khan wasn't entirely sure where they were. He found one not long after, letting out a victorious, "Aha!"

"Don't worry about it, Dad. I don't mind, really," Stacy called after him.

"No, no. You have come to the Drakethorn estate. You must expect the best service."

Stacy shook her head, smiling as her father reappeared in the kitchen. "You're not a butler, though. Thank God for that. You'd be awful."

Khan gave a hearty laugh. "I've figured that out, thanks." His expression sobered as he noticed bruises on Stacy's arm. "What happened here? Are you all right?"

Stacy didn't like the reminder of the attack a week ago. She had made a police report, and the cameras around her condo had been checked, but with the man's masked appearance, no one had been able to figure out who he was. Even the knife she had gotten away from him bore no fingerprints but her own.

She had kept the note to herself, intending to figure out what the hell Lenny was up to before sharing it with the police. With Lenny having the police commissioner in his back pocket, Stacy was less inclined to hand it over.

"I handled it. Nothing to worry about."

Khan's expression shifted from concern to something hard. He opened his mouth as if to object. Then, for whatever reason, he decided to let it drop.

What was that? Stacy wondered. *The great Khan Drakethorn respecting my wishes? Never!*

However, she could not ignore the flare of gold in his eyes. It always happened when he was annoyed. Khan cleared his throat, motioning to the living space. "Shall we?"

"Lead the way."

After they were seated, he added, "I wanted to let you know that I put more into the reserve account than I think you'll need, but do not hesitate to use as much of it as you want. I feel sorry for your client and her situation. If anything, I'd like to pay her attorney fees to you myself. You said you won't accept charity, but perhaps a single, widowed mother of four children will."

Stacy gaped. "Are you sure?"

Khan waved a dismissive hand. "It's a tax write-off anyway. A charitable donation and all."

There it was. Khan could always make a move of kindness that benefitted his legacy.

"Well, thank you, then," Stacy replied. "I'll inform Mrs. Denninson that it's taken care of."

"No need to tell her it was me."

Stacy hadn't planned on it, especially since she'd made an effort to make a name for herself while in the city instead of being tied to him. It was why she went by Stacy Drake in her personal and work life, leaving Anastasia Drakethorn to the past. "Thank you all the same," Stacy replied.

"Well, that was all I had to say."

Why couldn't he have told her this over the phone? She realized it had all been a ploy to get her to visit him again. Her stomach growled. "Let's warm up this lasagna," she suggested, standing. "The drive made me hungry."

Back at home, Stacy scrolled through social media and found photos of Jenna and Derek on the beach, drinking bottomless mimosas at brunch and going out dancing at night. Stacy wished she was on vacation now and vowed to make Jenna plan a trip with her when she returned.

She had left her father's house in enough time to make it back before midnight. She flew inside, hoping not to be pursued by another attacker. With no one else to see that weekend, she perched on her sofa and went through her socials before deciding to turn to another screen.

She propped her laptop on the arm and peeked at her bank account. The numbers were well-bolstered thanks to her father's loan, and she began calculating how she would pay it off.

The attorney fees, at least, were not part of the loan agreement. *If I hadn't been so bound and determined to bring Lenny down, we could have extended the matter to trial, and I wouldn't be dealing with this.*

She thought of Lora after that and remembered how glad she had been to finish it for Lora's sake and that of her children. *I wouldn't change a thing*, Stacy determined.

Sometimes, the fire inside Stacy concerned her. When it came to Lenny, all she saw was red. She had voiced her concern to Jenna once, but her friend had assured her it was nothing to worry about, simply Stacy's strong sense of justice and disdain for greedy bastards.

"I don't have anything against illegitimate children," Stacy had mumbled.

Half laughing and half hissing, Jenna had shot back, "You know what I mean."

"I can't believe I'm doing this," Stacy admitted aloud as she stared at the numbers. A mixture of relief and conflict filled her. The screen's glow illuminated her face, and she imagined anyone seeing her would have spotted resolve and underlying worry.

She wasn't someone who couldn't accept help, but something about taking her father's aid bothered her. She groaned. "I'll always have daddy issues when it comes to him. The problem now is how much is there?"

Her father had refrained from lecturing her about her life so far, with only a few snippy comments here and there. Stacy imagined a day would come when he'd break, and everything he thought about her now would pour out in a rage. She knew this because she was the same way. A lot of her avoidance had been a simple matter of not wanting to become like him.

"But if it's in my blood, what can I do about it?" she asked herself.

Stacy closed her laptop and set it aside. She had changed. Could Khan Drakethorn have done the same? If so, how long would it last? She felt exhausted and decided it was high time for a shower and bed. Before heading to her room, Stacy checked the front door to ensure it was locked. The last thing she needed tonight was an intruder.

CHAPTER FOUR

*"Claudius, though he sang of flagons
And huge tankards filled with Rhenish,
From that fiery blood of dragons
Never would his own replenish."*
—Henry Wadsworth Longfellow, Drinking Song

The buzz of the activity in the office was electric. Lawyers, their assistants, and secretaries flew about in a flurry of papers. Voices intermingled, some low and others high-pitched with exclamations of irritation or victory.

Someone in the far corner of the office growled about someone not cleaning the coffee grounds from the communal coffee maker. A squeaked "sorry" came from one of the office interns. Someone yelled about the bathroom needing more toilet paper and whether "that damn janitor" ever restocked shit.

Stacy blocked it all out by sequestering herself in her far corner office. It was small but organized, and she'd been lucky enough to secure one with a door so she could be away from everyone else's business. She often had her door open to be accessible to her colleagues, but she'd closed it today, needing to focus.

The legal documents for her next big case littered the desk. She pored over them, brow furrowed in deep concentration. Monday mornings were always busy, but much busier when a new case sat before her. Many lawyers in the firm had already taken a crack at the case, but it had proved too difficult for some, and the managing partner had suggested she take it.

Stacy wasn't more intelligent than the others in the firm, but she had less tolerance for injustice and more motivation to see a case through. Sometimes, she wished her boss didn't see that in her because it meant this kind of pressure.

Oh, well. At least it kept her distracted, and she liked to think she was well on her way to paying back her father's loan.

The ringing of her phone ousted her from her focused trance. "Stacy Drake speaking."

On the other end, a worried voice replied. "Attorney Drake? Yes, I wanted to speak to you about the case. Is there any more progress on the…what did you call it?"

"Subpoena, Mr. George. Yes, I'm making progress. We should hear back from the court by the end of the day. I'll email you the update."

"Oh, thank you. Thank you!"

Stacy smiled, making her voice sound as reassuring as possible. "I'll call or email if I need anything from you, Mr. George." The old man had retired years ago, leaving his small pizzeria to his son. Since then, a problem had arisen involving property status. Like always, someone was trying to take poor Mr. George's life-long venture away from him. Since the pizzeria was still under his name, the case was tied to him, not his much younger son, who was currently running the place.

After hanging up, Stacy checked her email. No updates on the subpoena had come through, but she was certain they would by the end of the day, as she had told her client. She focused again on the legal documents, a pen clutched between two fingers to take notes. She hoped to have this situation cleared up before it went to court, for her and Mr. George's sake.

A girl can dream, right? she thought with a small chuckle as she went to grab herself a cup of coffee.

Not many people frequented Bemelmans Bar on East 79th Street this early in the day, which was precisely the reason Lenny Dolos chose to have his meeting there. He checked his watch as he sat in a corner of the dimly lit upscale bar. It was nearly one in the afternoon, and the man he was meeting was supposed to be here at 12:30. He growled. What was keeping the damn man?

The bartender brought him a glass of scotch. Lenny barely nodded at the man before taking the glass in one heavily ringed hand and swishing it around, then knocking most of its contents back in one pull. For the past several minutes, he'd listened to someone prattle on the other end of the phone he held to his ear. Finally, Lenny had his chance to reply.

"She thinks she's won, but the game's just begun." A sly grin spread his lips. The cold edge to his voice was enough to tell the caller how he felt.

"Even so, Mr. Dolos, don't do anything rash," the person on the other end cautioned. "Slow and steady wins the race, eh?"

"We've been racing for fucking ever," Lenny growled.

The caller sighed and hung up.

Impatient, Lenny threw his phone on the table next to the hat he'd laid there upon arriving. He checked his watch again. Where was that damn man? Finally, the bar doors opened, and the man strode in. He wore a dark trench coat and a hat pulled low over his face so Lenny could only see the chiseled outline of his jaw.

The man spotted him in the corner and came over, sliding onto the other side of the booth and folding his large hands together. He said nothing. Lenny was tempted to berate the fellow for being late, but the man's largeness and mysterious, menacing quiet stopped him.

He muttered something under his breath, then fished an envelope from his briefcase. "Your payment for the last job." He extended it to the man, but before his companion could grab it, he snatched it back. "Do it right this time, or you won't see another payment."

The silent figure waited, hand open to receive the envelope. Finally, Lenny gave it to him. The figure weighed its contents, seeming satisfied with the weight of the bills inside. Lenny gave a jerk of his head. "All right, you can go now. You know what needs to be done next."

The man nodded, understanding the implied command. He arose and was gone.

Lenny watched him go with narrowed eyes, hoping his hire wasn't a waste of time or money. If that turned out to be the case, he'd be in hot water. He hissed, then downed the remainder of his drink.

After lunch, Stacy dove back into her work.

She was in the process of going through a pile of mail when a knock came at her office door. A young man's head poked in. "This is for you, Ms. Drake."

"Thank you, Conor." She received the envelope, assuming a document was inside. She hoped it had to do with Mr. George's case and that she'd soon have subpoena information in hand. The intern closed the door behind him, and Stacy sank into her desk chair, opening the envelope quickly to read its contents.

"What the fuck?"

The papers had nothing to do with Mr. George or any other case in the firm.

Stacy sprang to her feet. "Lenny is fucking suing me?"

The papers were served on behalf of Leonard Dolos by his representative. The cease and desist was ridiculous. Lenny had sent them to her, knowing she would deny them, and he could file a lawsuit from there.

Growling, she dropped back into her seat and buried her face in her hands. *This is the last fucking thing I need!*

It wasn't like she hadn't been expecting it, though. The rumor mill in the office had passed around stories of Lenny suing other lawyers before, even going as far as to claim lawsuits against whole firms. He had yet to win one, but it sure as hell was annoying that he tried anyway.

For Stacy, it would mean time taken away from her current cases and more money from her reserve account spent on something pointless. It was all a tactic to intimidate and exhaust her. She was more convinced than ever that he'd paid the attacker at her condo. "I might as well show the police the note I found," she decided. "Though they'll ask why I haven't shown it before." She didn't give a damn if Lenny and the police commissioner smoked cigars together. She needed help.

"Clearly," she muttered as she wadded up the papers and tossed them to the floor. "He's playing dirty, but he'll find out soon enough that I don't fucking back down." Her eyes flashed, the flecks of gold in the green, normally subtle enough for no one to notice, taking over.

The lawsuit stated that Stacy had caused issues with Victor Corbinelli's business, one with which Lenny was associated since he was the businessman's main lawyer. One of Victor's clients had tried to obtain the land Lora Denninson and her children lived on. Losing it had affected not only Lenny and his client but Victor himself.

Fuming, Stacy turned on her computer and opened a fresh draft in her email. Her fingers flew over the keyboard as she formed a response. It was one she'd have to draft now and sleep on later. Hitting send wasn't an option yet.

People in the city called Victor Corbinelli "The Titan." A hulking man nearing fifty, his presence filled every room he entered. Stacy remembered the first time she'd seen him. A year ago, she had attended a gala with Jenna, whose client had invited her. Stacy remembered everything about the moment she'd first seen Victor. Of course, she'd seen his face plastered on billboards throughout the city and heard his name whispered in her office, but seeing him in person had struck her differently.

His sharp, piercing blue eyes had swept over the room, taking in every man and woman in attendance. Stacy had somehow managed to stare back while holding a champagne flute to her lips. She'd wondered if he knew she wasn't wealthy enough to be attending this gala with an entry ticket, though she should have been with the last name Drakethorn. Good thing she was going by Stacy Drake then. The last thing she wanted was for someone like Victor to know she was "one of them."

I'll never be one of them, Stacy thought.

Despite his large size, Victor moved through rooms with an unsettling grace. He was like a predator among sheep, not even bothering to dress himself like the common person. He was charismatic, capable of being charming when it suited his purposes.

Beneath his façade lay a cold, calculating individual who rarely expressed emotion. It made his sudden outbursts of rage more terrifying. Stacy had heard stories around the office about those outbursts. One lawyer had gone to his office to hand something over to Lenny and fled when Victor threw a vase full of water and flowers at a secretary.

Stacy finished her draft and saved it before turning to a search engine. She knew a lot about Victor, but it wouldn't hurt to bolster her knowledge with more research. A quick search and several articles later, she'd learned Victor hailed from a family with a storied past in the city's development. The Corbinellis had been a cornerstone of the Upper West Side community for generations. Stacy doubted all their progress had been aboveboard.

Through her research, Stacy discovered Victor was not the first Victor Corbinelli. He was Victor III, with his father and grandfather preceding him in terms of both the name and ownership of Corbinelli Enterprises and several other smaller businesses. The Victors before the one Stacy knew had done well for the business, but things didn't flourish until Victor III came along. He had expanded his family's wealth to a considerable scale and diversified it into legitimate enterprises.

What goes on in the dark? Stacy wondered. Men like Victor didn't reach the top of the mountain without exploiting others, knocking them off cliffsides, or having shadowy dealings before and after office hours. How many Lora Denninsons and Mr. Georges were victims of men like Victor?

Perhaps the most interesting thing about him was his relationship with the law. Victor had been under investigation multiple times but never convicted. Lenny Dolos, his number one lawyer, had been instrumental in keeping him out of prison. "And now, filing a fucking lawsuit against me!" she groaned.

She turned off her computer and rose, knowing she'd need to pick up a bottle of wine on the way home. She exited her office, and a different idea came to her. Things were getting too heated to simply go home and ignore it. That's what Lenny hoped she'd do.

"It's high time I take matters into my own hands," she muttered. A plan began to form in her mind.

Stacy wore all-black clothing.

She pulled up a block from a building known to be a front for

Victor's operations. What operations, exactly, she did not know. She'd come here to find out anything she could. If exposing him got her out of a lawsuit and helped others, she was all for it, even if it meant being out this late instead of enjoying the comforts of her bed.

She walked down the street. When the warehouse came into sight, she crouched behind a dumpster several yards away to watch. Her phone buzzed in her back pocket. A message from Jenna blinked across the screen. She'd lowered the light on her phone before leaving the car, so when the message flashed, it was barely a glow. Stacy squinted to see it.

> JENNA
>
> Checking in. Everyone said you left the office in a huff today. Everything good? I was hoping you'd join us for happy hour, but you dipped.

Not wanting to worry her friend, Stacy replied.

> All good. Just doing some personal research.

It was enough of the truth without having to concern Jenna.

She returned her steady gaze to the building, scanning the windows up to the fourth story and the flat roof before sweeping back down to the front doors. As soon as her gaze hit the doors again, a figure emerged from the building. He was a tall man with nothing extraordinary about his appearance. He wore clothes suitable for working in remodeling or construction, and weariness marked his face.

Stacy stayed behind the dumpster, hoping his gaze wouldn't roam to her. Her heart raced as she spied the figure meeting another. The second man appeared from a sleek-looking sedan parked at the side of the building. Stacy had not seen it at first because it was parked in the shadows. The man who appeared wore a long trench coat and a hat pulled low over his face. He was much taller than the workman who'd exited the building.

The pair began a conversation, hushed but growing heated. The figure in the coat didn't seem to say much, but the workman gesticulated. His voice rose, indicating he was upset about something. Whatever it was, she couldn't hear them. They were too far away. How could she get closer without being seen? *An invisibility spell would be nice right about now,* she thought. Her dark clothes and quiet feet were not enough.

The two men spoke at length, then the workman stomped off, huffing. The figure in the coat and hat remained where he was, scanning the building as Stacy had done. He turned to view the parking lot, and his gaze went to the dumpster.

"Shit!" Stacy hissed, ducking away. She heard no sounds of him walking over. Eventually, she heard a car start and screech away. When she dared peek out from her hiding place, the car and the man were gone.

She stood. "Time to leave." She had gained little by not being able to hear them, but she'd made careful note of their appearances. It would have to be enough for now.

She spent the drive back to her condo going over the encounter. Her mind was abuzz with questions. What had the men been meeting about? How were they connected to Victor and Lenny? She was certain there was more to Victor's and Lenny's plans than met the eye. "I need to dig deeper," she resolved. She wasn't sure how she would do that yet. "I'll think of something."

Stacy was hardly inside her apartment before her phone rang. Who the fuck was calling her this late at night? She closed the door, and her eyes widened as she saw her father's name on her screen. "Hello?" she answered, hoping nothing serious was the matter.

"I'm calling to see how you are," Khan stated. "Have those bruises of yours healed?"

"Dad, it's past midnight. Why are you still up?"

"I could ask you the same thing."

He had a point. She sighed. "I'm stressed about a new case, is all. Nothing to worry about."

"I'm an old man who lives alone in the country. Please, let me worry. The least it'll do is occupy my mind."

Stacy paused, a hint of a smile on her lips. "The bruises are fine. They healed quickly. I've always healed fast, now that I think about it. Did I get that from you or Mom?" Saying the M-word was always a risk when it came to her father. Stacy had only dared a handful of times growing up, and it usually ended in an argument where Stacy declared she deserved to know, and Khan kept saying, "When you're older."

Well, she was older now.

Khan hesitated, then admitted, "Certainly from my side, but I'm thinking your mother might have had something to do with it as well."

Stacy plopped onto her sofa, still holding her phone to her ear. She liked the idea of having something from her mom. Khan seldom spoke of her on his own accord. It was a painful point for him.

"Tell me about this case," Khan invited.

"Trust me, you don't want to hear about it."

"Try me."

Stacy was tempted to tell him about Mr. George and leave it at that, but she knew there was no deceiving her father. He'd see right through her. She told him about the papers she'd received from Lenny's office that day but chose to leave out her nighttime sleuthing venture. She hadn't been in any real danger and saw no reason to worry her father further.

Khan's voice came back to her, tinged with concern. "You know I can help you with this lawsuit if you let me. I can make it go away in a day or two."

Stacy did know that. The Drakethorn estate and businesses were the only things that could stand up to Victor. However, she understood why her father had stayed out of it all these years. She admired him for staying away from the dark goings-on in the city. She hated the thought of putting the Drakethorns on Victor's radar by solving her lawsuit.

She hesitated, then told him, "Thanks, Dad, but this is something I need to handle on my own."

A pause followed, broken by Khan's last words for the night. "You're more like me than you will ever know, Stacy. The offer still stands if you change your mind."

They said goodbye, and Stacy rose to gaze out over the city from her wide windows. She was a lone figure against a sprawling cityscape. A rumble of thunder in the distance preceded rainfall. Lightning forked across the dark clouds. The rain would help her sleep, at least. "Time for bed," Stacy muttered.

CHAPTER FIVE

"Since the Gold Dragon's demise, only one other has arisen in comparable power. The Red Dragon could save us, but no one knows where it went. No one knows where it hides. Some fear it has gone away forever, slipped past the veil with no intention to bring humanity to peace."
—*Unknown*, The Dragon Codex History, Vol. IV

Police Chief John Turnbower knew Victor Corbinelli was in the building before the secretary announced over the intercom, "Mr. Corbinelli is on his way in, sir." Her voice contained a mix of respect and apprehension that the chief felt as well.

He was on the phone but stated, "I've got to go, Smith. I'll call you later for an update." He swiveled to a mirror on one wall, smoothed his black-dyed hair to one side, straightened his shirt, and fixed the badge on the right side of his chest.

The police department building was always busy as a beehive. Still, the normal chatter and office noise turned to whispered speculation and hushed tones of apprehension the moment someone spied Victor Corbinelli entering from the ground floor, flanked by two bodyguards who were more intimidating than all the police inside the department combined.

The whispers had mostly to do with Victor's mysterious presence overall. The whole city knew about him, had seen his face on billboards and signs in Times Square. He held galas almost every weekend, and various bars, restaurants, and museums boasted of his visits and donations.

The police department heard about him for other reasons, too. The shady dealings reached them often but with insufficient evidence to arrest the Titan. Although Victor seemed to be everywhere, something untouchable about him made those who turned their eyes upon him feel as though they were in the presence of a god.

Eyes followed him to the secretary's desk outside the chief's office. The secretary's throat bobbed. "The chief is in his office, sir. He's nearly done with a meet—"

Victor ignored her, nodding to his bodyguard to open the office door. The Titan disappeared, and the voices that had fallen silent in his wake began again, hushed questions about what Mr. Corbinelli wanted and why he was here.

Victor Corbinelli had visited the police chief's office before, but it had been several months since the last incident. Those in the department called it "the incident" because, for days afterward, John Turnbower had been a nervous wreck. Anyone who spoke to him found they barely had his attention or focus. He refused coffee in the mornings and went home early three days in a row. The whole department had fallen into a state of disorder as a result.

Everyone watching hoped they would not have a repeat of that. One of the department heads scooted his way over to the secretary and dropped his voice to a nearly inaudible whisper. "Susan, what did he say to you?"

"Not a word," Susan replied, typing away on her computer. She eyed the middle-aged man leaning on her desk. "Does Mr. Corbinelli have to say anything to me?"

The young man chuckled. "You're dazed. I've heard the Titan

has a certain effect on young women."

Susan, who was nearing forty-five, grinned. "I appreciate you calling me young, but it isn't only women." She motioned to a cluster of five middle-aged men around the desk nearest the door that wasn't hers. They whispered back and forth with smiles pasted on their lips. She caught bits of their conversation.

"Wonder what it'd be like to smoke cigars with the Titan."

"I hear he owns half the hotels in the city. They say when the President comes to stay at one, his suite isn't as nice as Corbinelli's. The Titan keeps that one for himself so he can be there at the same time."

One man whistled. "Hell, what a guy, huh?"

Susan shook her head. "Please tell them to get back to work. We wouldn't want anything falling out of order."

Susan cast a glance toward the Chief's office in time to see a bodyguard staring out the window at her. He closed the blinds, and Susan released a breath. Today was going to be a long day.

Chief John Turnbower wasn't surprised to see his old acquaintance, Victor Corbinelli, filling the doorway to his office with his hulking form, two bodyguards lurking behind him. It had been several months since Victor's last visit, and John had anticipated this one would come soon.

But why the hell did it have to be on a Monday?

John stood, pasting a smile to his lips. "Good morning, Victor." He motioned toward the chair on the other side of his desk. "Please, make yourself comfortable."

Victor strode into the room, wearing a charming smile with too-white teeth and passing his piercing blue eyes over the space. He drank everything in with a single glance and seemed to judge John's whole life on the basis of his office.

John noted how long Victor's gaze stayed on the small frame

sitting on his desk with a photo of his wife and two sons smiling at the camera. Victor's bodyguards came in behind him, one closing the door and remaining by it and the other closing the blinds before turning to pin John with a hard stare.

Fucking hell, John hated those bodyguards. Always had.

Victor did not sit right away. He turned to a cart in the corner of the room where wide windows overlooked the city and poured himself a glass of whiskey. It was a drizzly day, and the Brooklyn Bridge was visible, wreathed in fog. John liked a drink in his office every now and then, but not at ten A.M. on a Monday morning. Victor sipped the drink as he surveyed the city, then turned to John with a smile. "I'm doing well, John. Thank you for asking."

John didn't remember asking.

Victor remained standing, clearly aware that John was infuriated by his sense of dominance and familiarity. However, John didn't say anything about it. What could he say? He was powerful every day except when Victor came to visit. Around Victor, almost everyone felt powerless. John hated that feeling. It took everything in him not to squirm like a worm on a hook. What the hell did Victor want now?

John couldn't hold it all in. "What are you doing here, Victor? I'm busy today, as you can see." He gestured to the mountain of files on his desk. "We have cases piling up, messes everywhere. Some of them I'm sure you're well aware of." It was the closest John would ever come to outright accusing Victor of anything.

Victor uttered a low chuckle, finally turning and taking a seat in the wide leather chair. It was then John remembered the leather chairs in his office and the mahogany desk were gifts from Victor. Relics from his grandfather's old office. The bodyguards were as still as statues. John tried to ignore them.

Victor raised his glass in a mock toast. "My apologies, John. Got a bit heated over a project hiccup. You know how it is." His tone was calm enough to disarm John, and Victor had a way of speaking vaguely where you couldn't ask questions no matter how much you wanted to.

The soothing tone, paired with the use of his first name, made John feel less like a worm on a hook and more like a worm taken off and held in the palm of Victor's hand. He was safer than before but not out of danger yet.

John had done the same with the first name. "Mr. Corbinelli" wouldn't be coming out of his mouth anytime soon. Not with the decades they'd known one another.

"Have a drink, old friend," Victor offered as if this was his office and John was merely overlooking it. He gestured for his bodyguard to pour John a glass and set it on the table. John stared at it, wondering how the hell he'd gotten to this point.

The tension eased as they discussed city affairs and criminal activities. "Tell me your troubles, John," Victor invited. "These cases that are piling up. What are they about? The gang activity seems worse than ever. My men are dealing with incidents all over the place."

"Men" could include any number of people and their professions. Bodyguards, lawyers, the fellows who did Victor's dirty work. The fewer questions John asked, the more he could stay in the dark. Not that it would matter. Who was around to punish him if he made a misstep? The police commissioner was thick as thieves with Lenny Dolos, Victor's personal attorney. If anything, John was sitting pretty. *So why do I feel like I'm in the hot seat?*

"Well, John?" Victor pressed. "What do you think of the gang matter on the south side? I've heard about shipments going missing and what might be in them." Drugs, guns, whatever. Did it matter? Whatever it was, it wasn't good.

"We're working on it," John replied, not wanting to give too many details away. The truth was, he didn't have much detail on hand to give away. The case was fresh, and though he had several men on it, they hadn't been able to crack anything yet.

Victor leaned forward, his forearms perched on the desk and

his fingers intertwined. He was close enough for John to note the sprouts of white hairs on Victor's knuckles. Victor wore a slim gold wedding band next to a ring with a large, sparkling ruby.

The ring on his middle finger had long been in the Corbinelli family and bore their crest etched into it. It was old enough that John couldn't tell what the crest was, but he had the distinct idea it was something serpentine. Little marks that looked like scales flashed in the fluorescent office light.

"Let me take care of it, John," Victor offered. "You've got enough on your plate."

"You're not law enforcement," John replied with a weary smile. "Technically, I can't let you." *I also won't stop you* was the implied follow-up sentiment.

Victor shrugged his large shoulders, leaning back with a grace that seemed impossible with his hulking figure. "Consider it subcontracting. I'll have my private detectives on that matter and a few others. You're better for the city if you have less to do."

John had the sense he was having his arm twisted. This wasn't the first time Victor had made such an offer or casually persuaded John to turn a blind eye to certain matters. He felt his morality disintegrating every time he sat in his office with Victor, but he had a wife and two young sons at home to think of. Victor was right about one thing. The city was better off if he had less to do, and it would relieve him to have a few cases off his plate.

Victor chuckled. "It'll be like old times, John. Our shared past may be over, but we can have a shared future. Look at where we are now and think about how far we can go."

Long ago, the pair had run a number of gangs but ultimately chose different paths. They weren't young men anymore. John had gone into the police department, and Victor had turned to running his empire. They had helped one another climb to the top.

John didn't like to admit it, but he was the closest thing to the Corbinelli family's inside man. As police chief, he scoped out what went on in the city, from the smaller crimes in impoverished neighborhoods to big cases in the courthouses. He knew the names of almost every lawyer at every firm, who was in prison, and who had been bailed out.

"Toast to it, John, for old time's sake." Victor raised his glass.

John smiled with a hint of nostalgia and regret as he raised his glass and clinked it against Victor's.

"To your continued sacrifices for the Pack." Victor's words were heavy with unspoken meaning. John tried to push the word "Pack" out of his mind. The more he ignored it, the less likely he was to let it slip around his colleagues or, worse, his family.

John tipped his glass back and emptied it. He'd need another after Victor left.

As soon as John placed his glass back on the desk, Victor's demeanor darkened. The guards shifted, their first movements since Victor sat.

"John, I might need some…personnel changes soon. Ensure your men take care of the aftermath." It was a clear demand, no persuasion bothered with. The whole meeting had been ominous, but John wished Victor had at least kept up the façade that everything was fine and dandy, and they were on good terms. Now, John felt the ice thinning beneath his feet, a deep lake opening under him, and somehow, he didn't know how to swim.

He nodded.

Victor rose, pasting on another smile and buttoning his suit. "Thank you for your time, John, and I do apologize for how long it took for me to come here again. I'll be seeing you soon."

As soon as Victor departed, leaving a cold, unsettling aura behind, John rose and poured himself a second drink.

"I should have taken the fucking subway," Stacy growled. She preferred to make her morning commute in her car, but today's congestion left her battling frustration and impatience. What the hell was going on? Traffic was much worse on this route than normal, and she had even left early to beat it. She had a sense this wasn't the only thing that wouldn't go to plan today.

"Happy Monday to me," she groaned as she made another inch toward a green light. "As if dealing with a lawsuit wasn't enough already!"

A cacophony of honking and shouting filled the air. Pedestrians darted across the street. Taxis edged away from curbs into the crawl of traffic, and businessmen exited hotels, signaling for valets to bring their cars around. A slight rain pattered on her car, the leftover drizzle from last night's storm.

Stacy's phone rang, and she turned down the radio. She did not recognize the number and answered it with wariness lacing her tone. "Hello?" It was her personal phone, not her office number, so she didn't bother adding, "Stacy Drake speaking."

The voice on the other end sounded nervous but determined, as if the woman had worked up the courage to make the call. "Ms. Drake?"

Stacy hesitated. "Yes, this is she."

"Thank you for answering, Ms. Drake. My name is Amy Greentree. I'm a web reporter with a journal that reports on law enforcement and the court system as well as non-profits who work with disparaged citizens of the city."

Stacy had never heard of anything like it, but she didn't pay much attention to those things. "Go on."

"I'm looking into a Mr. Leonard Dolos, and after researching some of his cases, I believe you can help me."

Amy Greentree sounded nice enough, but Stacy could not deny the dread in the pit of her stomach or her rising wariness. She shook off her shock and wondered what to do. Amy did not seem aware of the danger she'd put herself in by calling Stacy. If she participated, she'd be putting this woman in more danger. *Is it right for me to pretend this never happened and have her dig deeper, possibly getting herself into something she knows nothing about?* Stacy wondered.

If Lenny made a victim of this journalist, Stacy wouldn't be able to bear it. "Why exactly are you looking into Mr. Dolos, Ms. Greentree?"

"Please, call me Amy. I've been assigned a piece on the city's most renowned lawyers, and since Leonard is so proficient in what he does, especially considering his age, he'd be a perfect subject for the column."

Why call me about it?

If Stacy had managed to beat Lenny, wouldn't that mean the journal wanted to write about her, too? "Does Lenny—I mean, Mr. Dolos, know you're writing the piece?" she asked.

Amy hesitated. "No, not yet. We wanted to gather some information before deciding if we're even going to publish it. You sound like you might need some convincing, Ms. Drake. I understand that, given your history of rivalry with Mr. Dolos."

Stacy's hands clenched the wheel harder.

"You see, our intention is not to elevate Mr. Dolos in any positive light but to expose the nastier dealings of lawyers toward underprivileged individuals. Some of these have been your clients, Ms. Drake."

This Amy Greentree had certainly done her research. The journalist went on. "I can understand why you might be hesitant to say anything, but I can promise complete discretion and confidence with us. Would you be willing to have a meeting? If you become uncomfortable, we can forget this ever happened."

Stacy saw the risks as clearly as the glowing red light ahead of her, but something about Amy's earnest tone and stated desires made her curious. "We need to talk, yes," Stacy agreed. "Be careful, Amy. You're stepping into deep waters. How about a meeting at Bluestone Lane Upper West Side Coffee at one?"

"See you there at one," Amy chirped and hung up.

Stacy sat in the quiet of her car, the chaos of the city humming around her. What would the meeting with Amy do for her? Would it help or get her deeper into the mess she was already floundering through? "What a Monday this is turning out to be," she groaned as she turned, and the office finally came into sight.

CHAPTER SIX

> *"The misty air and slush with granite maw,*
> *The sleet upon the griffins spits, and all*
> *The Saurian monsters, answering to the squall,*
> *Flap wings; while through the broken ceiling fall*
> *Torrents of rain upon the forms beneath,*
> *Dragons and snak'd Medusas gnashing teeth*
> *In the dismantled rooms."*
> —Victor Hugo, Eviradnius, Part III: In the Forest

Bluestone Lane Upper West Side Coffee was crowded when Stacy entered, exactly as she had hoped.

She wanted to meet with Amy in a busy place where they could look like old friends catching up, not newly associated young women taking a great risk. On her route there, Stacy thought about turning back and pretending she had never spoken to Amy. The same feeling had overcome her while going to her father's for the first time in years.

Something inside compelled her to go anyway, and the next thing she knew, she was sitting in a corner booth with a chai latte resting between her palms. What was her life as a lawyer if she didn't take risks, anyway?

"Ms. Drake?" a pleasant voice behind her stated.

Stacy turned to see a tall, willowy woman with soft waves of blonde hair and pretty brown eyes gazing down at her. The woman extended a hand. "Amy Greentree. Thank you for meeting me."

Stacy gestured for her to sit. "I'm glad I could make it work today." The truth was, since arriving at the office, Stacy had not been able to keep her mind off Amy. She had researched as much as she could online, learning they were around the same age, and Amy had gone to NYU for journalism.

Amy Greentree had been working for a small online news company for a year now, having started as an intern and quickly worked her way up. No doubt if she managed an exposé on Leonard Dolos with full evidence, she'd be their writer of the year.

Stacy didn't tell Amy any of this. She assumed the journalist knew as much about Stacy as Stacy knew about her. What was a journalist who didn't research the person they were meeting with? *A bad journalist,* Stacy thought. Miss Greentree looked like she knew what she was doing.

Amy scooted onto the other side of the booth and set a purse on the table. "I'm sorry I'm late. Traffic and all. It took me longer to get away from the office too."

"I understand." Stacy had given a flippant excuse about a small illness and needing to run to a pharmacy to get out of the office. She pushed her small mountain of work to the back of her mind and focused all her attention on Amy.

The coffee shop was full of pleasant smells, and the din of chatter, utensils against cups and plates, and food orders shouted into the kitchen. The occasional sound of the bell above the door rang out as patrons filtered in and out.

Stacy enjoyed the hum of the city. The quiet made her feel too alone.

"I know this isn't a conventional thing to meet about and has nothing to do with your current work," Amy started.

"You'd be surprised," Stacy returned dully, wondering if she should mention the lawsuit Lenny had filed against her. *Not now. Keep some cards close to your chest,* she told herself.

"You see, I've been researching Mr. Dolos for quite a while now and have come across some things that concern me. Suspicious connections and possible corrupt activities." This was nothing new to Stacy since she knew Lenny worked for Victor Corbinelli and had gotten him out of past legal entanglements. Not everyone knew these things, though.

A waitress stopped by to take Amy's order. Amy asked for a coffee and a muffin. "To be honest, I haven't had much of an appetite today. Greedy scumbags take that away from me," Amy commented when the waitress walked away. She gave a breathy laugh.

"I appreciate your work, Ms. Greentree." Stacy paused. "Amy, I mean. Normally, I would fully support what you're doing and help where I can, but…"

"But there are dangers in digging too deep. I understand." She leaned forward, folding her delicate hands together and lowering her voice. "I'm well aware of the dangers and of Leonard's more prominent connections. You see, I followed the case about the Denninson property pretty closely."

Stacy raised a brow. It wasn't like anyone to do that, even small journalists. The Denninson case, as far as she knew, was like most property cases involving underprivileged clients. Greedy businesses wanted to take them over and turn housing lots into businesses that could bring in more revenue than property taxes gave the city.

"The client Mr. Dolos represented has a company. You know

that, of course," Amy continued. "Do you know who owns the majority of the shares in that company?"

"I should have guessed already," Stacy replied. "Or at least done my damn research." She had been so caught up in defending Lora that she hadn't cared much who the adversary was. It hadn't mattered then with the evidence Stacy had.

"Mr. Corbinelli," Amy answered despite Stacy already knowing.

More pieces fell together, and Stacy began to fear Lora would soon find herself in trouble again. Her heart sank. *I won't let that happen or anyone else become a victim.* The biggest question was, what the hell was so special about Lora's land that Victor Corbinelli wanted it?

Stacy pondered the matter while Amy received her coffee, then remarked, "Fine, I'll do what I can, but we have to be careful. I won't be quick with it, either. I need to know I can trust you."

Amy nodded. "Of course. I plan to report with as many details as I can on the matter and spread the story quickly. Your name won't be attached to anything, so you don't have to worry about that. Thank you for doing this. It's not often I can find a willing ally in this field of work."

Stacy knew how that felt. "Me, too. It's good to have another girl I can count on, and I hope you feel the same."

"I do."

Stacy felt she could trust Amy but decided to be on her guard. She leaned forward. "How about this? I'll hire you as a personal assistant of sorts. You can shadow me on any cases involving Lenny and write what you find out during the process. We'll keep it under wraps for now, though. There's no need for Lenny to catch onto the fact that we're working together."

"Good thing he doesn't know I exist, then," Amy quipped.

"Yet," Stacy warned. "Lenny is a shark, and he smells all the blood in the water."

"Then it's best we don't start bleeding, right?"

Stacy liked her. "Right."

She checked her watch and realized the time. "I've got to get back to the office, but we can meet another time to strategize."

"Very well." Amy rose and handed Stacy a card. "This number here is personal. Call that instead of my office to reach me about this."

She was about to leave when Stacy asked, "How did you get *my* number?"

Amy smiled. "I'm an old friend of Lora's. Actually..." She glanced around, then lowered her voice. "I'm her niece, and I have been worried about her since this mess with her property began."

Stacy's eyes widened. This was personal for Amy, but did it change things for Stacy? Could she trust her more now?

"I want to continue helping her. I told her what I wanted to do and persuaded her to give me your number," Amy added.

Stacy wasn't sure how to feel, but if Lora trusted Amy, so could she. "Very well. I'll call you when I get the time."

Amy thanked her again. Stacy watched as the young woman stepped outside the coffee shop and melted into the crowd on the pavement. She glanced at the card and the elegant handwriting with Amy's name and number. *Have I made a new friend, or have I stepped into a trap?* she wondered.

She left the coffee shop feeling like she'd stepped out on thin ice, but it was a risk she was willing to take if it meant Lenny went under. *And I get out of my fucking lawsuit,* she thought. She was out on the street when her phone buzzed with a notification from Jenna.

JENNA

Coming to happy hour?

Stacy typed in her response, muttering, "Hell yeah. I need it today."

The sun set behind rows of buildings, their points piercing a darkening sky. The last light of the day burned on the horizon and cast an orange glow through the windows of Victor's office. This time of day was always his favorite. The time right before the sun disappeared and the real work began.

Victor checked his watch, frowning. It was high time Lenny called him about new developments in their plan. He hadn't heard from his lawyer all day. He finished his drink and set the empty whiskey glass on his desk, crossing his arms as he surveyed the city. Enough of it was his to make him happy for the time being. The time for expansion would come, but right now, he had to preserve.

They needed a new strategy for dealing with potential threats to the overall operation. Lenny's idea to send trained thugs after the young lawyer didn't seem fitting to Victor, who preferred more covert methods of turning things in his favor. Lenny had never been so adamant about someone before, though, so Victor had let him do what he wanted. "This time, Lenny. You had better not sink a ship."

The Titan sensed he would soon have to reel the lawyer in before he exposed anything in pursuit of the young woman. Victor was used to having enemies and nuisances, especially those involved in the law. He had learned long ago not to let petty vendettas get in his way and hoped Lenny would soon learn the same lesson.

Victor turned to his desk, where a file lay open. He sat and examined the photo of the young woman Lenny had filed a lawsuit against. Stacy Drake was pretty enough. Twenty-six and already holding an exceptional record of won cases, she was difficult to ignore. Victor had plenty of information about her, such as that she had gone to NYU School of Law. He knew what firm she worked for and how long she had been there.

However, he could not find who her family was. He hadn't done thorough research yet but would soon if matters developed further with her. He hoped Lenny would take care of it, and it would no longer be necessary. Ms. Drake was another person in a long list of small nuisances. Yet, as Victor examined her professional photo, she struck him as familiar. He couldn't quite put his finger on what it was.

He closed the file as the doors to his office opened, and a tall man wearing a trench coat and hat entered. The man removed his hat and set it on the desk, exposing a large face with small, piercing dark eyes and a mouth with a scar running over his top lip. He had a chiseled jaw and graying hair. His expression was perpetually stony.

Victor motioned for him to sit. "Thank you for meeting with me." He offered the man a drink, but the man waved his hand dismissively.

"Very well, then." Victor poured a second drink for himself. "Fancy a cigar?"

The man shook his head.

Victor wondered if the visitor ever had a good time. He decided to forego his cigar until the man left.

"Is Mr. Dolos joining us?" the man asked.

"No. I thought we should meet without him for once." Gone was any cheer Victor used when greeting the visitor.

The man in the trench coat remained still, waiting for Victor to tell him why he was here. "Leonard has taken it into his own hands to deal with the Drake girl, but I'm finding another plan is warranted. Something with direct action." He folded his ringed fingers. "I want to take over the land belonging to a rival family in a section of land with many docks."

He slid a map across the table with sections circled in red. Victor didn't bother going over the long, tumultuous history between the Corbinellis and the family who owned the docks. Instead, he tapped the red area of the map.

"This is why we have been looking into Ms. Drake. The case with Mrs. Denninson has foiled our previous plans."

"Right." The man in the trench coat shook his head. "Mr. Dolos told me that but didn't elaborate."

Victor leaned back, resting his hands on his belly. "Well, seeing as I hired you and not Mr. Dolos, it stands to reason that I should give you the details, not him."

The man nodded. "Tell me what you think is necessary."

Something about the man unnerved Victor, but he didn't show it. "I'm not exactly the kind of man who likes displacing a single mother, but we need her land. It's above an old subway station ending by the docks, where I have shipments coming in. The kind we don't need folks in this city knowing about." His blue eyes glittered. "I need my men working beneath the land, but if I don't own it, that damn woman will report our noise to the cops."

"I thought you had the cops wrapped around your finger," the man replied. "That's what they say in the Pack, anyway."

Victor bristled but managed a wide, knowing smile. "I have quite a reputation with the Pack, but that's not what matters now. I do have the police in my back pocket, but even so, the less attention we can bring to ourselves, the better. That is, we want attention, but we need to be able to control it."

It was why he held galas and ensured he was seen in public often. He needed people talking about his above-table business ventures and his pretty wife. He wanted them to discuss what dress his daughter would wear to her wedding and which paintings he'd be bidding on at art auctions. He needed to laugh during interviews when asked if he'd run for office, saying, "I don't want to climb that high." He had to lie through the best smile possible.

It was true that he had the police wrapped around his finger, but someone could always grow nervous and say the wrong thing. He had faith in John Turnbower's fear, but for how long?

"I'm sure you will be able to take care of everything, Mr. Corbinelli," the man in the trench coat commented. A crooked smile split his lips, the first hint of emotion Victor had seen on the man's face since he walked into the office. "Besides, it's not like there's anybody else in this city who can rival your power."

It was true. No one was as rich and influential as him. Once, there had been prominent rivals, but they weren't in the city anymore. "Go ahead with the plan Lenny devised involving the young lawyer," Victor instructed. "If things go south with her, report to me, not Lenny. She should be easy to handle, but Lenny can be flighty and impulsive at times. We don't need too much attention on the matter."

The man rose, taking his hat from the table and securing it on his head in a way that concealed most of his face. He stuffed his hands into the pockets of his coat. "Very well, sir. You should hear from me soon."

"I should hope so. Remember, report to me, not Lenny. I'll take care of him." He grinned. "We don't need a middleman involved every time."

The man nodded and left the room.

Victor smiled, thinking of Lenny. *Keep your friends close, but not that close.*

CHAPTER SEVEN

"Beings who can shift between human and animal shapes have existed since the earliest times, with carvings of serpentine creatures found as early as the Stone Age. Though most of the earliest evidence of such creatures no longer exists, tales and legends have carried the truth forward."
 —*Unknown*, The Dragon Codex History, Vol. IV

"It was perfect, Stace, exactly what I needed. You wouldn't believe how blue the water was. I think things with Derek might work out this time. Can you believe it? I can't believe those words came out of my mouth. Hey, are you okay?"

Stacy had zoned out for about the fifth time since sitting with Jenna at the bar down the street from the office. She'd only had half a drink despite being stressed enough to drink more. She had fiddled with her straw while gazing into the distance, Jenna's words floating in and out of her mind. She turned to her friend, forcing a tired smile. "That's nice, Jenna. I hope things do work out."

"But are you okay?"

Stacy nodded and dropped her gaze to her drink, swirling the straw in the dark substance.

Jenna frowned. "You're a terrible liar. Your old man isn't bothering you, is he?"

"No, it's not that, but I don't want to worry you." Stacy wished her only troubles had to do with the debt she owed her father. "I've got a lot going on at work, and I'm tired." Those things, at least, were true. She checked the time. "I should be getting home if I expect to be well rested before tomorrow. Thanks for meeting me here, though."

Jenna gave her a concerned look. "As long as you're sure going to bed early is all you need to feel better."

Stacy hated lying to her friend, but she hated worrying Jenna more. She squeezed her into a hug. "It will."

"Come out with me this weekend," Jenna insisted.

"I'll see what I can do."

Jenna's eyes returned to their usual sparkling bemusement. "I'll tell Derek to stay home if you want. It can be just you and me, like old times." Jenna and Stacy had been a duo since the first year of college when they met, two girls fresh out of high school, looking to become lawyers. They'd had big dreams and bright futures but also a sheltered past.

The two of them had jumped head-first into the party scene. Now that they worked in a professional place, it was time to reel the partying in. Nevertheless, Stacy felt she needed a good time out every once in a while. With everything going on with Lenny, maybe she needed it more.

"You don't have to do that," Stacy replied. She wasn't Derek's number one fan, but she loved Jenna and liked seeing her happy. Besides, Derek wasn't all that bad when he had a few drinks in his system and stopped explaining cryptocurrency or the plot holes in *Star Wars* to her, the latter of which she knew far more about than him.

Out on the street, Stacy hoped she could get away from work

for the weekend, but she wasn't so sure she could. She might take time off, but Lenny wouldn't. She was lost in a swirl of thoughts surrounding Lenny, Victor Corbinelli, Amy Greentree, and her father as she walked a block down to where she had parked her car. It meant going into a more rundown neighborhood, but the parking was much cheaper there.

Remember to take the subway tomorrow, she told herself as she rounded a corner onto the street and crossed it to the lot where she had parked her car.

She was nearly there when she halted, spotting a trio of thuggish-looking men mingling around her car. They muttered words she could not hear. One leaned close and peered into her car. Another's voice rose loud enough that the words, "You sure this is hers?" floated across to where she'd ducked behind a tree.

"Sure is," one of the other men called back.

What the hell are they doing around my car?

The dread curling in her gut and the strange series of events from the past two weeks told her exactly what was happening. Lenny had hired these thugs to track her down. She ground her teeth. The audacity, and in broad daylight, too!

She glanced toward the horizon. Well, not quite broad. The sun had almost set. How long had these guys been waiting around for her? Had they been tracking her all day? The thought that they might have seen her with Amy Greentree spiked her panic.

Stacy was so lost in her thoughts that she didn't notice one of the men turning until he spotted her and shouted, "There she is!"

Shit. She couldn't do anything but run. Taking on one guy was one thing, but three? No way in hell. She turned and fled in the opposite direction, her heart thumping faster than it had been a minute ago. She skidded around a corner and hurtled into another, more rundown street. A man taking out trash through the back door of a restaurant gave her a quizzical look, but Stacy continued.

The thundering boots of the guys following her came shortly after, followed by their shouts. They didn't seem to mind anyone noticing what they were up to. Lenny must have paid them well. With the sun setting and the area of town she was in, Stacy didn't see many people as she continued running through darkening streets.

I'll have to teach fucking Lenny Dolos a lesson for doing this, she thought. He had made it pretty damned personal now. She couldn't keep letting him put her life in danger. Stacy thought about calling the police as she fled, but she didn't have time. The men behind her were several paces away, but they were keeping up.

What the hell am I supposed to do? she wondered. She couldn't run all night. Stacy's anger built, and so did the pace of her feet. She found herself going faster than ever. She had never run so fast in her life. Stranger than the fact that she was easily outrunning the thugs was that she didn't feel the burn in her lungs or muscles. It was *easy*. *I'm in shape but not this good,* she thought, wondering what was coming over her.

Her veins rushed with heat, and she felt a tingling all over her body. This wasn't the kind of adrenaline she was used to. The heat inside her overtook her mind until she could no longer grasp her own thoughts.

Stacy veered into an alleyway without remembering why she was doing it or what she had decided to do next. The end of the alley had a fence too high to climb and a dumpster pushed up against it. The tall walls of two brick buildings were only three feet away, making it a narrow space to push herself into.

She wiggled between two more buildings, hardly large enough to fit her form. The stamping of boots and huffing breaths followed. The three men entered the alley, out of breath and cursing. "Where the hell did she go?"

"I swore I saw her run in here," another one stated.

The third man snickered. "She didn't climb the damn fence.

She's here somewhere, hidin.'" To Stacy, the third man called, "Come on out, girlie. We ain't gonna hurt ya."

"Aren't we supposed to—" another man started.

The third cut him off. "Shut the fuck up and look for her." He growled. "Where the hell did she go?"

The second man caught sight of something behind the third and gaped.

"What is it?" the third man demanded. The second man stilled, and he couldn't quite get the words "Behind you" out. Sounds fell from his lips in an incoherent jumble. What he'd seen was a dark figure emerging from a narrow space, eyes glowing an inhuman green and gold.

The second man didn't have time to warn his friend again before the figure slammed a brick on the third man's head.

When the two cops pulled up to the door and knocked, they were not expecting the story they would hear or what they would see in the alley when they investigated after speaking to Sofia Hernandez, the woman who had called.

The woman opened the door, her black hair as wild as her eyes. She was shaking, with four small children pressing in around her. Before either of the cops had a chance to introduce themselves, she started crying and shouting in Spanish. She pointed toward the alley, muttering words one of the cops couldn't understand.

The other cop, Maria, had been to this neighborhood more than a dozen times in the last month and was used to translating for other cops who came along with her. "Ms. Hernandez says she heard a fight in the alley next to her house."

The building Sofia and her children lived in was a rundown brick apartment complex, one of many on the street. Neither of the cops were surprised to hear about a fight breaking out in an alley, but Sofia's description made their brows furrow as they shared puzzled glances.

"She says she heard men yelling for someone to come out, then horrible screaming. Several other neighbors slammed their windows shut, but Sofia kept listening, then called us," Maria translated.

Sofia went on and on, fidgeting with her stained blue dress. Her eyes grew wider the longer she told the story. "She says the screams cut off one by one, then there was nothing. She looked out the window to see what had happened and saw a…" Maria hesitated, glancing at Sofia.

Sofia nodded vigorously, repeating one word under her breath. "*Demonio.*"

"She says she saw a demon or a monster who had attacked those men. Whatever it was, it disappeared."

The second cop surveyed Sofia and her children, noting how terrified they looked. "All right, we'd better have a look, then."

Maria thanked Sofia in Spanish, but Sofia was too scared to let them leave. "I'll stay here and calm her down while you take a look," Maria told the other cop.

Davis, the other cop, nodded. Whatever the story might have been, he didn't think he'd be coming into contact with a demon on the ground level. However, when he reached the alleyway, he wondered if he'd change his mind. The sight before him was not what he'd been expecting.

He stopped short, brows furrowing. "What in hell?" He turned on a flashlight and shone it over the alley. The normal sight of trash, a rat running into a hole, and worn brick walls met his eyes. He wasn't surprised to find the pile of three bodies, but the state of them made him draw in a sharp breath. He'd expected to find the men beaten, maybe even shot, but not bleeding so profusely from torn-off limbs that the ground was slick with red.

Maybe a demon or monster *had* come here. Whatever had done this must have been more animal than man. One of the men had his arm ripped off, and another's leg was shredded to bloody ribbons. All three had missing faces, or at least enough missing pieces that they couldn't be identified.

Davis' body went cold. Earlier, he thought Ms. Hernandez had been exaggerating. Now, he thought she hadn't described it enough.

He dialed a number on his phone. "Yes, Officer Davis here. No ambulance needed. They're already dead, but send someone to get the bodies." He hung up and took off toward the street as a chill darted up his spine. He no longer wanted to stand in that dark space alone.

Stacy awoke with a pounding headache.

It didn't help that she hadn't closed her curtains the night before, and bright sunlight streamed through her windows. She sat up, frowning at the TV she'd left on in her bedroom. The volume was jacked up to an ungodly level. She scrambled for the remote, turning it down with a muttered, "Fucking hell."

She found her phone, noticing the time and several missed calls and texts, the latest of which came from Jenna.

> **JENNA**
>
> Tell me you're not dead. Also, I covered for your ass today. When you didn't show up this morning, I told them you were sick. It helped that you went to the pharmacy yesterday. Boss totally bought my story.

Holy shit! It was one in the afternoon! Stacy leaped out of bed, then swayed as blood rushed to her head. Momentarily blinded, she quickly remembered her throbbing headache. Her head spun, her vision clearing slower than normal.

What the fuck happened yesterday? It wasn't like her to get

drunk with Jenna on a Thursday night, no matter how shitty her day had been. She didn't remember coming home, turning on the TV, and getting into bed. She didn't remember leaving the bar either. She texted Jenna back.

> I'm okay. Thanks for covering for me. I owe you one.

She wasn't okay, but at least she was home and with nothing apparently wrong with her except a raging hangover. Jenna's next message came seconds later.

> **JENNA**
>
> Thank the good Lord! As for owing me, how about an explanation?? You had half a glass of wine. It's not like you were too drunk to text me that you got home.

Only half a glass of wine? Why did she feel like she'd had two whole bottles? Stacy barely had the word "soon" typed in and sent before she sank back onto her bed, feeling woozy. Of all the days to miss work, this should not have been one. She had too much to do, and Fridays were always mayhem in the office. Her boss would be pissed, saying something like, "You had better have malaria or something to miss work today."

Stacy turned her attention to the TV. An afternoon news station was on, and the blonde reporter stood outside a rundown tenement building. She wouldn't have noticed the woman's words if it wasn't for the headline running across the screen.

THREE STRANGE DEATHS. WITNESS CLAIMS SUPER-HUMAN ATTACK.

"What the hell?" Stacy muttered. She turned the volume up.

"A witness, Ms. Hernandez, says she saw something monstrous in the night attacking three men in an alley beside her home. The culprit, who has yet to be named or apprehended, got away, and police say they have never seen victims in such a grotesque state before."

Stacy's heart thudded. Why did this sound familiar?

"Police are looking for whatever help they can get," the female reporter continued.

Her gaze wandered away from the TV toward a chair by her window. A bra lay there with a spot of blood on it. She frowned, rising to examine it. "How did this happen?" It was the bra she had put on yesterday morning, but she didn't remember taking it off. In fact, she was naked now.

Quickly, Stacy pulled on a robe to keep her warm and covered. She also noticed her window was open, so she closed it.

She returned to the TV and found the reporter with a new witness, a young man. "This witness says he saw a woman running in her underwear at an outstanding speed from the alley where the men died last night." She pushed the microphone into the man's face.

"The weirdest stuff I've seen in a while!" the man proclaimed. "She ran out of there faster than anything. If it wasn't for the dark, maybe I'd have made out her face. She sure did have a nice body—"

The reporter moved the microphone away to ask another question, but the witness leaned in, yelling, "I'm happy I saw my future girlfriend! I'm man enough to admit she's faster than me, and red underwear is sexy as hell—"

The reporter stepped away. Stacy would have stifled a laugh if it wasn't for the red bra she held in her hand.

Slowly, things started coming back to her. She remembered leaving the bar and walking down the street, then being pursued by three thugs. After that, she didn't know what happened. She had awoken this afternoon in her bed. Her heart hammered. *What did I do?*

Something had killed those men and tried to do the same to her, and she had gotten away. Her cheeks flushed at the thought of someone seeing her in nothing but her bra and underwear, but the chilling thought of almost ending up without a face like one of those men...

Unless it wasn't a monster who did it, but me.

She shook her head, shoving the thought away.

No, that's not what happened.

She checked her head for a bump. Maybe she had been knocked out at one point. No injuries there. Why did it hurt like hell?

Stacy started shaking. Something very, very wrong had happened, and she couldn't remember what it was.

Police Chief John Turnbower could not leave his office. Try as he might, he couldn't convince himself to get up and go home. His wife had already called, wondering where he was, and he had mumbled a lame excuse about having to work late. He knew a good meal and a comfortable bed awaited him at home, yet he couldn't make himself leave the damn office. Victor had that effect on him after his visits.

In the past, John had gone home earlier in the day. This time was different. Victor had made real threats, and he felt he had to sit in his office and devise a way out of this before allowing himself true rest.

For the past few days, John had been in a funk. He was unfocused at work and spent most of his time sitting at his desk, eyes trained on the New York City skyline as he slowly sipped a glass of whiskey.

Something had to change.

He was too damn tired of Victor and the pull he had over him. He was sick of keeping secrets and acting like a man of honor when he knew the reality wasn't anywhere close to that. He was letting a bad man get away with bad things. Simple as that.

Doubt and fear crept into his mind, further aided by the drink he'd been consuming the past few hours. Victor would not hesitate to take vengeance on John. First with his two boys, then with his wife. John's heart ached at the thought. He couldn't let that happen.

What the hell am I supposed to do about it? he wondered.

He felt lost, not knowing who to turn to. He had been loyal to Victor and the Corbinelli family since he was a young man in his twenties. He couldn't switch that off now, regardless of the threats Victor held over him. On the other side of the coin, he was a police officer. He had a duty to follow and a moral standard to uphold for himself and those he dealt with, whether they were his employees or a titan who had a rope around his neck.

John checked the time. It was getting late. He heard a rustling beyond his office doors. It was the first thing to convince him to leave his chair. He opened the door to find two police officers at their desks in the main office room. "What are you two doing here?" he asked.

The men looked up, and one answered for both of them. "Finishing up some paperwork, sir." John was not used to others being in the office at this time. Usually, the officers on duty were downstairs in the station part of the building.

He nodded and turned back to his office before something occurred to him. "You two come in here with me. I have a new assignment."

The police officers glanced at one another, then followed their chief as commanded.

John motioned for the pair to take seats, then leaned back in his chair, observing them. "For the benefit of the city, I have a name that needs to be dealt with. Can I trust you two to do it?" It was a rhetorical question. These officers worked here only because Victor had hired them. All day, John had been ruminating on whether or not he'd carry this plan out. The name had come from Leonard Dolos and, therefore, from Victor.

John hated that he was doing this right now, but he thought of his wife and boys at home. He didn't see another choice. *I'll think of a way out of this one day*, he decided. *I don't know what that is right now, though.*

John opened a locked drawer in his desk and drew out the piece of paper where he'd scribbled the name and address Lenny had called about that morning. He handed it to the men. They reviewed it, then nodded to one another and John. The last officer to look over it handed it back, refolded. John nodded for them to go, and they left.

Alone in his office again, John examined the folded piece of paper. He was glad not to read the name again. It struck him with a keen sense of guilt. It was easier not to feel responsible if he could ignore that the person had a name and a real identity. He felt cold, reminding himself it didn't matter whether he sent men after the person. If not him, Lenny and Victor would find someone else.

This city is rotten, he thought, pouring himself another glass. Earlier, he'd been sipping slowly. Now, he tipped it back and drank it all. After setting the glass on the table, John pulled a lighter from his pocket. He lit one corner of the paper and dropped it into a waste basket before watching it melt away into nothing. The evidence of his involvement vanished.

John rose, grabbing his jacket and hat, hoping his wife had kept dinner warm for him while he was gone.

CHAPTER EIGHT

> *"The dragons of the air,*
> *The hell-hounds of the deep,*
> *Lurking and prowling everywhere,*
> *Go forth to seek their helpless prey,*
> *Not knowing whom they maim or slay—*
> *Mad harvesters, who care not what they reap."*
> —Henry Van Dyke, Lights Out

By the time Monday morning rolled around, Stacy still hadn't been able to figure out what the hell happened to her on Thursday.

Instead of going out over the weekend, she recovered at home and told Jenna she needed to stay in to work on a case. It was true enough. Her attention was split between trying to figure out what the hell Lenny was doing and why, and her case involving Mr. George's property. She also had Lora Denninson and her niece Amy to worry about.

She hoped Lora wouldn't be pulled into court again soon. Stacy had a feeling her luck had run out, though. Why else had so many unfortunate things happened in a row?

She sat in her office at nine A.M. on Monday, jaw locked as she read over an update on her subpoena. It hadn't been implemented. How had Lenny done that? "I'll have to call Mr. George and let him know we've hit a roadblock," she muttered, picking up the office phone. As soon as Mr. George answered, Stacy opened her mouth to greet him, but he cut her off.

"Ms. Drake? Thank God you called. Something happened." Mr. George was the sort of older fellow who always sounded nervous, but this morning, he seemed at his wit's end. "Someone broke in last night. They left a note that I was to mind my own business. Place is in shambles, and there's no tellin' how long it'll take for repairs."

Stacy gripped the phone. "I'm sorry, Mr. George. That's awful. Did you file a police report? Was anything stolen?"

"Nothin' stolen, and yes, I called the police as soon as I got the alert. There's something else."

"Yes, Mr. George?" Stacy held her breath.

"I tried calling my buddy Henry a few days ago. You know 'im, the one who was gonna testify?"

"Yes." Stacy's heart rate increased. Henry was a key witness in the case for Mr. George. Without him, she wasn't sure she could win it.

"He won't pick up the damn phone. I went over to his house, and he wasn't there. Car was gone and everything. He lives alone, so there wasn't anybody to tell me where he'd gone. He hasn't been back since. That ain't like him, Ms. Drake. He's always around. He hasn't even taken a proper vacation in years, and he ain't got family anywhere. I think he's gone missing."

Stacy stilled. *Fuck.*

The whole thing reeked of Lenny's intrusion, especially since he'd sent thugs after her twice now. She'd always known he had reach and influence, but now she feared the scope of that reach was far broader than she imagined.

He has help from someone. Probably that fucking Corbinelli he works for, Stacy surmised. Into the phone, she stated, "Mr. George. I will take care of this as best I can. Please tell the police about your friend. It's up to them to figure out what happened to Henry and why your place was broken into. If we can find out who did this, we might have leverage in the case."

"You think so, Ms. Drake?"

I fucking hope so, she thought. Stacy didn't know how she did it, but she maintained a cheery tone to her voice. "Let me work my magic, Mr. George. Call me if you get any updates on either matter."

Mr. George promised he would and hung up.

Stacy sat back in her desk chair, bewildered at the turn of events. Everything was getting too strange for her liking. Part of her wanted to run away on vacation, maybe to the beach where Jenna and Derek had gone. She thought about Mr. George and his poor circumstances, Lora and Amy, and the debt she owed her father. She had too much tying her to this place.

This was the life you asked for, she told herself. *You wanted freedom, to be a Drake instead of a Drakethorn. Well, now you have it.* Stacy had wanted to go through her adult life without relying on her family name and wealth. She wanted to help without her family's legacy—whatever the hell that might be—looming over her.

She stood, grumbling about needing a second cup of coffee, but halted at the office door when the phone rang. Who was it now? "Stacy Drake speaking."

"Stacy?" The voice on the other end was nervous.

"Amy?" Stacy lowered her voice. "Why are you calling me right now?" They had a meeting planned for Wednesday and wanted to keep their interactions to a minimum. Stacy had told her not to call until then.

"You're my lawyer, and…" Amy hesitated, and Stacy heard a gruff male voice in the background telling her to hurry up. "I'm at the police station. They said I could call my lawyer. Stacy, I'm sorry. I didn't want to bother you today, but I've been arrested."

Stacy rushed into the police station, heels clicking across the tiles as she went to the front desk. The police officer standing there grunted. "Are you Ms. Greentree's attorney? Better come with me."

"What is she being held for?" Stacy demanded as she strode with him down the hallway. Amy had not explained over the phone. She'd only urged Stacy to come to the station as soon as she could.

"Trespassing," the officer replied.

Stacy's brows rose. Had Amy gone somewhere she shouldn't have during an investigation? She thought about asking the officer where Amy had been trespassing but feared that her concern for Amy would give away the fact that they were connected beyond Stacy being her attorney. *I need to focus on the legal aspects and nothing else.* At this point, she wasn't sure she could trust anyone. The police hadn't been an ounce of help in tracking down the thug who attacked her at her apartment over a week ago.

Divulging her connection to the arrested journalist could put the nature of Amy's investigation at risk. She'd been caught trespassing but had managed to hide her intent. At least, that was what she garnered from the officer. He told her they didn't know why she was trespassing, but they had gotten a call, and all the witnesses bore testimony to the same thing. Regardless, she'd been arrested, and Stacy was her sole hope of getting out.

"May I see the arrest report?" she asked.

Grunting, he handed it over. Stacy reviewed the charge and the consequences. A two hundred and fifty-dollar fine was on the table, along with Amy needing to stay in jail for fifteen days. *I'll pay the fine*, Stacy decided, then glanced at the officer. "What is the bail amount for Ms. Greentree? I'm happy to pay it, and she and I can leave today."

The officer arched a brow. "I'm not sure…"

Why did he hesitate? She was going about this as she always did. Aboveboard like any other respectable attorney. "What is the bail amount?" Stacy asked again, this time reaching into her purse for a pen.

The officer hesitated, then told her, "I'll go get the paperwork."

He returned not long after. This time, he had Amy in tow. "Oh, thank you for coming, Ms. Drake!"

Stacy kept her calm exterior intact, not letting the officer see they had a personal relationship. "It's my job, Ms. Greentree. Of course I would come." She didn't give Amy her normal friendly smile, and Amy caught wind of what Stacy was trying to do.

Stacy looked over the paperwork, careful to examine every detail so she could do everything by the book. The last thing she needed was more suspicion directed at her. After the incident last Thursday, Stacy had wanted to avoid the police, but the witness who'd seen her fleeing the alley scene had not glimpsed her face. So far, she was safe. *And whatever attacked those men and me better not come lurking around again,* she thought as she scribbled her signature.

Stacy handed the papers back to the officer, feeling uneasy about the amount she was paying. It wasn't much compared to the bail some paid for worse offenses, but she was still out more money than she liked. Her father would see it, too, since she'd have to dip into the reserve account again.

The officer reviewed the paperwork. "You're free to go, Ms. Greentree." He gave Stacy a curt nod.

The two women walked out of the police station, and Amy released a sigh of relief. "I'm not happy I have something on my record now, especially since it's tied to my work. As for the bail, I'll pay you back as soon as I can."

Stacy wasn't so much worried about the money as she was about her father seeing the transaction. "Let's go somewhere private," she told Amy, not wanting further personal conversation on the street where anyone who might have gotten Amy arrested could be watching them. Stacy had the distinct feeling Amy wasn't totally to blame, but she would not hear the story until they were somewhere else.

"What were you thinking?" Stacy demanded when they were in the coffee shop where they had met before. The hum of activity around them would let them talk without worrying about being overheard. Stacy had contemplated going somewhere quieter, like her office or home, but she didn't want to take that risk yet. It was better to talk where hardly anyone but the waiter would pay them any attention.

"It wasn't trespassing. Not really," Amy protested. She leaned back in the booth, sighing and looking like she'd been through hell. "I went to Mr. Dolos' office this morning. I knew he wouldn't be there because he has a case today at the courthouse. I fibbed a little, saying I was a journalist wanting to do a column on the city's most renowned lawyers for my university newspaper. The journalist and column part were both true enough, as you know."

She paused and stared at the hot cup of coffee between her palms. "His assistant let me in and told me it would be a while before Leonard was back. I told her I'd wait anyway. I used this time to observe what was going on in the office. It was weird. The people there seem afraid of Leonard, but they all talk behind his back when he isn't around. They say such nasty things, yet what happened later showed undying loyalty to him."

Amy's eyes swam with emotions. "I was sitting there, waiting for Mr. Dolos to return, when suddenly the police turned up and arrested me for trespassing. I tried to tell them the assistant had let me in, but the woman lied and said she hadn't. Someone told her to do that, Stacy! Someone must have called the police and made up the story. Several people told the officers it was true. I was trespassing, and it was my word against all of theirs."

Stacy ground her teeth. How infuriating! If there was a way for them to get ahold of the security footage in Lenny's building, she could prove Amy had been let in and allowed to stay. She had no idea how the hell she could do that, however. When Lenny caught wind of what had gone on, he'd probably destroy the footage. If he hadn't already learned of it and was responsible for getting Amy arrested.

"You took a big risk going to Lenny's office, Amy. What were you thinking?"

"That I'd find something out, and I did." She leaned forward, her tone dropping to a conspiratorial lowness. "He is indeed working for Victor Corbinelli, and his current slew of cases all have to do with procuring land for him. I don't know why he wants the land, but they all connect on a map. There's an area of docks over an old subway station that runs beneath a bunch of houses and land. One is my aunt's place."

"Can you show me this area?" Stacy asked.

Amy nodded and drew a folded map from her purse. She spread it on the table and traced her finger over the areas. Stacy's eyes went wide. Some of the land Lenny wanted belonged to Mr. George. *What a fucking snake*, she thought. She decided not to tell Amy this since she wanted to protect the journalist as much as she could.

"You have to be more careful moving forward, Amy. Lenny is onto you now, and I fear that with me coming to the station today, he'll know we're working together."

"I know, and I'm sorry. I didn't know who else to call."

"You were right to call me, don't get me wrong. It's just…" Stacy tapped her nails on the side of her coffee cup, remembering the two times Lenny's thugs had attacked her. This was no longer a workplace rivalry. He'd put her and her clients in danger. She was beginning to feel way over her head. Maybe it was time to talk to her father and get help. *Or the next thing I know, me, Amy, Lora, or Mr. George will be found dead in a ditch.*

Amy's voice broke through Stacy's thoughts. "What should I do now?"

"Lay low. You can do your work, but no more trailing Lenny. If you have other projects you can work on in the meantime, do those."

Amy gave Stacy a tired smile. "Thank you. I hope you know that if there's ever something you need, I want to help. You saved my ass today."

Stacy returned the smile. "There might be a time one day, Amy. I'm sure I'll need you to save my ass, too."

Khan sat at the desk in his study, the soap opera playing on TV reduced to minimal volume. It comforted him to have shows on throughout the day, especially without staff in the house. It grew lonely when he was the only one there.

His desk was large enough for several people to work at, but it was only him, surrounded by piles of papers yellowed with age, ink wells, quills, and miscellaneous trinkets he had collected over the years. He had old pocket watches and small clocks, sleek knives with ivory handles, music boxes that played haunting tunes, wooden pipes carved centuries ago, and a dozen other things.

Khan, normally a man of order, kept his desk anything but orderly. His hand passed over a document as his phone rang. He answered with a simple "Hello?" without bothering to introduce himself. Only those in his innermost circle had this number.

The caller's words on the other end were so low they were nearly inaudible.

A fire crackled in the hearth behind Khan, warming his back as the caller's message washed over him.

Though no one was there to see him, Khan kept his face a canvas of contemplation, intent on making his response measured yet noncommittal. "Yes, I hear you. Mm-hmm." His voice betrayed no emotion. "Thank you for calling. I'll talk to you later." He hung up, and a deep sigh escaped him. He felt the weight of the brief interchange like heavy stones placed on his shoulders.

Khan's unfocused gaze passed over the television and wandered to the windows. Rose bushes pressed against the panes wet with the residue from morning rain. The downpour had dissipated, and the roses glistened with drops of water. The sky was still overcast, and it would not be long before night arrived. Khan was glad for the fire, both for the warmth and the disruption to the silence.

Finally, resolving something within himself, he arose and strode through the grand hallway of his house, examining the art arranged there years ago. It was the one part of the house he had maintained himself. The rest had been arranged by his butler, various staff members, and former Drakethorns who had lived here long before he was born.

Much of the art had been put up before he arrived, but he had added to the collection. Each piece meant something and was valuable beyond words, both in price and emotionally. He eyed a photo of his daughter on the day she graduated, and a hint of a smile tugged at his lips. He had been so disappointed when he learned of her plans, but pride still swelled inside him. "My dear Anastasia," he murmured, passing the photo and directing his gaze to the large portrait at the end of the hall.

The stunning painting of his late wife always generated a fresh ache within him. His expression softened. He approached the painting as if the person in it was truly standing there, not confined by oils on a canvas. "I honored your request to hide while our daughter was growing up, Catherine. Believe it or not, she has grown up. Those years went by far too quickly. I wish I had…well, treasured them more." He chuckled. "Treasured is a funny word for people like you and me to use, right?"

The painting stared at him. Catherine Drakethorn had laughter in her eyes. She did not reply. Of course she didn't.

Khan continued anyway. "She's ready to change the world as we once dreamed." His voice dropped to a whisper, tinged with pride and concern. He'd hated the idea of this day coming. Not because he believed Stacy couldn't do it but because he had wanted to shield her from it as long as he could.

That shielding had been the downfall of their relationship. Khan had wrestled with himself for the past several years about what he could have done differently. The strain between him and Stacy was one thing. The thought of his wife despising him for his failure was another wound.

"Now, I fear it is time she knows the full truth." His gaze lingered on the painting. He remembered the day it was done. Catherine had sat in his study with the afternoon light pouring over her. She'd had laughter in her eyes, a pleasant smile gracing her perfect lips. She had been as beautiful as ever then, and Khan wanted to preserve that memory of her forever. She had been pregnant but not so pregnant that it showed in her portrait.

His wife had not known for certain she would have a daughter, but she always called the baby her "little girl." "My little Anastasia. I want you to name her that, Khan."

"*We* will name her that, if you insist."

He had not known then what Catherine suspected—that she would be gone before she had a chance to know her little girl. His heart ached at the memories. Tears pressed into his eyes, and he batted them away. *Now is not the time for emotion,* he told himself.

He reached for a small, hidden catch by the painting. It swung open silently, revealing a nondescript wooden door. Khan turned the knob. A yawning passage of darkness greeted him, along with a cold draft.

It had been some time since he last delved into this area beneath his house. He strode down the passage, his vision becoming used to the darkness. He approached another door, this one made of more solid materials. It shimmered with energy and secret substances even Khan could not name. This door had been here long before he was born, much like the house and the many things inside it.

Khan pressed his hand to the center of the door. A red light flared around it, then turned green. A synthetic voice filled the passage. "Drakethorn DNA recognized. Permission granted." The click of the door unlocking sounded, and it opened. Stone stairs stretched before him.

He inhaled deeply before descending into a world away from the one above.

CHAPTER NINE

"Wolves, vampires, dragons—these are but three of many creatures who roam the world. The were-shifters have been among us for longer than we can tell. They will remain with us for longer than we foresee. They are hidden, and we know not how to see them."
—*Unknown*, The Book of Were Creatures and Shifters

When Khan entered the room at the bottom of the stairwell, lights flickered to life around him. Making it happen was as easy as snapping his fingers. His brows drew together as he drank in the sights. It was cold down here, and the dozens of lit candles in the room did little to help.

The space was more like a cavern with stone walls and ceiling surrounding him. An array of rugs covered the floorboards. Some were hand-woven, others were animal skins. All were quite old. Books lined the walls on wooden shelves, surrounded by many small trinkets and relics he had either collected over the years or were already here when he first came.

A long stone table stretched through the center of the room with chairs arranged around it. If Khan stared long enough, he could almost see the vague outlines of the people who used to occupy those chairs on nights when they held secret meetings here. He could have sworn he almost glimpsed his late wife's ghost sitting at the head of the table in his seat, wearing a knowing smile with a look of warning.

Dust and cobwebs covered everything. Khan felt a weight in his chest. It had been years since he last ventured into this space. The emotion it caused him would've been almost too much to bear. "Well, I'm here," he murmured into the space as if his wife truly did sit at the table. The chair was empty, though. If she had been here, she would have risen, saying, "About time, Khan."

"I know you've waited long enough," he whispered toward the vacant chair. Still, Khan sensed he was not alone. He turned, his gaze alighting on the person who had crept down the stairs after him, no doubt wondering where the hell he was going and why she had never known about this room in their old house.

Khan gave his daughter a sad smile. "Hello, Anastasia."

He'd known she would come back to visit soon. He had guessed she was in more trouble than she'd let him know about and would come to him when she met the end of her rope. He had wanted to wait until she asked for his help, not force it upon her as he would have done a few years ago.

She looked tired. Her face was paler than normal, and dark circles shaded the spaces beneath her eyes. She cast those bright green eyes flecked with gold—*his* eyes—around the room. Her shock was evident in her face and her voice. "Dad? What is all this?"

Stacy had never been good at swallowing her pride, but as she sat in the driver's seat of her car, hands clenching the wheel, she knew she had to do it. She'd started driving out to the Drakethorn estate as soon as her meeting with Amy concluded.

Her father would want to know why she had taken money out of the reserve account and who she was bailing out of jail.

Stacy was afraid to move forward without support, while Lenny grew more audacious with his movements. *What a fucking prick*, she thought as she turned out of the city and headed north. When would he stop being a pain in her ass?

At her family estate, she would be safe, at least. Well, safer than she was in the city. It was a drizzly day, matching her mood. Stacy drove in dismal quiet, accompanied only by the patter of rain on her windshield and the whirring of her thoughts.

The Drakethorn estate came into view much sooner than she anticipated. Normally, dread made time stretch for her. Today, it went by too fast. She inhaled deeply as she parked the car in front of the house and bolted for the front door to avoid as much of the rain as possible. She knocked, but no response came. She tried the knob, and to her surprise, the door was unlocked. It wasn't like her father to leave his house so accessible.

She stepped into the hallway, careful not to drip rainwater on the floorboards. That was one easy way to piss off her father. The house sat in strange silence, seeming empty. "Dad?" she called. No answer came, and his staff did not appear to be back yet.

Her brows furrowed as she noticed something different about the hallway. Her mother's portrait at the end of the hall was no longer attached to the wall but swinging open, revealing a doorway. "What the fuck?" she breathed, edging toward it. She didn't care about dripping water anymore.

She found a hallway and, at the end, another open door. She descended those stairs, catching sight of glimmering candlelight and her father's back. What was this place, and why the hell was he down here? Why hadn't she ever known about this before?

She had often hidden in the family cellar during games of hide and seek or when her father had company she wanted to avoid. The way into the cellar was from a stairwell in the kitchen, though, not here. She thought this might be attached, but after reaching the bottom of the stairs, she realized it was a whole new space altogether.

Stacy took in the sight of the cavernous room and all its contents. Khan turned to her as if knowing she had followed him down here. He wore a sad smile. Shock was written all over her face as she turned her gaze from a wall full of books to meet his eyes. "Dad? What is all this?"

Khan gestured to the chairs as if he would suggest they have a seat, then remembered how dirty everything was and thought better of it. His low voice rumbled toward her. "This is where the Drakethorns have been gathering for years, Stacy. I knew you would be coming to me soon, and..." He hesitated, his eyes going everywhere but to her. "I think it is time you knew the truth."

Stacy crossed her arms, feeling indignant before he'd begun. "What do you mean 'the truth,' and why now?"

Khan's eyes met hers. "Anastasia..."

He always called her that when he was being serious. Well, so was she. Still, the sound of "Anastasia" instead of her nickname grated her nerves.

He went on. "There are things in this world, in our blood, that are far older and more complex than you can imagine. I've told you bits and pieces over the years, hoping you would one day put the full picture together for yourself, but then..." He shook his head as if not wanting to say the rest. "You left."

The words dropped like stones in water. He sounded bereaved but not angry. Disappointed, maybe, but not condescending or as if she had done anything wrong. That was a first. Years ago, when she first told him she was moving into the city, he had called her a traitor. Stacy couldn't figure out whether she felt disarmed or something else. She lifted a brow. "What pieces?" she ventured.

He beckoned for her to follow him to the far end of the room as he replied. "I told you stories of magic and all sorts of creatures while you grew up. Perhaps you thought they were fairy tales, but much of what I told you was the truth. An ancient truth, yes, and a lot of it legend, but real nonetheless." He halted with his back to her, hands locked together behind him. Before him was a landscape painting of a cliffside under an overcast sky, a sea churning far beneath it.

The longer Stacy looked at it, the more it changed until the whole image morphed from a landscape to scribbles of lines and words cascading from one another. The faint outline of a tree glimmered behind it. The words were…

"Are those names?" she asked, catching sight of hers near the bottom. *Anastasia Catherine Drakethorn.* Above her were two other names linked with a small drawing of a heart. *Constantine Edward Drakethorn. Catherine Diana Drakethorn.*

My mother, Stacy thought, fingertips tracing her name. A small jolt of something warm entered her fingers, and she drew them away. Her father had mentioned magic. Was that how the painting formed into this?

The branches of the family tree intertwined with a vague timeline, revealing dates stretching back to the Roman empire and key figures Stacy had learned about in school. The names of the Drakethorns shimmered and glowed as if written there with magic. *Or a super-cool glittery pen,* she thought.

Finally, Khan's words rumbled out. "The Drakethorn legacy is not simply a lineage. It's a guardian's vow to protect the world from shadows."

Stacy tore her eyes from the parchment family tree, settling her gaze on Khan with surprise and indignation. She had about a hundred questions and didn't know where to start. "I don't know what the fuck this is." She waved a hand at the parchment. "But I sure as hell want you to start being serious. No jokes. No more of your stupid stories. I'm not a child anymore."

The pain in his green eyes made Stacy wish she could eat her words. She glanced again at her mother's name, linked to Khan's, and it softened her anger, replacing it with a pained curiosity.

"I am being serious," came Khan's low response.

"What…are you, Dad?"

"What are *we*?" he corrected. "The Drakethorns have been a powerful family since the dawn of their existence in ancient times. We've held kernels of magic the world was built with and have shaped events throughout history as a result. There is much I could tell you, things that would take days and days to explain. I don't want it to be too much for you."

It already felt like too much. The word "magic" clanged around in her skull.

She struggled to decide what to ask next, but she couldn't take her eyes off her mother's name. "My mother, was she part of this too?" She waved a hand about the room. "Whatever this is?"

Khan's eyes glazed over with a tearful glimmer, and he nodded. "Your mother was the bravest and most powerful witch I've ever known."

Witch.

Stacy felt like something heavy had been dropped onto her shoulders with that word.

"Losing her was losing part of myself," Khan managed, voice thick with emotion. His sounding like that was more surprising than the revelations coming from his mouth.

What did it mean for her mother to be a witch? Stacy diverted to humor, wanting to avoid the emotion she saw in her father's face welling up in herself. "My mom never seemed like the old hag type who rode around on a broomstick and wore a pointed hat."

Khan chuckled despite himself. "No, she wasn't like that. She belonged to a coven and wielded magic gifted to her from other realms. She had a way with spirits, too. Some called her the Spirit Whisperer. She could calm unwanted spirits with a few words or a gentle song. She was quite useful to our endeavors."

Whatever the hell that meant. Stacy hoped her mother hadn't

been used, that she had chosen whatever a life marrying a Drakethorn entailed.

She sank into one of the nearby chairs, not caring about the dust. She couldn't stand anymore, not with a hundred questions weighing her down.

"I know this is a lot to process at once, Ana—" Khan halted himself. "Stacy. I want to answer everything as best as I can, but…"

She eyed him again. "Why keep the full truth from me? Why tell me *any* of this now?"

His face shadowed. "I wanted to protect you. I want to protect you now, too. I know you've run into some trouble, whatever that might be, and knowing the truth might help you."

Stacy's brows furrowed. How could that be?

He gestured for her to follow him to the opposite wall, where a pedestal separated the bookshelves. Upon it sat a very old book. Khan blew and wiped off the dust.

Stacy's brows rose. "Are those snake scales binding it?"

"Not quite," Khan replied. "Try something bigger."

She whipped her head toward him. "There's no way."

He nodded.

"Are they *real*?"

Khan smiled. "Yes. Real dragon, real scales."

Stacy wasn't sure she wanted to know how that was possible.

"These are from the soft areas," Khan added. "The main scales are too big and hard to use. Though for armor, they can—" He stopped himself, not wanting to overwhelm his daughter.

Whoa, dragon armor? her mind echoed. *Do I want to know?* How did he know, and how did one obtain dragon scales from the "soft parts?"

Khan continued, his voice shifting from one he used in natural conversation to something deeper. He sounded like a storyteller reciting a tale he'd told many times before. "Our ancestors have shaped the hidden magical society, fought wars in the silence of history, and kept balance where there could have been chaos."

Stacy had the distinct feeling she had heard those words before, probably uttered by her father over her as she fell asleep. Her finger hovered over the tome, a spark of energy connecting her to the legacy she never knew she had. Without meaning to, she touched it. A jolt, something hot and sharp, went into her finger.

"Ow!" She sucked on it as if burned, and the pain disappeared. Odd. It didn't work like that with normal burns.

Overwhelmed and on the brink of a breakdown, she stated, "It's like I'm living in a storybook. How the hell am I supposed to accept this?" She met her father's eyes, half pleading and half searching for answers or any sign she belonged to the world of shadows and legends he spoke of. She felt like she'd been handed four corners of a puzzle but no other pieces.

"Come upstairs with me," Khan suggested. "We can talk in more comfortable seats."

Stacy followed him in a daze, and it wasn't until she sat in his study with a warm fire crackling before her that she began to wrap her mind around everything. Khan selected a book from the mantle. It was old, but not as old as the one bound in dragon scales downstairs. He still hadn't explained what that book was.

She touched the leather-bound book on her lap, trying to make out the faded words.

"That book can tell you all about the various creatures who have roamed this world since the beginning," her father told her. "It's a good starting point."

Well, she had to start somewhere.

Khan sat opposite her, eyes glimmering with old wisdom. "Many supernatural beings have existed in our world for centuries. Ages, even, though most have managed to stay hidden either by keeping to secluded areas or blending in with the world."

"Like you?"

Khan nodded. "Like me." A weighted pause, then, "World governments have been aware of a few beings for some years. Mainly witches, a few fae, and the occasional shifter. They track them the way they would terrorists, so many hide as well as they can. The covens that do exist in our country do not cooperate with the government and are punished when found out. Anyone else with magic is closely monitored if the governing forces happen to discover them. We prefer that doesn't happen."

"Are there any magic users who work with and in the government? I mean, what's a better way to blend in than by doing that?"

"You're right. Some do, but most work alongside the government in less-than-good ways. Under the guise of Black Hat operations, as one example."

Stacy felt like her head might spin off her neck. She was hesitant to ask again, but she dared to speak. "And…what are you?"

Khan swallowed but did not answer her directly. "Werewolves and vampires are known to the government, but the existence of other were creatures, including dragons, remains a secret."

Earlier, the word "witch" had made Stacy feel like she was teetering on a tightrope. Hearing her father say the word "dragon" felt like being pushed off a cliff edge.

Her father continued. "There are only seven dragons left in the world, though I do not know where the other six are."

Other six. Stacy sat back, eyes wide. It couldn't be. How?

Khan nodded, reading the realization on her face. "Yes. None have been seen for a long time." He paused as if deciding if he should continue. "The last dragon, the ancient Red Dragon named Constantine Drake, was last sighted in 1666 in The Białowieża Forest."

"What the fuck? How old are you? How old am *I*?"

"You are twenty-six."

"And you?"

"I am quite old, Anastasia."

Stacy's blood thrummed. He looked good for...well, however old he was. 1666 made him at least a few centuries, but it was possible he had lived long before that, too. *I'm fucking dreaming. I have to be.*

"I have a long and storied past I can tell you more about later," Khan continued as if what he'd said was as simple as declaring what the weather would be tomorrow. "I've spent centuries building my empire. For years, I traveled the world with the other dragons, but we split due to unfortunate circumstances. I've been laying low since then. Eventually, I met and married a powerful witch named Catherine Thorn. Together, we formed the Drakethorn family with you, our only child, to grow up and take on our legacy."

"Fuck," Stacy breathed.

"I wish you wouldn't use that word."

Stacy glared at her father, her mind going back to one word he'd used. *Eventually.* What did that mean? Had her mother been centuries old, too? Had they been married a hundred years before she was born?

A tense silence passed between them until Stacy finally asked, "What am I? A witch or a..." She couldn't make the word "dragon" leave her tongue.

"I don't know. You never manifested powers as a child. I suspect you might soon, though. I wanted to tell you in case something happened and the wrong people bore witness."

Stacy's heart pounded faster. She stood, blood rushing to her head. "Is that the time?" The sun had gone down. Their conversation had taken longer than she thought. It was easier to leave, easier to run away and make sense of all this shit later. She had come for help and gotten what? A load of bullshit? Was this her father's way of confusing her into his good graces?

"Wait," Khan pleaded, also standing. He returned to the mantle, opened a box, and drew out a sealed envelope. He handed it to Stacy. "This is for you. It's a letter from your mother."

Stacy stared at it, then took it, stuffing it into her purse.

She was halfway to the door when she thought of another question. "If all this is true, why the hell leave the door unlocked?" She waved a hand at their general surroundings. "Don't you have immortal enemies or some shit you want to keep your secrets from?"

Khan nodded. "Of course." She had been half joking, but he was serious. "But the grounds are warded. They always have been. Only those with the warder's blood—myself—and those I choose can gain access without complications."

"Right. Of course." Stacy didn't know what to think. She turned, shutting the door behind her, and fled into the night. She sensed her father watching her from the window, sadness written on his face.

Stacy felt like she was in a dream the whole drive home, then while walking into her apartment. Her clean, minimalistic, and simply decorated living space felt sterile and dull compared to where she had been. The clutter of her father's house, especially the secret room she'd discovered for the first time today, had spoken of a long and detailed legacy. Her apartment only showed her vague interests over the past few years.

She sat on the edge of her bed and pulled the letter from her purse. Her hands trembled as she held it. What had her mother written to her and when? She didn't want to read it. She wasn't sure she could handle any more of the truth tonight. She rose, legs wobbling more than she liked, and wandered toward the window where she overlooked the city, arms folded. She kept the letter clutched in one hand as if it were a lifeline.

The city sprawled out, lights filling the space beneath a cloudy sky. How many magical creatures and people lived in New York City now, blending in and hiding in plain sight? *Am I one of them?* she wondered.

Stacy certainly had never thought she possessed a shred of magic. She wondered how many people she had helped as a lawyer and if any had been keeping a secret like that. Further, she conjectured there might have been enemies she'd faced in a courtroom with the same secrets. Her heart thudded faster. *Am I in danger?*

She didn't mean Lenny and the thugs he'd sent after her, though she now wondered if he knew more about her than she did. She'd forgotten all about Lenny after finding her father's secret basement. Now, she wished she had brought it up and sought his help. It wasn't so much about money anymore as it was about protection.

I can take care of myself, she thought. Then why was there a niggling at the back of her mind that she was being stupid by keeping all this to herself? It was about more than her. She had acquaintances and friends in trouble, too.

Stacy remembered the blurry encounter in the alley from the other night. Had whatever attacked her and killed those men been a shifter or a were creature? Something else? *What if it was...*

She let the thought trail off, shaking her head. *No, it wasn't. It couldn't have been. So why do I feel guilty about something I don't remember, let alone had no fucking control over?*

The whole thing scared her. She hadn't been scared like this since she was a kid who believed monsters crept under her bed. "So much lost time, so many lies," she murmured. "How do I reconcile this?" She wasn't sure where the words came from, only that she knew to say them.

She paced back and forth, blood thrumming and restless energy building. Her reflection appeared in the window like a ghost against the city lights. The sharp feeling of betrayal stung her heart. How dare her father keep this from her until now?

Deeper down, she felt something different: compassion. He had kept this to himself for so long. Stacy knew secrets made a person lonely. It was why she felt she had to tell him.

Not tonight, though, she thought. *I need to process all the shit from today.* Bailing Amy out of jail this morning felt like eons ago. Though she was exhausted, she doubted she'd be able to find sleep tonight.

Her indignation rose. *I can't do this. I've got too much shit going on.*

The feeling fused with frustration and boiled over in anger. She crumpled the unopened letter into a ball and tossed it to the floor.

The second the paper hit the carpet, the room trembled.

"Whoa. What the hell?" Stacy steadied herself.

A book or two toppled off her nightstand. A lamp crashed from somewhere in the living room.

She froze. Was there a fucking earthquake in the city? Nothing else happened. Nothing else seemed out of place. She stared at the letter with equal amounts of horror and puzzlement. "What the hell happened?" Whatever it had been, she could not bring herself to admit it had been her fault. Breathless, she picked the letter up off the floor. She unfolded it, smoothed it out, and laid it on her dresser. Let it collect dust for all she cared.

The ring of her phone jolted her. "Hello?" Stacy answered, not bothering to check who was calling.

An urgent, worried voice reached her. "Stacy? I'm sorry to call this late, but I figured you would want to know. I found some things on Lenny. We should meet up soon. Tomorrow morning, if you can."

Stacy glanced at the clock. Amy wasn't getting any sleep either, it seemed. The time read 10:00 P.M.

She didn't want to meet at either of their homes. "I trust you would only call if necessary. We can't let that bastard get away with anything."

"I thought the same, but I'm sorry for waking you all the same," Amy replied.

"You didn't wake me." Stacy was glad she'd kept her shoes on. "What do you think about meeting right now? We could go to a bar or something and talk things over."

"Sounds good. I'll send you an address."

Stacy was out of her apartment a few minutes later. She paused when a shadow flitted across the rooftops. *Probably a bird*, she thought, but she sensed a presence somewhere. Despite having no evidence, she knew without a doubt she was being watched.

Let whoever the hell it was watch her. Stacy turned down the street toward the place where Amy wanted to meet. She pulled her coat around her, muttering, "I'm not only Stacy Drake, attorney at law. I'm Anastasia Drakethorn, and it's time to face whatever comes with that name."

She strode off into the labyrinth of the city, her silhouette merging with the darkness as her mind worked, preparing itself for the battles ahead. It was time, despite how much she didn't want to admit it, to take the battles beyond the courtroom.

CHAPTER TEN

*"In deep water I heard tell,
Of lofty dragons belching flame,
Of the hornèd fiend of Hell."*
—*Robert Graves*, Mermaid Dragon Fiend

Stacy had spent many late nights at Fred's, an all-night diner known for its strong coffee and the solace of neon-lit booths. At this hour, it felt like stepping into another dimension, but Stacy had felt like she was in another dimension since seeing her father that evening. She'd come here after midnight movie premiers with Jenna or to take the edge off the alcohol on nights out with stacks of pancakes.

She entered, hit with the smells of frying bacon and fresh coffee. Not many people were inside. The jukebox in the corner played quiet jazz. Amy sat in a corner booth, her laptop open with the blueish-white glow making her pale face look paler. Around her were scattered loose pieces of paper. She had a cup of coffee nearby, too. Since Amy had chosen this spot and many notes were scattered around, Stacy guessed she had been here since before she called.

The clattering of dishes in the kitchen and the clinking of change in the cash register provided comforting background noise. Anything was better than the dead silence of her apartment. A light rain pattered against the window. Streaks of water ran diagonally down the pane, gathering in one corner before finally falling to the street.

Stacy slid onto the other side of the booth and set her purse down. It felt heavier than normal, but she decided it was because she was tired. Amy raised her eyes to meet Stacy's, and they shared a weary but determined look. "What did you find?" Stacy asked, keeping her voice low.

"I found a lead that might expose a critical link between Mr. Dolos and an underground network." She slid a small pile of papers to Stacy. "These are names of men Mr. Dolos has been in contact with in the past several months. A few names have emails attached to them going to and from Mr. Dolos for years."

Stacy glanced over the names, not recognizing any of them. "Who are they?"

"Part of this underground network, like I said," Amy replied. "Some of them are random people, but others are...well, on domestic terrorist watch lists."

Stacy paled. Were they truly terrorists or simply magic-using people or creatures the government didn't want anyone to know about? What did they have to do with Lenny, and why were they working together?

Shit.

Stacy didn't tell Amy what she was thinking. She simply nodded before handing the papers back. "If that's true, you have to be more careful than ever. It might be worth it to give this up, Amy."

Amy's face hardened. "I'm not going to. The more I look into this, the more it confirms I'm supposed to be doing this."

"How did you get all this information?" Stacy asked.

Amy paused, hesitating, then answered, "I have other skills

I've been using that don't exactly fall under normal journalism measures."

Stacy had the sense Amy was holding back to protect herself, and she understood. It wasn't like she was keeping Amy fully in the loop herself. She decided not to push it for now. Regardless of what Amy had done, she was trying to do the right thing. "Be careful," she insisted. "And take breaks in your research when you can. We can't let something like this consume our whole lives."

Stacy knew what secrets could do to a person, how lonely they could make someone. She also knew what obsession could do. She'd seen Lenny in courtrooms, half mad with it, and assumed it was only the tip of an iceberg.

"I will," Amy replied. "I bet you and I are similar in that regard. We like to continue a job until it's finished, even if it does us in."

Stacy showed a hint of a smile. "You're right about that."

"Then I hope you will take your own advice."

Stacy almost wished she and Amy had met under different circumstances, that they had become friends not through a common enemy but more naturally around shared interests. She leaned closer. "This underground network. What do you think they're dealing in?"

Stacy considered a number of things. Drugs, trafficking, guns, or something as simple as a lot of cash. Whatever it was, it affected the city, and they needed to find a way to stop it.

Amy didn't know. "I've only found out who Lenny is in contact with and what land he's trying to obtain. It seems to link together," she explained. "Do you think we should get the law involved? I mean, not another lawyer but the police."

Stacy hadn't told Amy about the thugs who'd come after her. She shook her head. "Not right now. Not after what Lenny did to you this morning. I do have someone who can help if we need him, though." Her father's face flashed into her mind.

"Who?" Amy asked.

"Trust me on it," Stacy replied. "I don't want to tell you his name until I've asked him for help."

Amy waggled her eyebrows. "Got a boyfriend in a powerful place?"

Stacy chuckled, glad for the moment of amusement between them. "Definitely not a boyfriend."

Amy feigned a sigh. "All right, keep your secret. I'll trust you." She gathered her papers. "I'm going to take your advice and go home to rest. I hope you'll do the same."

Stacy rose with her and saw her to the door, then stepped out onto the street and into the drizzle. She shivered, pulling her coat tighter around her. She wished she had brought an umbrella.

As she thought it, Stacy's body warmed. How did that happen? She ignored it as she watched Amy walk off into the night.

Her protective instincts kicked in. She wanted to make sure Amy wasn't followed or attacked, so she decided to trail her. She followed at a safe distance, keeping close to buildings and out of sight. The reflections of streetlights danced in the puddles. The occasional car swept past, sending water onto the sidewalk. Stacy avoided it, her body remaining warm beneath her coat.

Finally, she spotted Amy entering an apartment building. She was relieved to see the woman safely inside and turned to make her way back home. Her mind remained a whirlwind of questions and theories. She wasn't sure what to think about more, Lenny or her father's revelations from earlier in the day.

It was after midnight when Stacy returned to her apartment. Her coat was covered in rainwater, so she hung it up by the door to dry. As soon as the coat was off, she shivered and went to check the thermostat. She busied herself with getting ready for bed, but the day's events would not leave her mind.

Her mind drifted between what Lenny had done to Amy that morning and what she had discovered at her old home. Then, finally, to what Amy had revealed less than an hour ago. She also considered the thugs who had chased her. First one man, then three. She paused while brushing her teeth and gave herself a long look in the mirror. She appeared tired, but something about her eyes seemed different. The green in them seemed brighter.

I'm so fucking tired, she thought, finishing with her task and putting her toothbrush away. She padded into her bedroom, her gaze falling on the city skyline. She thought of men working in an underground network and what harmful things they could be doing at this moment. Were Lenny and Victor awake right now planning something malicious? Who would find themselves a victim when dawn broke?

She couldn't make herself get into bed. Her anger, paired with every other overwhelming feeling she had acquired throughout the day, boiled over. She felt raw and unchecked. Something warm inside her stirred as if awakening for the first time. She felt it build to a near-explosive degree. Her TV stand trembled. Books dropped from nearby shelves, thumping to the carpet. A deep rumble traveled through the floors.

She froze, eyes widening in horror and realization. *There it is again! I did it. I must have.* If she had caused the minor earthquake earlier as well as this one, it wasn't too far of a stretch to assume something had happened in the alley a few days ago. Maybe she hadn't been attacked. *She* was the attacker.

She edged into bed, trembling. *Get a grip,* she told herself. *Don't panic and make this worse.* She breathed deeply, centering herself with techniques and patterns her father had taught her years ago.

The tremors and intense warmth in her body subsided, but the fear remained cold and sharp in her chest. She could no longer deny she had magical power coursing through her veins.

Why had it awakened now? What had changed for this to happen? She needed answers.

She glanced at her phone, wondering if she should…

Yes, just fucking do it.

She typed in a message to her father and sent it before she convinced herself not to.

> I want to know more. Can I come over tomorrow to work on it?

She didn't tell him what happened or what she suspected about the attack. If the government was reading her texts, the last thing she needed was to be put on their watch list. She turned onto her side, groaning. "I'm certainly not a fucking terrorist." Witch? Maybe. Dragon? She didn't want to think about it. Where had the days gone when she could simply be a friend and a lawyer?

A prickling sensation crossed the back of her neck. She turned toward the windows and peered through the streaks of rain. What the hell was that down there? She slipped out of bed and roamed toward the window, where she caught a shadowy man wearing a trench coat and hat standing on the street below. She could not make out his features. He watched her building for a minute or two as if considering something, then turned and wandered away into the rain and darkness.

A new fear pierced her. *They're here for me,* she realized. *They're waiting for their moment.*

She stepped back from the window, heart pounding. The backs of her legs hit the bed, and she sank onto it. The warm magic she had felt before stirred again, like something great and ancient inside her opening one eye. *Not now,* she told it.

She pulled the covers over her, feeling like a child again who would be safe as long as the blankets kept the monsters out. She shivered there, wishing the warmth she felt earlier would come again.

Her phone buzzed with a message. Khan's reply was short.

KHAN
I'll be here.

A swell of gratitude passed through her. *I guess tomorrow I'm Stacy Drake, attorney at law, and Anastasia Drakethorn, daughter of a fucking dragon shifter.* The idea was so ridiculous that she nearly laughed. So much was on her mind that she did not think she would find slumber, but the day's exhaustion won over, and she slipped into blissful darkness.

The hum of activity in the law office was background noise to Stacy as she worked the following morning. She had her office door closed for privacy and quiet. It didn't matter much, though, because people popped in and out of her office all morning. Jenna swung by with a muffin and to ask how she was doing. Stacy forced her best smile, hoping her friend would not guess she was troubled. "Everything's good, Jenna. Thanks."

Jenna frowned. "You still owe me an explanation about what happened last week."

"Good things come to those who wait," Stacy chirped.

"You've picked one of the most impatient people in the world to be your friend." Jenna glowered, then raised a coffee cup to her lips. "Oh, well. Keep your secrets. You are stressed, though." She waggled her eyebrows as she lowered her cup. "Maybe you need a boyfriend or a one-night stand to take off the edge."

Stacy shot her a look. "I don't think so. I don't—"

"Have time for it. I know, I know." Jenna grinned. "I remember the slew of almost-boyfriends you blew off in college so you could study."

"I had to pass. Look at where I am now."

Jenna shrugged. "I passed and had time for guys." She cocked her head. "You could call one up. A few of them stayed in the city. How about that one nerdy guy, Jonathan? He's not the hottest of the bunch, but he sure knew how to—"

"Can we not do this right now?"

Jenna flashed a smile. "I'll see you at lunch."

After that, associate attorneys and interns drifted through, looking for resources and papers or seeking to ask questions. For a few hours, Stacy was able to forget about most of her troubles. At one point, she searched for a document regarding Mr. George's case and couldn't find it. She groaned, slapping her palm to her forehead. "I hope I didn't leave it at home!"

She had awakened that morning feeling groggy and out of sorts, almost like the not-hangover she'd had the other day after dealing with the three thugs in the alley. She had forced herself out the door regardless. It had taken a cup and a half of coffee to shake the feeling off. She had been frazzled, too, with thoughts of the previous day whirling around her head. It was no wonder she had forgotten some of her paperwork.

Stacy reached for her purse and dug around, looking for the folder. Instead, her hands landed on something smooth and leathery. Frowning, she pulled out the worn leather book her father had handed her when she was at his house. The one about magical creatures with the title so worn she could hardly make it out.

What the hell was it doing inside her purse? Her father must have slipped it inside when she was in a hurry to leave. It was like him to leave a silent command like this. He intended for her to read the book.

Stacy sighed, but she was too curious to put it back. Maybe it would give her answers. She opened to the first page and found it yellowed and crinkled with age. The words were in a language she did not know. It didn't look familiar in any way. Was it a magical language? If so, why the hell had her father thought she could read it?

She flipped through, hoping something in English would pop up. She found several pages with drawings. One had thirteen robed women standing in a circle, a pentagram drawn in the ground between them, and trees rising in the background. The illustration had been drawn with charcoal or a very old pen.

"Witches," Stacy murmured. The women had their eyes closed and palms open, fingers laced together. Something about the image felt haunting and beautiful at the same time.

She turned to other pages and found one of a human shifting into a wolf, his back arching in agony as the transformation overtook him. "No, thank you," she murmured. Was it the same for dragon shifters?

She felt like a child who had stolen away to read a book of fairytales instead of focusing on math problems like they were supposed to. She couldn't help but glance through the book longer despite not knowing what it said. Finally, she came across words she could read. One page had margins full of cramped notes. These were almost as faded as the actual text, showing similar age.

Stacy's fingers traced the notes, wondering if she'd feel a jolt of magic. She didn't. She scanned the words.

What this book misses are the details surrounding a were creature's coming into their magic. One who possesses kernels of magic this world was built with may one day find it awakening within them.

Sometimes, it occurs gradually, forming over many years and giving the person time to adjust and control their innate power. In other circumstances, the magic may lay dormant for a long time, then suddenly erupt into existence with a series of unpleasant side effects and small disasters. When this happens, the shifter may find their surroundings collapsing or small earthquakes occurring with the slightest outburst of emotion.

It is imperative for the person experiencing this to seek help and control over their—

She ceased reading when footsteps sounded outside her

office. She snapped the book shut and was shoving it back into her purse when the door swung open, and a bright-eyed associate attorney peeked in. "Ms. Drake? I was wondering if you would look over this document for me."

Stacy pasted on a smile. "Sure, set it here on my desk. When do you need it back?"

"By five, please."

"No problem."

The attorney closed the door, and Stacy was left alone again. Something about being caught reading that book made her feel uneasy, so she vowed not to look at it more until later. She checked her watch and realized she had a few hours before meeting her father at the family estate.

Maybe he could help her figure out how to read the book, though the last thing she wanted were more language lessons like the ones she had endured growing up. Latin was one thing, but an ancient language that had nothing to do with English and was rooted in magic…

"I don't think so," Stacy murmured, returning to the work before her. She couldn't stop thinking about the notes she had read, though. They hadn't been in her father's handwriting, so who wrote them? The description in the notes was exactly like what she'd experienced the night before. Magic was awakening inside her. She was turning into something new and different. *Or it's been there all along, and I'm only now beginning to realize it,* she thought.

She downed the rest of her coffee, knowing she'd need all of it to get through today.

CHAPTER ELEVEN

"The poets, historians, and songwriters have long spoken of our kind. Some of their sayings, proverbs, and songs tell the truth; it is but a shred of the whole. We have done well in hiding the parts of ourselves that would make us monsters to them."

—*Unknown*, The Book of Were Creatures and Shifters

Stacy strolled across the grounds of the estate, looking for her father. His last message to her as she drove out of the city was that he would meet her outside. That was a broad scope, given how much land was on the Drakethorn estate. However, it did not take her long to catch sight of him. He stood at the edge of a forest that stretched over most of the property, his back to her and hands in front of him.

She wound her way down the path through a garden and a small orchard, then a space of trimmed grass and nothing else until she reached his side. The walk was long enough that she was out of breath by the time she halted. At least she'd had the common sense to put aside her work clothes and heels before coming here. She had traded them for athletic wear and gym shoes.

Khan glanced sidelong at her. "You won't be wearing that."

Stacy glowered. "Hello to you too, Dad."

"You will need proper fighting clothes."

"Fighting?" She gaped at him.

He nodded, then unfolded his arms to reveal garments draped across them. They looked far too small for her, but Khan handed them over anyway. "Boots, too." He picked them up off the ground.

Stacy thought about arguing, especially since she had to climb back up the hill to the house to change, but she refrained. After she changed, she was surprised to find the fighting leathers, vest, and boots fit her perfectly. They hugged her every curve, providing warmth or cooling sensations depending on what she needed. The whole thing thrummed and made her skin feel pleasant. She had no doubt magic was threaded inside it.

When she returned to her father, he turned, smiling with a hint of sadness and longing in his eyes. "You look…"

Stacy arched a brow. "Let me guess. Just like my mother?"

Khan swallowed. "That was hers, you know." He gestured at her clothes.

Stacy didn't know how to respond, but it didn't matter because Khan continued before she could. He motioned toward the trees. "We'll train in there."

"Why?" Stacy asked. "Don't tell me there's another secret underground place beneath the forest."

A hint of a smile touched Khan's lips. "No. This is a place where our dragon sides won't attract prying eyes."

Stacy stiffened when he said "our" but decided it wasn't worth bringing up.

Khan started down a path leading into the forest, and Stacy saw no choice but to follow. Trees towered over her, old and rich with life. The branches spread overhead, creating a canopy blocking most of the sky. Still, sunlight found its way in, alighting on fallen logs and large stones protruding from the ground among lower vegetation. The narrow, rutted path wound through as if no person or animal had traversed it in quite some time. Now and then, she caught sight of wildlife. Birds, squirrels, chipmunks.

She had not ventured into these trees since she was a child and came here to play or hide. This didn't feel like either now. "I own the whole forest," Khan informed her. "About fifty miles of it span from where we are now to the border to the south."

Stacy gaped and cast a glance behind her shoulder. They had already walked about a mile. "Why so much land?"

Khan gave her a knowing look. "I cannot always stay in this shape, Stacy. To do so would cause me to eventually be stuck in my human skin."

Would that be so bad? Stacy thought. She was still coming to grips with the fact that her dad was a dragon and couldn't help admitting it was hard.

Khan's face softened. "I know, but I hope that by learning all this, you can get some help."

Right. Help. It was why she had come.

"You're probably wondering why I haven't told you what has been going on."

"I didn't want to force it out of you," her father replied.

Well, that was a change, and a good one if he meant it. Stacy chose to leave out the bits about Lenny and Victor, deciding to discuss it another time. It was better to focus on what was changing inside her.

She told him about the three thugs pursuing her, citing that she had been in a dangerous area, which was true, and leaving out the part where her rival in the workplace had sent them after her. She explained how she had lost her memory after ducking into the alley and what she had seen on the news. She mentioned the small earthquakes from last night.

Khan listened with thoughtful bemusement as they continued. He walked the path as if he had done so a thousand times before. Maybe he had. When Stacy finished, she added, "So, there it is. Your daughter went off to the big city and fucked up bigtime, exactly what you said would happen."

A hardness came into Khan's face, but he didn't feed into her self-deprecation. "Everything you have told me about how your body is changing is normal for the transition you are going through. I wish I had told you before so you could have better prepared for it."

Stacy's gait slowed. "I feel horrible about what happened if it was me who attacked those men. They were pricks, and there's no telling what they might have done to me, but..."

She wasn't a murderer.

Khan settled a weighted look on her, then replied with the soft wind joining his voice in the trees. "It was your dragon side that attacked and shredded those men, Stacy, not you at your core. It's like you said. You don't remember it. You didn't make the choice."

Stacy wasn't convinced. She folded her arms tightly and rubbed them above her elbows like she was cold, though she wasn't. The clothing made sure her body stayed at an even temperature. "Shouldn't I be staying the hell away from magic, then?"

Khan shook his head. "That's not possible anymore. It is part of who you are, and if you do not accept it and get it under control, it will overtake you."

Cold fear doused her. Could she be capable of worse actions than what she'd done in the alley? She thought it was high time to turn the conversation away from herself. "What do you look like when you're in your...other form?"

Khan's eyes glittered. "I haven't seen myself in a mirror, though I have flown over rather large lakes and gotten glimpses of myself. I'm red, for one."

"I guessed that." He was called the Red Dragon. Were the

others named after colors, too? Was there a rainbow dragon? Stacy buzzed at the thought of flying.

"I won't be taking my shape today," Khan assured her. Stacy wasn't sure if she felt disappointed or relieved. "Depending on who wrote about me, I could be described as death incarnate or a fuzzy, if large, pet."

Stacy arched a brow. "Who wrote that about you? The fuzzy pet thing, I mean."

Khan's lips twitched. "Your mother. She was influenced by her feelings for me, though."

"Right." Stacy shook her head, fighting off a smile. "So, if you're not going to show me your full dragon glory, what are we going to do?"

"It will be quite some time before you are able to take on the full form of a dragon, Stacy."

Thank God, she thought.

"That doesn't mean you can't use the power manifesting inside you in a human body."

"So we're training today?"

"Yes. This won't be like the self-defense I taught you when you were younger. You will let your magic well up. You're safe here to make the ground rattle and whatnot. I want you to learn to control what comes out of you."

"With breathing patterns or something?"

"Not quite." Khan gestured to a wide clearing they had reached. "Stand in the center there."

Stacy gave him a questioning look but did as he commanded. She stood where she thought the center was.

"Close your eyes and sense what is around you. This forest is rich with magic. Let it flow through you like your blood does. It might awaken your magic."

His suggestion sounded better than letting herself get so emotional that she erupted.

She closed her eyes. The wind was soft. The rustle of the

leaves around her was gentle to her ears. The warm sun made her want to lie down and take a nap among the moss and vines. Instead, she listened to the thrum of her body until a new kind of warmth threaded through her. It started as a faint tingling sensation, then increased until it felt like a new layer of something in her veins.

"Anything?" her father asked.

"Is magic supposed to feel like pins and needles but nice?"

He chuckled. "Good magic does."

Was there bad magic?

Stacy didn't ask. Her mind began to feel foggy.

"Focus," her father told her. "When you open your eyes, you'll need to move quickly. Give in to your magical instinct. Don't be afraid of it. Most importantly, rein it in when you need to."

"I don't know what that means."

"You will."

Stacy began to grumble something, but then a cold gust of wind blew over her. She opened her eyes. Khan was nowhere to be seen, and the sun had disappeared behind a cloud. Everything before her was shadowed. She yelped as something hurtled out of the trees and zipped toward her head. She ducked in time, and a second object came flying toward her. She ducked lower, rolling on the ground. "What the fuck was that?"

Stacy hurried to her feet, stumbling, and lurched from the clearing as a third object went past. This time, she got a glimpse of what was attacking her. Someone—or *something*—was hurling spears wreathed in magic.

Instead of feeling cold fear, she sensed burning indignation. "Not funny, Dad."

Something snapped from the brush behind her, snaking around her ankles so quickly she didn't have time to realize it until she crashed to the ground, landing on her front and emitting a low groan.

Stacy whipped her head to find vines digging into her ankles.

She struggled away, tearing with her hands until she was free. Something in the wind hissed to her. *Run if you want to make it.*

Make it where? Out alive?

She gritted her teeth and bolted. She was certain now that her father had set these traps to train her. As long as she evaded them, she would pass. She zigzagged through the trees as more spears hurtled toward her. She stumbled over a root at one point, falling to her face and earning a few cuts and scratches.

The vines on the ground took the opportunity to attack by snaking around her. Stacy battled them away, scrambling up again and continuing on. The magic inside her grew warmer. It welled up like a wave, beginning to crest. Her mind felt muddled.

Focus!

She wasn't sure if the command was from her father or herself. It had the same voice. The trees grew blurry and dark. *What the fuck is happening?* she wondered. If she slipped too far into her magic, she would forget what was happening. She would lose all control. It was the last thing she wanted. She remembered what her father said about reining her magic in, but she still didn't know how to do it.

What if I tug on it? she thought and reached inside her. She felt the searing warmth of her magic like bundles of threads floating through her. She gathered enough in an invisible hand and tugged. They moved. She felt her head becoming clearer. *It worked!*

Her feet carried her onward as if driven not by her brain but something else. The magic felt…good. She had not expected that. She was on the edge of victory and euphoria when she slammed into something hard. Her head throbbed as she stepped back, blinking. "What the…"

She glanced in front of her, but nothing other than the trees stood there. She had not run into one. She reached out a hand and felt something hard and smooth, though she still couldn't see it.

"The wards," a voice rumbled. She turned to see her father behind her.

"I thought you said because I had your blood, the wards wouldn't be in my way."

His eyes glittered, the gold flecks in them shining brighter than normal. "That was yesterday. I altered the ones on this part of the property for your training today."

"Oh, well, fuck you—"

The sentence was halfway out of her mouth when Khan whipped out a .22 and fired.

The bullet punched into her leg with force. She cried out more in shock than pain. Then, gritting her teeth, she ground, "What the fuck was that for?"

"Your mouth," he replied with enough nonchalance to make her simmer.

Stacy considered letting her magic take over and hurling every bit of it at him. Let him see what good a gun would do with that!

Khan pointed to where he had shot her. "Look."

The bullet oozed out of her body and fell with a soft *plop* onto the ground. Her magic was already driving away the pain, and her skin closed. Stacy's eyes widened. Her magic could heal her.

"You have to know what it feels like," Khan told her. "To take the knowledge that you can heal and to continue fighting. You aren't human, Anastasia. Not *fully* human, anyway."

She noticed the cuts and scratches she had acquired earlier were also healed. "Yeah, well, I might not be wounded anymore, but there's blood and dirt on my clothes."

Khan gave her a half-smile. "Your mother had a spell that could clean her clothes. I always thought it was inside the garment itself, but I see now that it wasn't."

"Would be nice if I could use it," Stacy grumbled.

The clouds moved away from the sun, but by this point, that burning star was low on the horizon, and long shadows seeped through the trees. Khan gestured for Stacy to sit with him on a fallen log and handed her a water bottle. She drank until she was gasping for air.

"I might have had a shifting form, but your mother could always outlast me," Khan mused, his eyes wistful and glazed over as they roved among the trees.

"Did you two come out here to practice and train?" Stacy asked.

"And to release built-up energy, in more ways than one." A smile tugged at the corner of Khan's mouth.

"Gross."

He chuckled. "Catherine had a contagious laugh and the fiercest spirit of anyone I ever knew. She was old, not as old as me, but she had many years on her. Yet every time she laughed or teased me, she seemed so much younger." The fondness in Khan's voice made Stacy's heart ache. "You remind me a lot of your mother. You always have. You have much of the same spirit."

They relaxed into a momentary silence, and Stacy considered what it might have been like to grow up with a powerful witch for a mother. Would she have found out sooner about her legacy? Would she have spent her teenage years in this same forest, learning how to shift and cast spells?

The thoughts generated grief for a time she had never known. She had cried a few times growing up when she thought about her mother. It had always been a sadness about never being able to know her, not one about losing her, to begin with.

Khan spoke again, his voice thick with emotion. "Though your physical abilities are remnants of my power and blood inside you, you might become adept at wielding raw magic and casting spells like your mother once did. There's nothing that doesn't say you might have witch power, too."

The concept boggled Stacy's mind.

He turned to her. "What did you feel when you were running?"

"Almost euphoric," Stacy admitted. "I started sweating, but I didn't run out of breath. My muscles didn't hurt."

"They will later."

"Great."

He chuckled. "That's what your magic does. It keeps you going in the moment so you don't get stuck in a life-or-death situation."

"Is it the same in dragon form?"

He nodded.

"Is flying like running?"

"Better."

Stacy grinned despite herself.

"As for the witch thing," Khan continued, but she interrupted him.

"One thing at a time. I can only take so much at once."

"Very well."

Stacy thought of the letter at home, the one written by her mother that she had left on her dresser. *Maybe I will read it.*

"Are we done for today?" she asked her father as she leaned her head on his shoulder.

He stilled in surprise, and his slow reply came in a gentle tone. "Yes, we can be finished for now."

Stacy raised her head to see the sun had almost disappeared. "Good, because I need a bath and something to eat."

CHAPTER TWELVE

"Deep in th' abyss where frantic horror bides,
In thickest mists of vapours fell,
Where wily Serpents hissing glare
And the dark Demon of Revenge resides,
At midnight's murky hour
Thy origin began:
Rapacious Malice was thy sire;
Thy Dam the sullen witch, Despair;
Thy Nurse, insatiate Ire."
—*Mary Darby Robinson*, Ode to Envy

Stacy stood by the water cooler as people in the office chatted and worked behind her. Jenna stood beside her. "It's so fucking cold this morning," Stacy commented. "Who the hell decided it was a good idea to turn the AC down so much? It's like they're training us for a trip to the Arctic." She pulled her cardigan tighter around her body.

"Stacy?"

"Yeah?" Stacy glanced up absently.

"Got enough water there?"

"Oh, shit!" Her cup overflowed, some of the water splashing to the floor.

Jenna laughed. Stacy tipped the cup to her lips and drank so no more would spill.

"Thirsty?" Jenna asked.

"I think I'm getting a migraine."

"Here, sweetie." Jenna rummaged in her desk drawer nearby and drew out a bottle of painkillers.

Stacy thanked her as she unscrewed the lid. A new sensation came over her, a chill creeping up her spine and making the hairs on the back of her neck stand on end. It was cold in the building today, and the pressure building behind her eyes wasn't helping.

She had been up most of the night poring over the notes left in the book on magical creatures and ignoring the letter from her mother still sitting on her dresser. Somehow, she could face what was written in a book whose author she did not know, but reading her mother's words was too much for her.

She didn't dare risk reading it in the office, so at home it was. She thought an evening of training would have done her in, but the magic inside her had its eyes open, and that meant she was awake longer than she liked. She hoped it would go away and she could return to a normal sleep cycle. For now, she'd have plenty of coffee and painkillers to fight off the headaches.

It wasn't only the cold and ache in her head, though. She had the distinct feeling she was being watched by unwanted eyes. Jenna didn't seem to notice. She was going on about something.

Stacy glanced around with no small amount of alarm on her face.

"You okay, Stacy?" Jenna asked. "You look like you're about to bolt."

Stacy turned back, deflecting with an awkward smile. "I thought I saw a…spider. That's all."

Jenna shivered. "I hate spiders. You see him, step on him for me."

"Was it making a web?" one of the interns at another desk asked.

"Does it matter?" Jenna asked him.

"Female spiders are much better at making webs. Depending on the design, maybe you shouldn't be calling it a 'him,' and—"

Stacy didn't hear the rest of his sentence. Alex was always babbling random facts no one cared about. It came in handy only when he could recite obscure laws many of them had forgotten after college. She excused herself and returned to her office, where she closed the door. In the quiet and privacy of the four walls, she sat at her desk and opened her laptop. She didn't want to use the firm-provided PC for what she was about to do.

She'd been contemplating whether she should do this all morning and finally decided that she would. "Time to put Dad's emergency fund to good use." If someone was watching her, she needed to figure out how the hell they were trailing her everywhere she went. Had they followed her out to the Drakethorn estate or caught onto the fact that she left the city every few days?

She logged onto a few tech websites, searching for someone who might be able to help her conduct a different kind of research into Leonard than she had done before.

Stacy scanned several options before it dawned on her that she probably knew someone, and she might not have to use her father's funds. She recalled what Jenna said about an almost-boyfriend from college, about knowing someone who could help and not in a sexual way.

She searched her phone for his contact. They had exchanged happy birthday texts since leaving college and seen one another on a night out once, but that had been the extent of their friendship. Would it be weird to call him for this? Stacy considered that she would have to explain her need without pulling him into a dangerous situation.

She dialed his number. A cool voice reached her on the second ring. "Well, if it isn't Stacy the Straitlaced calling at…

eleven in the morning? Don't tell me you need to be picked up from a random frat guy's house again."

"That was four years ago, Jonathan!" she hissed. "I'm at work anyway."

He chuckled. "Good to hear from you, Stacy, even if it is an odd time."

"Stacy the Straitlaced" had been her nickname in college because of how dutiful she was regarding classes, tests, and exams. She never missed a study session or a class, even when she was sick. She was the friend at parties who made sure girls weren't roofied and told shithead guys off like it was her daytime profession.

Jonathan had been a steady friend throughout those years, and they might have kissed once. Twice. Fine, three times, but they had been drunk for two of them, and the third was before they graduated, and both pretended it never happened. Stacy wasn't sure if there were feelings between them, but that wasn't why she called.

"Tell me, Jonathan, are you still a giant tech nerd?"

"I can't tell if you're being a dick or not."

Stacy grinned. "I could use your help if you are. I'll pay in Chinese food and beer."

"And here I thought I was finally getting a booty call."

They had always teased and flirted with one another shamelessly. Stacy, Jenna, and Jonathan had been a trio throughout college. They had done everything together, from bar-hopping on Fridays to study sessions throughout the week. Stacy had split her holiday time between Jonathan's family home in New Jersey and Jenna's in Boston, not wanting to return to her home.

After college, Jenna ended up at the same firm as Stacy, while Jonathan took a high-end tech job elsewhere in the city. Life had taken over, and she had only seen him once since. That time, he had a girl wrapped around him all night. Someone he was "going steady" with. If he still had that girlfriend, Stacy doubted she would be a fan of Jonathan's "booty call" comment.

"Not this time," she chirped.

"What's this about?" he asked in a serious tone.

"Can I tell you tonight when you come over?"

"Send me the address."

Stacy had chosen to take the subway to work that morning, not wanting to fight traffic for half her day. She took the subway back and had to walk a few blocks to her apartment when she got off. The city was as busy as ever, but she couldn't help feeling that among the many cars, one was trailing her.

Let's test him, Stacy thought, turning down a street in the opposite direction of her destination. The nondescript gray sedan she had noticed since exiting the subway station turned as well. She made a second turn. The sedan followed. Stacy returned to the street that led to her apartment. With how many encounters she'd had, she guessed they knew where she lived. *Maybe I should find somewhere else to stay for a while,* she thought.

Where that would be, she did not know. She didn't want to worry Jenna or put her in danger, and her family estate was too far from work. She turned again and ducked into an alley. Hidden in the shadows, she watched the car pass by.

"Gotcha," she whispered as she memorized the license plate. "Should have tried harder, fellas." A slight smile played on her lips. She didn't see how she could go to the police. They wouldn't do a damn thing about it. Still, having the information would help in some way, she was sure. At the least, she could keep track of the car.

She set off toward her apartment. She remembered the food and beer she had promised, and she crossed the street to enter a Chinese takeout restaurant.

Stacy made it back to her apartment and barely had time to change clothes and set the food out before the bell rang. She smiled as she opened the door for Jonathan. "You haven't changed a single bit."

His floppy brown hair nearly hung past his brows, and he swept it aside to reveal pleasant brown eyes and a slow smile. "Hey, Stace. You haven't changed, either."

He entered with a black bag in hand and scanned her living room. "Got enough gadgets to start a spy shop, eh?" His eyebrows rose as he surveyed her setup. Her laptop wasn't the only thing she had procured for tonight. "Did I need to bring anything?"

"Only that tech wizard brain of yours."

Jonathan sighed but grinned. "You only ever wanted me for my brain."

"Careful there. You might start sounding like an incel."

"Maybe I've become one. People change after college." He sounded serious enough that Stacy had to glance at him. "I'm joking."

She handed him a beer and a takeout carton of his favorite Chinese dish. "I hope you still like this."

"I eat it every weekend. Thanks." He sat on the couch and opened the container. The scents filled her apartment.

Stacy slumped beside him, digging into her food. She didn't want him asking how she was, so she jumped in. "So tell me what's been going on in the Life of Jonathan since I last saw you."

Jonathan reported that his job paid well, and he loved it. Stacy guessed by the business casual clothes he wore that he'd come to her apartment right after work. It was a nice upgrade from the worn Star Trek T-shirts and strange-smelling Converse he wore every day in college. All he needed now was a haircut.

"Still got that girlfriend?" Stacy teased.

Jonathan's eyes glittered. "Wouldn't you like to know? But no, Brooke and I broke up. That night, actually, after I saw you last."

"I figured you were too drunk to remember seeing me."

"God, no. You were wearing that... Well, it doesn't matter."

Stacy noted the flush in his cheeks and had to fight a blush of her own.

Jonathan continued. "Anyway, she was pissed that I wouldn't move in with her, but I had just gotten a job and wanted to be close to the office. Her place was on the other side of town, and she didn't want to live where I was. She left me, and I've been okay with it ever since. What about you? Got a boyfriend?"

"I couldn't be more single if I tried," she shot back. "But I'm okay with that. My life has had plenty to keep me busy."

"Like what?" he prodded.

Stacy figured it wouldn't hurt to tell him some of it. She explained the case of Lora Denninson and two new ones she was working on now. Her trial for Mr. George would come any day now, and she'd been chipping away at a case involving a Native American tribe fighting to keep their land that had landed on her desk last week. "Plus, I'm talking to my dad again," she added.

Jonathan's brows shot up. "Whoa. Something bad must have happened."

"Not bad, exactly, and it's going all right." Stacy absently moved her fork around in the food carton. "He's not as stuck up as he used to be."

Jonathan chuckled. "I always thought you were like, this super uptight person with a stick up your ass, and you got it from your old man."

"That would be all types of painful," Stacy quipped, grinning.

Jonathan was a nice enough guy but not very suave. Not with women, anyway. Her comment made him blush. "Well, should we dive into the task at hand?" he suggested after an awkward pause.

At this point, Stacy had to admit some of the truth to

Jonathan. He had to know what he was looking for. "With these cases I've told you about, my opponents have the same lawyer. All three have to do with land being seized by someone who wants to use it for some purpose or another. These 'clients' my opposing attorney represents are all different, but I have a feeling they're posing for someone else, someone bigger who is behind it all."

"Sounds like you're dealing with a real prick," Jonathan commented.

"The prickiest of pricks. Victor Corbinelli, actually."

Jonathan raked a hand through his hair. "And you want me to do what, exactly?"

Stacy rifled through a pile of papers. They contained notes she had taken, and some Amy had sent her. She didn't mention her work with the journalist to Jonathan. The less he knew, the safer he was. The papers showed a list of shell companies, dummy accounts, and cryptic transactions. She needed help arranging the points of the web in whatever way things made sense.

"I can take a crack at it," Jonathan announced after looking everything over. His optimistic tone made Stacy feel like she had a chance to discover something. "Let me set up some of my equipment, and I'll get to work."

An hour later, he had hunted through a web of digital trails with Stacy sitting behind him, suggesting things he could try here and there. More than once, Jonathan commented on her unexpected tech-savvy side. "Don't get too savvy, though," he told her with a mock smile. "I can't have you bruising my ego by becoming better at this than me."

"I would never," she teased back. "What excuse would I have to call you?"

It felt fun to flirt and tease, though Stacy didn't want to take it any further tonight. To her surprise, many of Victor Corbinelli's actions were easily trackable online. Stacy wondered if he was leaving a dummy trail for people like her to follow. "Maybe," Jonathan hedged after she mentioned it to him. "But it's showing us things anyway. Here, look at this. Interesting, huh?"

"That *is* interesting!"

Jonathan had discovered a series of transactions and messages between Police Chief John Turnbower and Victor Corbinelli. "And here's the two in Facebook posts from years ago. Having holiday parties and all," Jonathan pointed out.

Stacy wasn't surprised to find out the city's chief of police was friends with Victor Corbinelli. Not after what had happened with Amy and how unhelpful the police had been in catching the first stalker. Stacy hadn't gone back to them since, knowing they didn't plan to help her no matter how bad things became. It was clear to her now that the police were not on her side as long as she had to deal with Lenny.

She didn't say this to Jonathan but asked instead, "The question now is, does the chief do what Victor tells him to because they're friends or because Victor is holding something over his head?"

Jonathan shrugged. "Could be both."

A few hours later, Jonathan couldn't stop yawning and rubbing his eyes. Stacy checked the time. It was nearly midnight. "Go home, Jonathan. You've been a great help."

He gave her a tired smile. "This was fun, Stace. If you ever need me again…"

"I might." She piled his arms with leftover food and beer before walking him to the door.

Before he left, Jonathan turned, his brows pulled together. "Hey, when I got here earlier, a man was sitting in a car by the building. Looked like he was watching your door. Any idea who that might be?"

Gray sedan? Stacy guessed inwardly. She forced a smile, not wanting to worry her friend. "Oh, that's my stalker. He's obsessed with me."

Jonathan's expression was serious. "Stacy…"

"Don't worry about it. I was joking. It's probably nothing."

Jonathan held her stare before nodding. "All right. If you say so." He turned to leave, then lingered a second longer, a smile breaking out across his face. "Though if you do have a stalker, I don't blame him for his choice."

Stacy shook her head, laughing. "Go home, Jonathan, before you get yourself in trouble."

She did not spot the gray sedan or any shadowy figures in the parking lot, but her protective instincts made her want to watch Jonathan until he'd driven away. After he was gone, she returned to the papers spread across her kitchen counter. She wanted to go through their findings again. They had discovered a series of places in Victor's surveillance network, but she hadn't pieced it together yet. She felt like she was on the brink of completing a full puzzle.

"I'm not seeing anything yet, though," she muttered.

Stacy settled down. Her eyes grew red and tired, but the time passed quickly. It wasn't until the soft gray light of dawn peeked through the windows that she realized she'd spent the whole night sleuthing. She was surrounded by a sea of papers, and about twenty tabs were open on her laptop.

Finally, she hit a breakthrough.

The locations of Lora Denninson's, Mr. George's, and the Native Americans she was representing were not in close proximity, but a network of underground tunnels ran beneath all their land, connecting to docks outside the city where several barges came in. "Got you now," she whispered, a determined glint in her eye as she leaned back in her chair.

Stacy was exhausted but triumphant. As she glanced toward the rising sun, she muttered, "Good thing today is Saturday."

CHAPTER THIRTEEN

"Humans believe us to be monsters; they do not know we are their saviors."
　—*Unknown,* The Book of Were Creatures and Shifters

Amy's heart raced as she crouched among the towering containers of the shipping yard. She was out of sight, and the shadows grew long with the setting sun, making it easier for her to remain concealed. With her phone, she filmed the exchange between the two men.

One wore a trench coat and a hat pulled low over his face. His hands were shoved deep in his pockets. The second man looked like he worked at the shipping yard. He was greasy and dirty and tired. He grumbled something to the man in the coat about a late shipment.

"It'll come soon, though. I promise."

The man in the trench coat appraised him with a sharp look. "It better, or else…"

Amy didn't catch what he said, but his tone spoke of a threat. She would enhance the audio on her recording later and find out what it was.

She had found clues that Leonard Dolos was connected to the man who owned this shipping yard. He had won a case for him last year. Stacy had told her to be careful, but Amy hadn't been able to help herself. She had come down to the shipping yard hoping to talk to a manager and had seen the two figures talking.

So, instead of going inside, she crouched behind two large containers and whipped out her phone. As long as her boss didn't find out, she couldn't be fired. Besides, she had come after work hours.

She edged closer to better pick up what the men were saying, but she didn't make it far before they finished their business and parted. The manager went inside while the man in the trench coat got into a nondescript gray sedan and pulled out onto the street.

Amy was beginning to think it was time to go inside and speak to the manager when a shift somewhere nearby had her turning. A hulking figure emerged from behind another container. He was a full two heads taller and as greasy-looking as the manager. Their eyes met, and Amy's heart thundered. *Shit.*

She lowered her phone but didn't stop filming.

The hulking man advanced toward her. "You're in over your head, girlie."

Amy darted to get out of his way, but she wasn't quick enough. A dirty hand closed over her upper arm, and he jerked her toward him. Amy released a pained sound, and her phone clattered to the ground. The man's grip on her arm tightened enough to leave bruises. He got in her face, snarling, "What's a pretty bitch like you doing here?" His breath smelled awful, and it was clear he hadn't brushed his teeth in a long fucking time.

"Let go of me," she demanded.

A sneering smile widened his mouth. "I don't think so."

He threw her against one of the shipping containers. Her back slammed into it, and air whooshed out of her lungs. Amy groaned when she caught her breath. Her head throbbed. The man's hands gripped both her arms, hauling her away from the shipping container and moving to throw her into it again. Blood dribbled down the side of her face. The whole world spun. Darkness encroached on the edges of her vision. She figured it didn't matter what the hell he did to her after she became unconscious. He might drag her away, hurt her more, or…

Another form hurtled from the darkness to their left. Amy's heart leaped, afraid another assailant had come to join the man throwing her about. Instead, the second figure shot out a fist, connecting with the side of the man's face.

The figure landed with feline grace and shot out a leg, sweeping the man off his feet. He crashed to the ground, and the figure kicked. Another second, and they were over him, their fists hitting with perfect precision. The man howled and snarled. The figure attacking him—Amy's savior—didn't make a sound except for the scuff of their boots on the concrete.

Amy staggered, bracing herself with a hand against the shipping container. Blood still seeped down her face, but she no longer felt like she was about to pass out. She watched in amazement while the dark-clothed figure beat the man to a bloody pulp. The mystery figure was much smaller than the man but also much faster. They had a quiet, quick precision to their movements and wore all black with a hood.

Finally, the figure stood, panting but not as much as Amy thought they should, given their effort. The figure turned, and Amy's heart pounded faster. Had the person saved her, or were they planning on beating her ass too?

"Are you okay?" came a low voice from the hood.

Amy blanched. "Holy shit, Stacy."

What the hell was she doing here?

"Are you okay?" Stacy asked again, edging closer to her and checking for wounds.

"I'll be okay. I just need cleaning up. Where the hell did you learn to fight like that?"

"Shh, not here. It's a long story." She glanced around to make sure no one was looking. "Let's get out of here."

Amy looked for her phone. She found it lying a few feet away. Her screen was cracked, but the video she had taken was saved. Stacy put an arm around Amy's shoulders, and they stole away into the darkness outside the shipping yard. The night chill and shadows gathered around them like a shroud, keeping them out of danger's sight.

Gradually, Amy's adrenaline faded, replaced by the sharp, cold reality of her dangerous endeavor. If not for Stacy, she wouldn't be awake right now. Maybe not even alive. "How did you know I was here?"

"Not yet," Stacy warned, glancing over her shoulder to ensure they were not being followed.

"Thank you," Amy breathed. "I owe you one." Her voice grew shaky. "We need a plan, a real one. Or anything better than what we have been doing."

"Agreed," Stacy replied, her voice a little louder. She pointed down the street. "Let's talk over coffee. I know a place." She finally lowered her hood and gave Amy a dismal but reassuring smile. "I have a first aid kit in my car. We can fix you up first."

Stacy had tracked the gray sedan here. After returning from Saturday errands, she'd found it at the far end of the parking lot. As soon as the guy driving it left, she followed. Maybe this way, she'd find out what the hell was going on. When he drove out of the city onto a road flanked by forests, she wondered how far she would go before she gave up. Then he turned into a shipping yard parking lot and exited his car.

Stacy parked closer to the tree line and followed on foot. She wore the clothing her father had given her and slipped a hood over her head. She hoped she wouldn't need to stay hidden, but...

"Just in case," she murmured as she followed the man wearing the trench coat at a safe distance.

She trailed him to a small lot by a building where he talked to someone who looked like they managed the place. The conversation went on for about ten minutes, and Stacy couldn't hear a damn thing. She tried filming, but she was too far away. She didn't dare step closer and risk them seeing her.

The man wearing the trench coat soon left the manager and returned to his car. Stacy slunk farther back behind the building so he would not catch sight of her. The manager grumbled something under his breath before heading inside.

She was about to return to her car when a male voice rumbled, "You're in over your head, girlie." A woman's yelp of pain rang out.

Stacy whirled, alarm ringing through her whole body. She peered around the corner of the building to see a large man throwing a blonde-haired woman against a shipping container.

Amy! What the hell was she doing here?

She was half inclined to be angry with the journalist for putting herself in danger, but Stacy had come here too, so she had no room to talk. She cracked her knuckles. "I'll take care of this bastard."

When they arrived at Joe's Diner, Stacy told Amy her version of the events. This was the only place to eat besides a gas station this far outside the city. Stacy had driven through darkness and fog until they reached it. The restaurant was several miles from the shipping yard. After Amy was no longer bleeding, they wandered inside.

Night patrons spoke on bar stools and in booths. The clattering of dishes became soothing background noise. They sat in a corner booth under a neon red sign that read, "Cup of Joe." The waitress came by, and they ordered coffee and something light to eat. Neither of the women had much appetite after what happened. They kept to small talk until they were served and could speak without the waitress interrupting.

"I can't believe the timing. It was divine intervention or something," Amy remarked, shaking her head.

"Tell me what you were doing there," Stacy asked without trying to sound reproachful.

Amy shared the connection she had learned between Lenny and the owner of the shipping yard, then gestured at her phone. "I got their conversation on film. I've seen the guy who spoke with the owner meet with Lenny on multiple occasions. The video is evidence, but golly, Stacy, this whole thing is bigger than I thought. I knew Leonard was a crook from the second I began researching him, but I never imagined it went this far."

Bruises marred the side of her face, and Stacy was sure she had them elsewhere, too. She wished she could lend the healing properties of her body to Amy, but she couldn't. *If I have witch powers, I need to learn a spell for that,* she thought.

"It does," Stacy confirmed. "I have the legal and, let's say, physical means to help you, though." A hint of a smile played on her lips despite the situation. Avenging Amy like that had made her feel good. Euphoric, almost. She couldn't figure out if it scared her or if she loved it so much that she could shake any fear off. It wasn't like she would go after anyone merely to have a fight, but if it happened again, she wouldn't be mad.

"I've discovered a lot more I haven't told you about," Stacy admitted. "I think it's time we share the full scope of what we have found and make this more of a partnership, not you hiring me and whatnot."

Amy nodded. "I'd like that."

Stacy told her what she and Jonathan had discovered and the connections between Victor's and Lenny's movements with the cases she worked on. However, she did not tell Amy anything about magic or her father's involvement.

Amy listened with a thoughtful expression. When Stacy finished, she raised her mug. "To taking down the big bads."

Stacy clinked her mug with Amy's. "And staying alive while we do it."

"And better threads?" Amy asked. When Stacy gave her a questioning look, she nodded down.

Stacy glanced at her clothes, which were streaked with dirt. What had the waitress thought when they walked in? She decided to ask her father if any more of her mother's fighting clothes were lying around somewhere.

"I have an idea," Stacy told Amy as they finished their coffee. "Let's make sure you can handle yourself better if things go south again. How about some self-defense lessons?"

"If it means I can fight like you, count me in." Intrigue shone in Amy's eyes at the prospect. "Lead the way, sushi."

Stacy frowned. "Do you do that on purpose? Fuck up words for fun?"

Amy grinned. "It *is* fun." A pause. "Sushi."

"Sensei."

"Whatever." Amy stood. "Thanks for saving my ass for a second time. I'm sort of hoping something happens to you so I can return the favor."

An idea came into Stacy's mind. "Actually, would you mind if I stayed at your place every once in a while? I know we agreed that being seen together at our homes was stupid, but we're linked now, and Lenny knows it. I have a stalker or two, and it would be nice to have somewhere in the city to go. It doesn't sound like you're being followed yet."

"Yes, but I'm not sure how long it'll last. Do come and stay tonight, though."

Stacy smiled and thanked her. "You know, I might have to keep saving your ass, Amy, but I'm beginning to like you."

"Maybe you're co-dependent."

Stacy snorted. "Let's get out of here. I want a shower and a change of clothes."

Stacy took Amy to her favorite gym the next day. To both their relief, no one followed them. They did warm-up stretches and exercises before Stacy began walking Amy through the basics of grappling. Amy was getting the hang of a defensive stance when a muscular man a few years older than them sauntered over. "You're teaching it all wrong," he told Stacy. He stepped onto the mat, smelling like he'd been in the gym all morning.

Stacy gestured, unfazed. "I doubt it. Maybe we have different styles."

"I'll show you."

She gave him a mocking smile. "Sure. Amy, watch what I do and take note."

Amy's eyes glittered. "Yes, ma'am."

Stacy took the same defensive stance she'd been teaching Amy while her new opponent took another one. Right away, she realized where he was going wrong. He lunged for her after Amy counted down from three, but Stacy evaded him easily.

He swung an arm out, but she ducked, then lunged toward him, taking him down around the waist as she had done the first time a thug attacked her in the parking lot of her apartment complex. This was much safer since this guy didn't seem intent on beating her up.

The man crashed to the mat, with Stacy pinning him down. She swung her legs until she had him in a chokehold. "Yield?" she crooned.

The man struggled against her, but when he realized there was no way out, he tapped the mat. She released him, and he panted for breath. Stacy stood, wearing an uncontrollable smirk. "Nice," Amy chortled.

The man remained lying on the mat. "I was trying to impress you, is all," he admitted, eyeing Amy. "But your teacher beating my ass probably killed any chance I had."

"Probably," Amy replied, though she still smiled. Stacy didn't miss how Amy's eyes lingered on the man's pectorals and upper arms. If he could manage more humility, he might have a chance. The tension from before dissolved, and Stacy chuckled as she extended a hand to pull him up.

He gave her a look of gratitude before taking her hand. Stacy pulled him up with more ease than she should have shown. "You're faster and more experienced than me, but there's no way you're stronger," he commented. "How'd you pull me up like that?"

She flashed her most charming smile. "Don't worry about it." Amy had wandered away to get a drink of water, and Stacy leaned closer to the man. "As for your impression, don't feel too bad about it. Give her your number. She might still call you."

"You think so?" Hope shone in his pleasant blue eyes.

"What's your name?"

"Spencer."

"Stacy."

Amy returned. "Spencer, meet Amy. Amy…"

She shook his hand, eyes sparkling. They spoke with Spencer for a few more minutes before Stacy saw the time. "I should go now. I want to pick up groceries before heading home." It was part of her Sunday routine.

"Are you coming back to my place?" Amy asked.

"Not tonight. I need to do some things at home."

Stacy was heading out of the gym when she heard Spencer laugh, saying something about how Stacy might not be going to Amy's, but he knew someone who would like to.

Stacy wandered the produce section, wondering how many cartons of strawberries she could eat before they went bad.

She was still in her workout gear, a favorite pair of leggings and a sports bra with a zip-up cropped jacket over it. Sweat glistened on her forehead and made her ponytail stick to the back of her neck. Anyone passing by would have seen the mixture of post-workout fatigue and unspoken strength on her face.

Stacy glanced up, searching for another item as she placed one carton of strawberries in her basket. A twenty-something pair of men on the other side of the aisle met her eye. Stacy glanced away, but not before one of the men glanced over her whole body. A smile pulled at the corner of his mouth. He murmured something to his friend that Stacy barely heard as she strolled toward a robust selection of lemons and limes.

The first guy sauntered up to her, hands in his pockets and blue eyes glittering. A playful grin remained on his face. "Never seen someone make gym wear look so professional."

Normally, Stacy would have ignored this type of advance unless she was at a bar. Today, however, she was in a good mood and in need of a distraction. She turned, returning his grin. "You should see me in a courtroom. It's less sweaty but just as intense."

The second man, tall and with dark features, had a more reserved expression and tone of voice. Even so, an amused glint came into his eyes as he joined in. "I bet you're as formidable with a gavel as you are with barbells."

Stacy laughed, surprising herself. She felt lighter and more carefree than usual. *Maybe I should get to the gym more. Blowing off steam is doing wonders for my personality*, she thought. Aloud, she told the young men, "I prefer lifting legal briefs to barbells. They're heavier with all the lies and secrets people keep."

Both men chuckled, and Stacy knew she had their interest piqued. The taller of the two leaned toward her. "So, what's your workout routine? I could use some tips to…strengthen my argument in court."

Stacy felt a flicker of enjoyment. She seldom allowed herself this kind of attention. "Well, it involves a lot of chasing down the truth and knocking aside legal obstacles. Not sure it's for everyone." Her tone was light but edged with the thrill of the flirtatious exchange. First with Jonathan and now with these guys. It felt nice every once in a while.

But don't let yourself get distracted, she told herself. A little flirting was fun, but she didn't have time for anything more. She gave the boys a dismissive wave, bidding them goodbye as she wove her way toward the checkout counter. She shook her head when she exited the store a few minutes later, amused and a tad bewildered with herself.

The playful energy faded when she entered her apartment. She put her groceries away and showered before draping a comfortable robe over her body. Hair damp and body clear of sweat, she re-centered her mind.

It was Sunday, but this work against Lenny had to be done. The evidence spread across her desk demanded her attention. From Amy, she had collected photographs of covert meetings, documents littered with the language of corruption, and notes linking back to Victor's sprawling network.

Stacy sat, running fingers through her hair as she narrowed her eyes over the contents of her findings. "Victor won't know what hit him when I get through with this," she muttered. A determination settled within her, driving away every last bit of enjoyment from the day. Her fingers danced across the laptop keyboard as she cross-referenced data and highlighted every discrepancy she discovered.

Elsewhere on her desk sat files pertaining to the case involving the Native American land. Shortly after beginning Mr. George's case, her firm had foisted this new case onto her and turned Mr. George's over to another attorney. Stacy had hardly been able to give it her attention the past couple of weeks, but with everything involving Victor and Lenny, she felt it was high time she dove in.

The longer she read and searched, the more in over her head she felt. Having Amy in on the case helped since it meant she wasn't doing anything alone.

Her phone buzzed with two messages. The first was from her father.

KHAN
Another training session this week? Let me know what days work for you.

Stacy had a court hearing coming up and would have to spend all week preparing for it. She texted back.

Swamped right now. I'll get back to you.

The second message was from Jonathan.

JONATHAN
Need my tech wizard brain again? I'll bring dinner this time. Pizza?

Stacy hesitated, then thought it might be nice to have company.

I like mushrooms on mine. Is that a deal-breaker?

JONATHAN
Yuck, but sure. 5?

5.

She returned her attention to her laptop screen, where she was currently looking through the background of the shipping yard manager she and Amy had seen yesterday. She had a copy of Amy's video on her phone and played it over and over.

This prick in the trench coat kept showing up, but none of the names on the list matched his appearance. Not that she could pick up on much of his appearance anyway. Sighing, she clicked out of the tab and returned to the pages scattered in front of her.

This was far more than a battle of legal wits. It was a fight against a deeply entrenched empire of corruption. *I'm going to need more than Amy and Jonathan helping me before long,* she realized. Dragon and witch magic or not, Victor was far better connected than she was.

She stewed, deep in thought, with her eyes fixed on the screen. The weight of the task ahead sat on her shoulders. *I feel like a dragon lurking in the shadows,* she thought with amusement. *Ready to strike with precision and power.*

In the reflection of her screen, she caught a glimpse of her eyes. They were still green, but the flecks of gold were larger and brighter.

CHAPTER FOURTEEN

"When in thy petrifying car
Thy scaly dragons waft thy form,
Then, swifter, deadlier far
Than the keen lightning's lance,
That wings its way across the yelling storm,
Thy barbed shafts fly whizzing round,
While every with'ring glance
Inflicts a cureless wound."
—Mary Darcy Robinson, Ode to Envy

Stacy answered her phone on the second ring, trepidation in her heart. "Everything okay, Amy?"

"Yes, just checking in with you. Haven't heard anything from you in a few days."

"I've been drowning in this case, and if I don't get inside the courtroom in fifteen minutes, I'll be late."

"Good luck," Amy responded. "Call me after if you need to. We could go to the gym to blow off steam or share a bottle of wine at my place."

Jenna had said something similar this morning, knowing

Stacy was about to go up against Lenny again in court. This was the biggest case of the year so far, and the land Stacy was fighting for on behalf of a Native American nation was much larger than any she had defended for past clients. Stacy told Amy that she'd asked Jenna to join them after. She thought of Jonathan and Derek, too. "It might be nice to do something with a group."

"I won't say no to meeting new friends," Amy replied, a smile in her voice.

Stacy promised to call when the trial was over. She had arrived at the courthouse. She inhaled deeply and gathered her courage before stepping out of her car.

The courtroom buzzed with activity when she entered. Another attorney in her firm greeted her. The young man had been appointed to the case first and had gone through pretrial but now acted as Stacy's partner in the real thing. "Seen Mr. Dolos yet?" she asked when they were seated.

"Not yet, but I know he's here."

Stacy surveyed the room, then organized her papers and files for the upcoming trial. Not long after, her clients arrived. They hadn't had many meetings to prepare, but Stacy was glad to see them again.

The two middle-aged men were representatives and members of the Shinnecock nation who had land in Southampton. With their lands threatened by a corporation Stacy had no doubt Victor Corbinelli was behind, it came as no surprise to find Lenny Dolos as her opposing attorney. She shook hands with them, and they sat to await the judge and the jury.

Stacy took this time to observe the other attorneys, a slew of corporate lawyers, sleek in their tailored suits. The younger lawyers were gathered around their table, whispering back and forth. Occasionally, a few would shoot looks in her direction. Stacy was tempted to grin and wave. *Hello, boys. Yes, it's me you have to beat.* However, she had little desire for the judge to consider her unprofessional.

The air was heavy as Lenny entered. His eyes met hers, and he started. Stacy wore a smile she couldn't control. Lenny hadn't known she'd been given the case. He headed to the front, his face turning red with fury. After that, until the trial began, he didn't spare her a single glance.

Stacy was called forward to give her opening statement. "Your Honor, ladies and gentlemen of the jury, thank you for being here with us today. My name is Stacy Drake, and I am representing the Shinnecock nation in their efforts to maintain their rights over the land they were given federal recognition and status over in 2010. For thirty-two years, the people of the Shinnecock nation endeavored to become federally recognized as a tribe and to take possession of their ancestral lands, some of which include the Southampton area of our state. It is this land and the rights of the Shinnecock people that is being argued for today."

Stacy held her head up, barely glancing at her notes to give the statement. She'd been working on it for days and had it nearly memorized. "For the past two decades, The Shinnecock nation has been trying to open a casino in the Southampton area in hopes that it will become an economic engine to lift them out of poverty. This business would also fund many social programs that are beneficial to the community."

Emotion rose in her voice. She spoke with logical rhetoric as always but allowed her voice to plead with those listening. This wasn't only about land and property rights. It was about the lives of people who had been trodden on for centuries.

"They have been prevented from doing this for many reasons, but the one we will focus on today has to do with the corporation present today whose members seek to seize the land that is not rightfully theirs and use it for their benefit, thus not only destroying chances of a better life for the Shinnecock nation but also impoverishing them more. Several of the tribe's neighbors have united against the Shinnecock people because they want their summer getaway to remain their own.

"Regardless of their feelings on how the land should be used, it is wrong for corporations to step into this matter. With the evidence my team and I bring before you today, we will prove the corporation against the Shinnecock people is not attempting to seize the land for business purposes but because they want to keep their precious summer homes and expand where they spend the holidays."

Stacy thanked the judge and jury for listening and sat back down. She felt she had done well. She must have because when Lenny stepped up to make his opening statement, he shot her sharp, heated glares. Stacy kept her expression neutral. It would do her no favors to look angry in court unless she was giving an impassioned speech on behalf of her clients.

Lenny gave the normal opening remarks, then drawled in a low tone, "Ms. Drake's plea for the Shinnecock nation is admirable." He said this as if he didn't admire her words in the slightest. "However, she has failed to see that the Shinnecock people are not in need of a casino. They are doing well financially despite what two of its representatives have told her."

Stacy boiled. *Bullshit.* How would he know that if it was true? Forged subpoenas? False evidence? She wouldn't put it past him.

Lenny continued with a sly smile parting his lips. "Furthermore, we must look at this from a property rights perspective. The corporation I am representing today has plenty of legal rights to develop the land the Shinnecock people wish to build their casino on. We will prove this with contracts and purchases."

Through third parties or shell corporations, Stacy thought. The shit kept piling up.

"The development of this land will be for the greater economic benefit. It will provide jobs for the Shinnecock tribe, who can earn money to take back to their families."

Stacy's hand clenched around her pen as she jotted down notes. Simply giving her clients jobs would do nothing but put them under further control of Victor Corbinelli and the corporation. It would give Lenny endless cases to win for the remainder of his career. Lenny continued for a few more minutes, then closed his statement with a pointed look at Stacy.

"What the other side wants is to create economic prosperity for a small group of people and ignore the larger population. My clients' plan to develop the land in the Southampton area would reap benefits for all, not one group."

He sat, looking smug and childish.

Stacy was ready to burst, but she managed to control herself. The judge called for her to rise and bring her first witness forward.

You've got this, she told herself. *You know what you're doing.*

Stacy meant to call Amy as soon as the first court session was over, but as soon as she was in her car, she found several messages from her father.

"Sorry, Dad. Afraid there won't be any training this week," she told him when he picked up the phone. "I'm swamped with this case."

"Anything I can help with? I've dealt with my fair share of court trials."

She raised a brow. "You have?" On the way home, she recounted the day's details and how it had ended with an electric sparring match of legal terminology between herself and Lenny, neither able to gain the upper hand.

Stacy had presented most of her case, including witnesses. Tomorrow, it would be Lenny's turn. She had walked away with a solid sense of purpose but unsure if she would be able to get ahead. "I guess I'll find out tomorrow," she told her father when she finished.

His tone was somber when he replied. "You do have abilities that can help you, remember."

"Are you saying I should literally beat their asses?" Stacy recalled what she'd done to the man in the shipping yard. As much as she would like to give that sort of lesson to Lenny, the courtroom wasn't the right place.

Her father chuckled despite the situation. "While that would be amusing, no. What lies within you can enhance your intuition. Use that."

He was careful not to refer directly to her magic or dragon lineage over the phone.

She thanked him and promised to update him later, then hung up.

"The precedents of eminent domain must also be considered," Lenny stated to the judge and jury the following day. "The government can allow for the transfer of property from private to public use regardless of past decisions and relegations. If the corporation is considered beneficial to the overall economy, the governing authorities may make this transfer for redevelopment by a private entity."

Stacy felt like banging her head against the table as Lenny made his rebuttal against her arguments from yesterday.

"In this, I challenge the validity of the historical treaties made." Lenny's voice carried a sharpness that matched his eyes sweeping the room, gauging the attention of the jury and those watching from the public gallery. Many from the Shinnecock nation and several wealthy-looking businessmen had come to witness the case unfolding. Victor Corbinelli was nowhere to be seen, which didn't surprise her.

"I have referenced clauses, as you might remember from yesterday, in the 2010 allowance of the Shinnecock people as a tribe. Though this was done, it does not mean they have full rights to their ancestral land. Why not share it with corporations who can help them?"

Because those corporations will drive them clean out of the area with their bullshit developments, Stacy thought. All they wanted to do was build more summer homes and private beaches. She jotted down a few notes as he continued.

"Various state and local regulations allow my client to continue their work. I have presented these already, but I would like to remind the jury of these regulations."

All he was doing was taking up time. Stacy finished a series of questions for cross-examination while he prattled on. Finally, Lenny called the corporation's CEO to testify on the stand. He asked a series of vague questions, and his client gave vaguer responses. He finally finished, and the judge invited Stacy to rise.

"I'm afraid you haven't disclosed all the necessary details for your plans, Mr. Wentworth." Stacy kept her tone light, her expression unreadable.

Let him weave his web to fall into.

"It doesn't matter what their plans are," Lenny snarled from where he sat.

"I'm afraid it does since the jury cannot make a decision without knowing all the facts." Stacy directed these words to Lenny but kept her gaze on the judge.

"Answer the question, Mr. Wentworth," the judge directed tersely.

The man shifted and stared at the floor. After a pause, Stacy added, "I have documentation of transactions between your corporation, Mr. Wentworth, and various builders who plan to break ground and turn the Shinnecock ancestral land into housing areas. They're nice homes, I must say, with views of the beach and all. It would be a nice place for you and your friends to spend the summer, right?"

Mr. Wentworth grew flustered.

Stacy turned her attention to the jury, presenting the evidence she'd brought. The legal battle felt more complex than ever. Stacy felt like she was wading through a swamp full of constitutional, property, and environmental law as well as the specialized field of Federal Indian Law. She was more thankful than ever to have chosen the specialization near the end of her studies. The court's decision would fall based on how they interpreted the laws.

Use everything you know, she thought as Mr. Wentworth was dismissed from the stand. Stacy searched the faces of the jury, allowing the reassuring warmth of her magic to test them, dig deeper for the emotions swimming beneath the surface. Stacy didn't want to manipulate anyone, however. They had to see what was at stake for a whole group of people, and drawing on their emotions was the way to do it.

"I have presented the Tribal Sovereignty and Federal Indian Law, wherein we all can see the Shinnecock people have inherent authority over their lands and resources regardless of what purchase agreements may have come between corporations and third parties since."

She cited the agreements made and portions of the Constitution that upheld it. She spoke with a fluid grace, punching her words with emphasis when she found the jury waning. She felt their rapt attention throughout and spoke well enough that nearly everyone forgot about the witness on the stand.

It wasn't like Mr. Wentworth cared. He looked as if he preferred to melt into the floor over facing Attorney Drake.

"I am not alone in this fight, either," she went on. "The Indian Child Welfare Act and The National Environmental Policy Act uphold the same treaties and agreements. We must protect the financial abilities and opportunities of these people as well as the welfare of their children and the environment their lands create. Allowing the Shinnecock people to keep their land does benefit the broader society, despite what the opposing side might be trying to convince you of."

Stacy cast Lenny a sharp look as she continued. "The defendant's tactics are exactly what I expected. They're using legal loopholes and questionable land deals that do not hold up to the 2010 federal agreement with the Shinnecock people. In this courtroom, truth outweighs power." Her gaze was unwavering on the opposing counsel. Many of the lawyers gave one another uneasy looks while Lenny kept his heated, penetrating stare pinned upon her.

She returned her attention to the jury. "I am pleading with you today to understand what is at stake. Either a handful of wealthy families miss out on more opportunities to gain luxury real estate or a whole community of people fall further into poverty. What is more important? Can we consider the former a loss?"

Not long after, the judge called for an end to the day's session, declaring they would reconvene the following day for final statements. Stacy blew out a breath of relief. She might have gained the upper hand.

Let's hope there's only one more day of this, she thought as she left the courthouse. She considered going home, but with closing statements tomorrow, she chose instead to head back to the office. The marathon was almost over. *A little more now,* she thought.

Stacy arrived after work hours and found she was the only one at the office. She preferred the quiet and shut herself away to finish her task.

The glow of the city night poured in around her, joined by the light of her monitor cascading over her. Stacy was the figure of determination. Her hands flew over notes and the keyboard. She had everything she needed, every shred of evidence necessary to win this. She had to put it together in the right way, say the right words at the right time to win the jury's favor.

"Emphasize the tribe's sovereign rights and the unethical practices of the other side," she told herself. Every piece of evidence and argumentation had to boil down to those two things. Stacy hoped the jury would see everything and do their moral duty to uphold justice over corporate greed.

She paced with the final draft of her closing statement, practicing line after line. "This case is a testament to the enduring spirit of a people's fight against the relentless tide of exploitation." Her voice echoed in the stillness of the office.

She didn't leave until close to dawn when the barest hints of gray touched the sky, and she stole toward home. To her relief, no one followed, and she entered her apartment safe and sound. *I can manage a few hours of sleep*, she thought as she tumbled into bed. She would reward herself after she won the damn thing later that day.

"Since 1978, the Shinnecock people have endeavored to be recognized as a tribe and to obtain the rights over their ancestral land. Many of those who first began this endeavor are no longer with us and will not see the outcome of this trial," Stacy began with her closing statement.

"Their children and grandchildren will, though, and I know those who are gone would want nothing more for their families than the right to keep and maintain their land as they see fit. Who are we, corporations or lawmakers, to take that away from them when it was theirs to begin with?"

Stacy restated a slew of evidence and key highlights garnered from questioning her witnesses. She'd sat through a tortuous time of Lenny giving his final statement and now stood before the jury to expose his lies. Raw emotion filled her voice. Warm magic welled up within her, though she didn't mean to draw upon it. The magic was like a reassuring blanket, and she pulled it closer around her shoulders.

"We must think of the good of the Shinnecock people, not the corporations who are already successful and can provide for their families. There are many other places Mr. Wentworth and his associates can become prosperous, but there is only one Southampton ancestral land for the Shinnecock nation to preserve. I urge you, Your Honor and members of the jury, to take the side of justice in your decision."

After a pause, she delivered her final line exactly as she had practiced. "This case is a testament to the enduring spirit of a people's fight against the relentless tide of exploitation. Honor that today with your decision."

The courtroom was silent as she took her seat, the impact of her words resonating not only with the jury but the public sitting in the gallery. *Now we wait for the verdict,* Stacy thought. She felt Lenny's heated gaze upon her, but she ignored it.

"We won!" Stacy declared into the phone. "Oh, Jenna, you should have seen how happy my clients were!"

"And Lenny?" Jenna chortled. "I bet he wanted to melt into the floor."

Stacy shared with her friend how Lenny had reacted. The moment of triumph for her had been a significant blow to Victor's plans. Lenny had approached her with a venomous glare and hissed, "You've made the biggest mistake of your career."

She had met his gaze. "No, I've upheld what is right. That's never a mistake." Her voice held self-satisfaction and warning. She had exited the courtroom with her head held high, aware this was one battle in a war that had been going on for months. She doubted it would be long before she faced Lenny in the same courtroom again. Until then, she would celebrate.

Back at the office, her boss shook her hand, wearing a broad smile. "Well done, Stacy. Take a few days off. You've earned it!"

"Thank you, Mr. Chadwick. Maybe give me a light case when I'm back." She winked.

Jenna looped her arm through Stacy's. "We're going out for drinks tonight! The whole team is coming. You all deserve it."

Eyes shining, Stacy asked, "Mind if I ask a few more people to join us?"

Jenna arched a brow. "Who?"

Stacy smiled. "I was hoping I could invite a new friend of mine so you can meet her, and I've reconnected with Jonathan."

Jenna's smirk had Stacy batting a hand at her. "Not like that!"

Jenna agreed with a roll of her eyes. "As long as you and Jonathan don't sneak off and leave me stranded, and this new girl isn't replacing me as your best friend."

Stacy called Amy and Jonathan not long after. As she and Jenna made their way out of the office, Stacy imagined Lenny at Victor Corbinelli's, receiving a tongue lashing for his failure to gain the land the Shinnecock people had possession over. *Don't think about him,* she told herself. *He doesn't matter right now.* Still, she couldn't shake the feeling that no matter how much she put Lenny out of her mind, he wouldn't be too far.

CHAPTER FIFTEEN

"While most with the ability to wield magic and use it to change their form learn at a young age, the rare occurrence of one not discovering their power until adulthood has occurred."
—*Unknown,* The Book of Were Creatures and Shifters

Stacy stood alone in the chill of the night, but she wasn't cold. All the alcohol she drank at the bar kept her warm. She was still riding the emotional high of her courtroom victory that day and was tipsy enough that she had walked here.

She had set off on foot from the bar, knowing she'd be walking several miles to reach here. She hadn't cared. The magic inside her allowed her to go longer distances without becoming tired. If she needed to jog back to where her car was after she was sobered up, she could. It was a freedom Stacy was still adjusting to but one she wished she'd had sooner.

The quiet of the small graveyard was a relief compared to the business in the city. Her heart was heavy with unspoken words. While out with Jenna, Derek, Amy, Jonathan, and several members of her firm, Stacy had been able to forget all about her troubles. Everyone had bought her drinks, and with her dragon magic coursing through her, the alcohol burned much faster. Jonathan made comments about Stacy the Straitlaced being no more with each shot she put down.

She was twenty-six and kicking ass in her career. She needed to have fun sometimes. However, she didn't feel like having fun anymore as she stood in front of a tombstone, scanning the inscription.

Catherine Diana Drakethorn
Beloved Wife and Mother

Stacy doubted the dates marking her mother's life were accurate since they stated Catherine had only lived to thirty-five, and Stacy knew better.

The moon's soft glow shone over her as she knelt, fingers tracing the letters forming her mother's name. "Did I do right today?" she whispered. The rustle of leaves in the gentle night breeze was her only answer. She settled onto the ground, crossing her legs. Her whole body felt warm and pleasant, but an ache built in her heart.

She'd had one hell of a journey so far with legal battles, moral dilemmas, and personal sacrifices. But hadn't her parents gone through so much more in their lives? She had barely scratched the surface and felt as though she knew nothing.

"I wish I had known you," she added, choking on the words. "I wish you could have stayed longer, if only so I could have learned how your voice sounded or what made you smile."

Stacy caught a stray tear drifting down her cheek and wiped it away. The stillness of the night was far different than the clamor of the city and her friends. Stacy felt she could think clearly here. "I wish…"

She trailed off, shaking her head. What good did it do to wish for things she could not make happen? Her mother was gone and had been for twenty-six years. She hoped her mother had lived a long, full life before that. She stood, gaze still fastened on the tombstone. What had life as a witch been like for Catherine

Thorn? What had it been like when she met and fell in love with Constantine Drake? They must have loved one another a lot to join their last names and create a new family.

Here she stood, going by "Drake" and nothing else in her professional life. *It might be time for a change,* she surmised. She wanted to honor her mother, too. She wasn't merely a Drake, only a dragon. She had witch blood inside her. It was time to find out what that meant and what her full, real last name could do for her.

She left the graveyard, wondering if she had been watched or followed coming here. She didn't care because if anyone tried anything, they would learn a lesson about crossing her. *I'll need more training,* she decided. Now that the big case was over and she had some time on her hands, she might as well. She made a mental note to call her father in the morning after she finished fighting off a hangover.

The fight was far from over, but as Stacy strode back toward the city, she thought of her mother. The dragon had given her the will to fight today, but her witch blood would come to her as well. "One day," she whispered. "I'll honor Mom, too."

The clock read one A.M. when Stacy returned to her apartment, but she wasn't ready to sleep yet. She slumped at her desk by the dim light of the lamp, hearing the soft hum of the city beyond her windows. She had been wrestling with a question all day but had pushed it to the back of her mind to be fully present with her friends and colleagues. Yet, after seeing her mother's grave, she couldn't avoid it any longer.

Did I do the right thing by using magic in the courtroom?

While she had used it for good, she wondered at the fairness of having a hidden advantage. She didn't want to become like Lenny, using secrets to gain the upper hand. Back when she'd chosen to attend law school, she hadn't considered that one day, she might be battling between two sides of herself. The magic that came from her parents was part of her. She couldn't ignore it. She had a feeling it was responsible for the strong sense of justice that had taken her into law, to begin with.

Stacy drew a journal out from her desk. She used to write in it every day but had slacked on the habit since becoming entrenched in her case. She scribbled her thoughts and feelings onto the paper, ignoring the slight cramping in her hand. She had a lot to think through.

Although nothing had come of Lenny's lawsuit against her, she couldn't ignore it. She had to deal with the fact that he had men trailing her, and she had beaten a guy to a bloody pulp in a shipping yard. She had attacked the three thugs who chased her. People were dead because of her. Her heart thudded with each realization. She could write each one off with a slew of justifications, but it all boiled down to one thing. She might have powers, but she could not compromise her integrity.

Is it too late? she wondered.

Finally, she tore the paper out and closed the journal. She took a lighter to it, then dropped it into a waste bin to burn. Writing it down had helped, but she wasn't stupid enough to leave the confession lying around.

When the paper was blackened and crumbling away, she fixed her gaze through the window, watching for the gray light of dawn to break over the city. *I've got to stop staying up this late.* She had won a case and deserved a full eight hours of sleep.

She rose and prepared for bed. While sliding clothes from the top drawer of her dresser, she spied the letter from her mother. She had forgotten all about it. She reached for the envelope, fingers trembling as she opened it and extracted the paper inside. She sat on the edge of the bed and drank the words in.

It wasn't much of a letter. Her mother had only written two lines.

The world will need you one day, Anastasia.
I love you,
Mom

Tears pricked her eyes. That was all? What made her mother think the world would need her?

"No pressure, I guess," Stacy mumbled. Despite the letter's brevity and vague nature, Stacy clutched it to her chest. An inexplicable connection to her mother's spirit filled her. It was as if Catherine's presence had found a way to fill the room. Stacy closed her eyes, breathing in and out. She didn't believe what her mother had written about the world needing her, but maybe some parts of it did. For those people, she would fight.

She drifted to sleep with the letter still in hand.

Khan was not at the Drakethorn estate when Stacy arrived the following day, late in the afternoon. She had slept until midday. Then, feeling the need to be out of the city, she drove to her old home. She hadn't let her father know she was coming ahead of time, wanting to surprise him. She guessed he was out running errands and wouldn't be long, so she explored the library he was so fond of.

She had spent many hours in the library as a child, but it had been years since she walked the long aisles with numerous stacks of old books. She had never wondered how old the books were, but she thought about it now. She traced spines as she passed, wondering how many had magic woven through them. The room itself was warded and protected with magic that preserved the books and artifacts. Otherwise, pages would crumble into dust beneath her fingers.

She wondered how many secrets of her family's lineage lay within this library. She could search for hours, days maybe, and not get through much. Her father had only collected a fraction of this library. Many of the books and artifacts had been here since before he was born, placed within these walls by the former members of the Drake family.

Stacy considered returning to the hidden basement to examine the family tree, but a new idea occurred. If there was a secret basement, who was to say there weren't other secret rooms? This library seemed like a perfect place to tuck a secret space away.

She strolled past shelves lined with books and wandered to the far wall. It was paneled with ornate wood, and several paintings hung at regular intervals. Her mother's portrait in the hallway had a catch behind it. One of these paintings might, too.

She reached the end of the gallery wall and peered at an image of rolling hills with a river running between them. She had the distinct feeling the place pictured was somewhere she had been before, though she could not remember it. Did something in her magic remember?

Stacy peered at the side of the painting and found a small catch. She chuckled. The house was consistent, at least. With a gentle pull, the painting swung to reveal a loose panel, which she moved aside. It did not open into a room but a shelf with several leather journals stacked on it. Among the journals were scrolls tied with ribbon and a small box full of intricate talismans.

What was this? She chose a journal from the top of the stack. Upon opening it, she was hit with the scent of jasmine and something earthy. She had smelled the same scents on the clothes her father had given her. Did it mean these journals had belonged to her mother, too?

Stacy opened to the first page and found her mother's name scrawled across the top. The journal was full of her mother's elegant script and sketches of arcane symbols. Stacy turned to better see the book's contents in the light. She settled in an armchair by one of the windows. The setting sun cast red and golden glows into the room, making the words on the pages look brassy.

Half the journal was written in the same ancient tongue as the book on magical creatures she had glanced through. The other half was in plain English, so Stacy focused on those pages. Near the book's center, she found a diagram of an unfinished symbol with notes scrawled around it. The top read:

I have been working on a shielding spell for some months now. It is a complex weave of incantations and magical diagrams. The picture below is what I have so far. The missing gaps are proving difficult to close, but I am speaking with those in other realms who may give me the pieces I need to complete it.

The page was not dated, so Stacy had no clue whether or not her mother had finished the spell. Whatever the case, her mother had been developing something using powerful magic. Half the diagram seemed to have an image of a tree inside a circle, with the branches sprawling out.

Stacy rubbed the hidden birthmark on the back of her neck. The drawing in her mother's journal looked similar, though they were not quite the same. Had her mother simply not finished what was in the journal? Had she managed to put a shielding spell on her own daughter? If so, what the hell did a shielding spell do?

A combination of awe and uncertainty played inside Stacy, and she reached for her phone. Her voice echoed off the stone walls of the library when her father answered with a low, "Hello."

"Dad, I'm at the house. I went exploring in the library and found some of Mom's things."

She paused to see if he would be annoyed with her.

"Go on," he prodded.

"Have you gone through her journals?"

"Some of them, yes."

"There's this one with…tips inside it," she told him. "I want to know about the projects she was working on." Reverence and apprehension tinged her voice. "Can witches create their own? I thought they simply learned how to use ones that have always been around."

Khan's voice held hints of amusement when he replied.

"They're all invented somewhere, Stacy. And yes, your mother attempted a few of her own. I wasn't going to teach you anything regarding your mother's abilities until you asked, but I see you're ready now. You might as well embrace both halves of your heritage."

"How can I learn? These journals talk of things that aren't in some of the other books you showed me. I wouldn't know where to start, and I don't expect you to show me how to wave a…stick around." She had to use another word for "wand."

"Hopefully, you won't need one," her father responded, catching her drift. "Those are for lesser kinds." He meant "witches."

"That doesn't sound very kind." Stacy frowned despite her father being unable to see it.

"I mean lesser as in less powerful. Some people need something through which they can send their power. You should be able to send yours directly from your body. But you're right. I can only teach you so much. Your mother was remarkable, Stacy. She left things behind for you to use, including a contact."

"A what?"

"We have an old family friend. I'll put in a word to him today and see if he will meet with you. He doesn't live far from our house."

Our. Because the Drakethorn estate was hers, too. One day, when her very old father died, she would inherit this place. Did dragons die of old age? Stacy decided not to ask. She wondered about the letter her mother had left. She would ask him about that later. The whole "you'll save the world one day" was too much for her to think about now.

"What is the name of this friend of yours?" Stacy asked.

She heard a smile in her father's voice. "Remember that case you were working on with the Shinnecock people?"

"Yes." What did that have to do with this?

"My friend is one of their elders. He's been watching you in court, Stacy, and he agrees that you're ready for new lessons."

Khan had once taught his daughter that everything was connected. He'd always spoken of it in vague terms, though. As Stacy traveled with her father to meet with the elder of the Shinnecock nation, she saw what he meant by connections.

"I can't believe you didn't tell me about your connection to them earlier," Stacy grumbled in the car as Khan wove them through winding roads leading south.

He gave her a knowing smile. "I knew you would be angry if you found out I was involved."

Stacy raised a brow. "Wait a second. You said connected before. Now you're telling me you were involved?"

"I may or may not have covered all the Shinnecock's court and attorney fees."

Stacy stilled, unsure whether to feel indignation or admiration toward her father. She placed her attention on the road ahead of them. If this was true, it meant the fight in court had been about a lot more than property laws and people's rights. It had been about magic, too.

"As soon as I heard you were taking the case, I contacted my friend," Khan shared. "I told them I would help them pay for the court fees if they promised to watch you in court and let me know if they thought you were ready to wield magic."

"I don't understand. What about these people has to do with magic? Are they witches and shifters, too?"

"Not quite," Khan replied. "There's a long history between the indigenous people and the raw magic in the land. They have long considered the land sacred and sought to protect it. In the process, they have learned much about magic. Some of them wield it in ways similar to your mother. I know them because your mother was a close friend of theirs for many years."

"Is this elder as old as you are?"

Khan chuckled. "I don't know anyone as old as me. The elder is eighty."

"That's young in magic years, I guess."

For the first time since learning about the Drakethorn lineage, Stacy wondered how long she would live. She wasn't thrilled with the prospect of outliving every single friend she had. What if she married a non-magic person one day and had children who might also not have magic? *I don't think that's something to worry about now,* she told herself. She had to get through this meeting with the elder first.

Khan drove them into the reservation from a road most people outside the place didn't use. The tribal lands sprawled out, lush and green. Towering trees rose around them, and with the windows rolled down, Stacy heard the distant roar of a river. It was early in the autumn, and the chilly air brushed her skin, turning it pink.

She closed her eyes, drinking in the feel of the wind and the smell of the trees. She had loved the city for the past several years, but something about being surrounded by nature felt necessary to her. It might have been the magic, but Stacy felt it was also a basic human need.

Khan parked the car before a long, pale wood building. Outside, an old woman greeted them, ducking her head toward Khan. "Welcome, Red Dragon."

"Thank you." He dipped his head toward her in return. "Can you take me to the elder?"

The woman clucked and nodded before turning toward a path among the trees. Stacy glanced over her shoulder at the homes around the reservation. It was quiet and peaceful here. Many eyes strayed in their direction. Instead of wariness, the

Shinnecock people gave Khan long stares of respect. They knew who he was.

Stacy followed Khan and the older woman into the trees. Not far past there, they reached a clearing where a man in light-colored linen clothes stood in the center, his eyes closed. He seemed to be meditating. Not a bad place to do it, Stacy thought. All there was to hear in this clearing was the soft breeze and the distant chirping of birds.

With his eyes still closed, the elder greeted them. "Khan, the Dragon Guardian. Your aid in our battle was invaluable. I am glad you have come to see me today so I could thank you in person."

The elder opened his eyes. Deep wrinkles marked his skin, and his eyes reflected wisdom and kindness. He gestured toward Stacy. "The representatives of our people speak well of you, Anastasia Drakethorn." They knew her full name, which surprised her, but it shouldn't have. They knew she had magic, and they'd gauged she was ready to learn how to use it. Her battle in the courtroom yesterday hadn't been only a test of her professional endurance and wit but also of handling the power stirring within her.

If you had told me a month ago that my life would look like this, I'd have thought you were crazy, Stacy thought. She had never imagined being in contact with her father again, let alone visiting the Shinnecock reservation to learn about...

Well, she didn't quite know what.

Stacy dipped her head in greeting as the old woman and her father had done to one another.

"Your actions have echoed the values we hold dear. Your journey into magic is a path back to these same values, as your father has pointed out to us," the elder continued.

Khan offered a humble nod. "The fight was far more my daughter's than it was mine. She fights for justice exactly as we always said, carrying on her mother's legacy."

How much did this elder know? He seemed to know far more about Stacy than she knew about him.

Stacy decided it was best to be honest. "I'm beginning to see the connection, but there's a lot I don't understand yet. What does my magic have to do with being here?"

"Walk with me." The elder motioned for her to join him.

Stacy glanced at Khan, who nodded. She fell into stride beside the elder, and they took a path leading away from the clearing. Soon, the trees gave way to open land that sloped downward. "Hear the wind, see the animals around you," the elder instructed. "At night, watch the stars. Everything comes from the same source: the earth."

"Including magic," Stacy added wryly.

A knowing smile graced his lips. "Especially magic. Not all cultures call it that, though. We do not call it magic but life source. For your sake, I will call it what your mother and father always did. We believe in balance in everything. Justice is part of that, and so is mercy. We must strike a balance in ourselves and thus the world. Between the dark and light, the physical and spiritual realms, the magical and the non-magical."

Stacy had a vague understanding of this thanks to stories her father told her growing up, but she felt she didn't have a full grasp of it. "I'm not sure why I'm here," she confessed. "What am I supposed to be doing?"

The elder released a low laugh. "Not everything is about what you're 'supposed to be doing,' young one. Here, you can learn to simply…be."

Stacy shifted. "I have a difficult time doing that."

"I'm sure you do. I've seen what you do for a living."

Stacy felt a wrong sort of pride welling up inside her. She had fought in the courtroom, but that didn't mean she should have all the credit. These people had fought far longer than her.

"I want you to keep coming here when you make time," the

elder told her. "I want you to connect to the earth and search for yourself in it. Search for your power and learn to wield it for good. Come here when you need quiet and allow yourself that time more often than you do now."

It was a command, not a suggestion. "I'll try."

The elder's face became like stone. "Don't try. Do."

After a pause, she nodded. "Can I ask you something?"

"Yes."

"Did you know my mother?"

"I did, but not as long as I would have liked."

"Can you tell me anything about her?"

To her surprise, the elder shook his head. "Not now, young one. Learn to be still and rest, to let your power grow and become good. Then, I will tell you the secrets you came here to discover."

Stacy turned from the shelf, holding a journal in her hands. "Are you sure all these stories are true?"

Khan sat in an armchair by a fireplace at the front of the room, scribbling something on a pad of paper. He glanced up at her, a smile playing on his lips. "I hope so. I wouldn't be surprised if some of them are embellished to make certain people look better and others worse, though."

Stacy peered at the pages. The journal in her hand was not her mother's but a collection of writings from past people in her father's family. It wasn't clear if the authors were always the ones talked about in the stories or someone who had heard them later and chose to write them down. The exploits in magic and politics spanned centuries and places. She could hardly wrap her mind around it all.

She turned to one story, laughing as she asked, "This one man accidentally turned a banquet hall into a winter wonderland, or so it says here. Do you think that's true?"

Khan chuckled, and light filled his eyes. "Yes, and it was midsummer! The whole town was talking about it for months. The Drakes spent much time in Russia before the 1600s."

Stacy shook her head, still unable to believe her father had lived back then.

Khan added, "Your great-great-grandfather had quite the flair for dramatics and magic."

"So it might have not been an accident?" Stacy drawled.

"He always said it was, but no one believed him. Anything he could do to get the attention of the woman who eventually became your great-great-grandmother, he did. No one was happy about the cold, but the place did look beautiful."

"Says who?" Stacy demanded.

"Says the woman who was wooed by the show."

Stacy laughed. "He's set a standard. None of the guys I've gone out with would do such a thing." That is if they could. It boggled her mind to think there were others out there like her, magic-using people hiding in plain sight.

"There are more feats and misadventures than I could tell you about," Khan admitted, rising from his seat and strolling through the shelves. "One time in Babylon—"

"Excuse me, *Babylon*? You've got to be kidding."

"I am quite old, remember?" Khan chuckled. "For many decades, centuries even, I roamed the world in my dragon form without shifting into my human one. I also spent much time in other places. That is, locations beyond the Veil." That was what separated their world from a more magical one where spirits and creatures like dragons roamed in unending darkness or light. At least according to some of her mom's journal entries.

"I guess you kept to your human form more after you met Mom."

Khan's eyes glittered. "She took plenty of rides on the Red Dragon."

"Ew!"

He sent a glare in her direction. "I mean when I was in dragon form! She loved to fly."

"Didn't she have a broom for that?"

He shook his head. "Oh, Stacy. You have so much to learn."

A comfortable pause followed, and Stacy's mind stayed on the word "Babylon." She wished she had paid more attention to her history lessons growing up. "The dragons fought in many wars, didn't they? All seven of you?"

Khan nodded. "The world deemed us monsters, but we were their saviors. Many times, we took the forms of great human warriors, our dragon magic making us capable of feats no normal human could accomplish. Other times, we were actual dragons, but those tales have become myths and legends. Hardly anyone today believes them."

She imagined her father in his full, red, majestic glory, soaring over burning cities as wars transpired. She imagined him in the World Wars, flying in the sky and being mistaken for a fighter plane from far away.

She wondered at the extent of his experiences and the losses he had endured. She wondered about the other dragons and where they were now, if her father was sad to no longer have his friends. She remembered things he'd said about the other dragons. That not all of them were here anymore, and that some were no longer good.

She decided to change the subject.

"Mom loved these stories, didn't she?"

Khan turned. "She did. This collection wouldn't be nearly as well-rounded if not for her."

"I thought you collected most of the newer additions."

"I did after she died. She had a running list of the tomes she wanted to collect. After she was gone, it was the only thing I felt kept her memory alive. Now I have a daughter who looks almost exactly like her and has the same spirit."

Despite the ache growing inside her, Stacy smiled. "I hope I can live up to her name."

CHAPTER SIXTEEN

"Out of the earth engendered men of arms
Of Dragons' teeth, sown in the sacred sand;
So this brave town, that in her youthly days
An Hydra was of warriors glorious,
Did fill with her renownéd nurslings praise
The fiery sun's both one and other house:"
—Edmund Spenser, Ruins of Rome

Khan led his daughter into the basement, wearing a sheepish expression. "There's something I must confess, Stacy."

She eyed him. "Go on."

"I showed you one room, but there are several hidden places down here."

She shook her head, chuckling. "Of course there are. I only wish you had told me about them when I was younger."

"Perhaps then you would have been better prepared for—"

"No, it's not that. I would have been much better at hide-and-seek if I knew about the dragon cave." Her eyes shone with amusement. Her father had always had his secrets, but she never thought having his own version of the Bat Cave would be one of them.

Khan glowered. "We dragons have lairs, not caves." He sniffed, and it took Stacy a second to realize he was joking. She laughed, shocked that her father had cracked a *joke* with her.

"Let me guess. Your lair is full of stolen jewels and gold from all over the world, too. What have you been doing the past five years to loosen you up like this?" she teased as they descended the stairs into the secret cavern.

"Doing my best to hold the world together." His tone was serious enough to tell Stacy his amusement had died out. Khan forced a weak smile. "One has to amuse themselves somehow so as not to go insane. Being a dragon can be…"

"Maddening?" Stacy guessed.

He nodded, then motioned to a far wall where he showed her a catch next to another painting. A second doorway opened to reveal a tunnel winding down into darkness. "How many are there?" Stacy asked.

"This is the only other secret opening. Through here will be a few more tunnels and several rooms," her father answered. "You might want to put this on. It gets colder the farther down you go." He handed her a cloak.

Stacy felt like she was on a secret mission. Wearing a cloak made her feel like she was stepping back a few centuries, but she accepted it. The garment felt comforting around her shoulders, and the scent of jasmine wafted up from it. "Another one of Mom's old things?"

Khan nodded. "It is a witch's cloak. It will help you compress and control any magic you might need for the spellwork. She made this cloak herself. She selected the materials and sewed it together. She wove enchantments through it to keep the wearer warm, agile, and focused."

Stacy blew out an impressed breath. "She was a woman of many talents."

Khan's green and gold eyes sparkled. "Much like her only child."

Stacy knew she was talented in law but wasn't sure about the magical side of things. This was today's purpose. She and Khan had decided it was time to try spellwork, and he'd said he had a place she could start. Stacy had expected him to take her back into the forest, but he'd stated that she needed a place where, if she lost control, her magic could run rampant without damaging her surroundings.

Stacy recalled what had happened in the alley when Lenny's thugs chased her, and her stomach turned queasy. The last thing she wanted was to lose control again.

They descended into the tunnel. It twisted and turned until they emerged into a large cavern. Khan pressed his hand into the wall, and lights shimmered across the walls and ceiling. They glowed a soft blue.

Stacy moved to the center of the room, carrying a satchel full of things the elder at the Shinnecock reservation said she might need to work the spell. She had also consulted her mother's notes.

She opened the bag and took out one item after another. The elder had helped her select herbs and plants that could root her to the magical energies naturally existing in the ground. He had also given her several crystals for containing and transferring magic she could not keep inside herself. The last item was a talisman Khan said her mother used to wear. She'd moved to place it around her neck, but he had stopped her.

"You will fashion your own at a later time. For now, use this as a point for your spellwork, like the other items. Let it bring your mother's spirit into the room," he had instructed.

"The talisman you will make for yourself one day will replace the items you have arranged now. A witch should be able to produce magic without needing a whole setup. This will be good for the beginning while you learn to summon and form your power. Over time, however, you will need to learn to do everything within yourself without the help of these aids."

Stacy wasn't sure if his words encouraged her or put more pressure on her. She did as he said, arranging the items at the points of the star etched into the stone floor of the cavern. Her mother must have conducted and formed many spells here. Signs of her were everywhere.

She had been a painter as well as a witch, and her art was all over the walls. She had painted fields full of flowers, flowing rivers, a night sky abundant with stars, and the shining rays of the Northern Lights. "This was where she came to practice," Khan told Stacy in a low tone that bordered on reverence.

Stacy felt a tinge of reverence herself as she stood among the items selected for the spellwork. Her mother had been talented and wise. After glancing through her mother's writings and consulting with the elder, she decided to try a shielding spell. As her father had explained, she would do no good with offensive strikes of magic if she could not first form a shield around her.

Her mother's notes indicated that when she could master a shield, it would be like putting on another skin. She wouldn't have to think about defense in combative situations after it became that easy.

Stacy had to wrap her mind around the fact that witches could walk into combative situations. It wasn't all rituals in the forest with coven sisters or speaking to spirits through a veil. Sometimes, it was as simple as taking an enemy down with a stunning spell or two. The more she learned, the more her expectations were blown out of the water.

Khan stood back, observing as she opened her mother's notes. The incantation for the shielding spell was written out. She would have to learn to say it and channel magical energy into the items around her. After she mastered the words, she would not need to speak the incantation. The message would move quickly between her brain and her magic. It all boiled down to teaching her brain to do something new.

"This is the moment of truth," she murmured. "Let's hope I'm as good at magic as I am in the courtroom."

Stacy memorized the incantation, then shut the book. She closed her eyes, focusing on the feeling of the warm magic stirring within her. She drew it up like water out of a well and sent it trickling into the items around her. Her mother's talisman flickered with light, a promise that Catherine was here in spirit, if nothing else. More magic filled the crystals, acting as stores for what Stacy could not contain. The scent of the burning herbs filled the room, holding her to the raw magic as if she were clinging to the earth itself.

Finally, she spoke the incantation, willing the magic to form a translucent shield around her. The air filled with a charged energy, and Stacy was sure she was on the right path.

This didn't last long. A burst of sparks had her eyes flying open. She yelped and sprang back before the sparks could hit her.

"Try again," her father instructed. "We're in this stone cavern in case you start a fire or anything else. You're safe."

Stacy steeled herself and tried again. She failed again, but this time, the results were less damaging. A rain of flower petals cascaded out of thin air. One landed on her head, and she opened her eyes, wincing at the possibility of fire or cracked stone. Instead, she smelled the fresh scent of lilies.

Khan chuckled. "Your mother's favorite. It might be her talisman causing that."

"I don't want flowers, though," Stacy muttered. "I want results." At least it wasn't boring. Her mother sure knew how to make things interesting. The thought both warmed her and filled her heart with an ache. What she wouldn't do to have a moment with the woman who had birthed her and died.

"Try again, then."

The third time, a small whirlwind swept through the cavern, scattering loose pieces of paper and almost putting out the heat in the herbs. *This shit is real,* Stacy thought. What disasters could happen if she had more magic? She sensed that she did but had not tapped into it yet. The magic was buried deep, yet to be dug out. *One step at a time*, she reminded herself.

According to her mother's journal, the shielding spell was an amateur step. The weakest of witches could form one. Stacy didn't feel confident as she tried for a fourth time. She centered herself, probing deeper into her magic. A warm surge of energy answered. She recited the spell, her voice growing stronger with each word.

"By the ancient blood of the Drakethorn, let this shield form and protect."

A shimmering aura formed around her, stable and strong. She opened her eyes, gawking at the thin veil of magic encasing her body. She'd done it! "Holy shit." The magic so close to her skin felt like static. It prickled, making the small hairs on her arms rise. *Did it feel like this the first time you did it?* she asked, glancing at the glowing talisman.

The magic folded around her, feeling more like a warm blanket and less like static. Stacy took that as a gentle "yes" from her mother's spirit. The paintings along the walls, awash in the soft glow of blue light, seemed to shimmer anew.

She experimented with the shield by moving her arms and focusing her thoughts. The magic expanded and contracted as she willed. Her heart leaped with joy first, then apprehension.

Her father's rumbling voice had her turning to him. "The shield is more than a magical construct, Stacy. It is an extension of your will and emotions, fueled by your dragon heritage."

Stacy allowed the shield to drop, her heart pounding with excitement and satisfaction. "So this is about controlling emotions, not only magic?"

"Consider them one and the same," Khan replied.

She couldn't help but quip, "Is that why you're so stone-faced all the time? Gotta keep those emotions in check?"

Khan glowered. "I don't know what you're talking about."

Stacy's laughter made his eyes glow.

She sobered and glanced around. "I've been thinking about taking a few days off from work. My boss suggested it after I won the case for the Shinnecock. Maybe I could stay here and learn what I can about the wider realm of magic. I should be reading Mom's journals more, and I can keep practicing here." She paused. "Is that okay?"

Khan's expression held shock at first, then delight. "Of course it's okay." He seemed on the brink of adding further elation but, not wanting to overwhelm her, retracted it and added instead, "I only hope my lousy cooking won't make you regret that decision."

His wry smile had Stacy producing one of her own. "Can't be worse than mine."

He chuckled. "We may not burn the house down with magic, but we might by using the oven."

"Everyone else I've sent after her has failed," Lenny growled from behind his desk.

The dark city sky and lines of buildings beyond glass windows rose behind him. In front of him, across the desk and shrouded in shadows, was the man he'd called to meet him here.

Lenny leaned forward, intertwining his fingers. "She's become too much of a liability and must be irrevocably lost." He produced a savage smile. "Your reputation precedes you, sir. You can guarantee success, right?"

"Of course." The man's tone was emotionless, almost bored. "But I'm not cheap."

Lenny waved a hand dismissively. "I'm not worried about that."

The man *tsk*ed. "Perhaps you should be."

Lenny shifted.

After a pause, the man added, "However, I can't guarantee how many pieces the body will end up in."

"I want a decapitated head, that's all. I trust you'll give me the real picture. If not, you will have to deal with those above me."

"Not you?" the man drawled. A flash of white teeth appeared in the darkness. One of the man's hands sat in the light, resting over the arm of his chair. He had large hands with bristles of hair on his knuckles.

Lenny snarled out his response. "If I say she's gone, and she shows up, I'll be the first swimming with the fish. And you'll be next."

The man whistled. "Oh, it's *that* kind of boss."

He sounded like he had much more experience with people like Victor Corbinelli and his unnamed associates than Lenny. It was why Lenny had hired him. The thug muscle from his previous attempts had done nothing but draw unwanted attention.

Lenny had continued his work in the courtroom, but Victor suggested he drop his suit against Stacy Drake and her firm. If and when the young lawyer ended up in a ditch without a head, Victor didn't want anyone tracing it back to the lawyer who hated her guts enough to file a senseless lawsuit against her.

Lenny remembered Victor telling him this, then feeling like a beaten dog. First by that stupid bitch, then by his boss. He had relented, and now he was here, seeking the aid of a guy with a reputation for making pesky people disappear forever.

"Yes," Lenny answered at last, despite the man's last words not being a question. "They're not very…forgiving."

The man cracked a smile as if he had heard this sort of thing before. "When is good?"

"As soon as fucking possible?"

Lenny could hardly make out the man's features. The fellow had wanted to meet in near darkness. A flicker of flame ignited out of nowhere, allowing Lenny to see the lower half of the man's face. He was clean-shaven with a wide mouth and slight scarring on his chin. The flame was from a lighter, which the man guided toward the end of a cigarette.

He placed the cigarette to his lips, then proposed, "How about the night of the full moon? I'll have better light to make sure of the kill."

Lenny's brows furrowed. "I don't see what that has to do with anything, but you're the expert."

"Don't forget it." The man's words were soft, almost a purr like a cat's, yet tinged with warning.

Lenny's palms became sweaty. "That's when?" he asked, swiveling to glance at a calendar. "Three nights from now?"

The man nodded as smoke curled from his mouth. Lenny waved it away, coughing. It was high time for this man to be out of his office.

"You'll have to pay me now, though."

"Crypto or cash?" Lenny asked, growing more nervous by the second. It was late at night. He had stayed here long after his normal work hours because the man across from him had insisted on meeting after nine P.M.

"The former." The man rose.

Lenny swallowed. "I'll make the arrangements now."

CHAPTER SEVENTEEN

"The First Age of Dragons was recorded long ago in scrolls enchanted to keep the words hidden from unwanted eyes. These scrolls have long been lost, and hope for their recovery is vain."
—Unknown, The Dragon Codex History, Vol. I

"Not coming into work?" Jenna chortled over the phone. "I hope this means you're taking a well-deserved vacation."

"Sort of," Stacy answered as she settled into an armchair in her father's study. He had long since retired to his room for the night, though she doubted he was asleep yet because she'd heard the low sounds of a soap opera on TV as she passed his room earlier.

"Going anywhere nice?" Jenna asked.

"I'm staying at my dad's for a few days."

Jenna laughed. "You two must be getting along again. I'm bummed I won't see you, but I get it. Things were hectic at the office today."

"Spare me the details."

"What will you be doing at your dad's?"

Stacy felt it was time to clue Jenna in to at least some of what she was going through. She inhaled deeply and organized her words before saying, "I'm taking time off to dive into something different. You could call it a new hobby." She had to inwardly admit that it was much more than a hobby.

"Like what?" Jenna prodded, sensing Stacy was holding back.

She paused. "Witchcraft."

"Witchcraft?" Jenna echoed. "Should I start calling you 'Salem' instead of 'Stacy?'"

They laughed, but Jenna added, "Fine. I bet you're going to be doing the walk of shame, but you're telling me witchcraft as a cover. You tell me you're at your dad's, but I know you've been talking to Jonathan again." She pondered for a moment. "I will get the truth out of you one of these days!"

"I *am* telling you the truth," Stacy replied firmly. She didn't want to elaborate, especially over the phone. Later, she could sit Jenna down and explain everything, whether Jenna wanted to believe it or not.

Khan had explained to Stacy earlier that it was difficult for humans to see the truth of the supernatural world. They were resistant to it by nature, and there was only so much she could do if she wanted to share it with others. This made her decide not to call Amy and tell her the same thing.

"Do you mean to say if a big-ass dragon is flying in the sky, humans won't see it?" Stacy had asked her father.

He had shaken his head. "They'll see it, but most might be inclined to believe it's a jet plane, not a dragon."

Stacy wondered if she'd ever mistaken supernatural beings for ordinary surroundings before her magic stirred within her.

"Whatever," Jenna replied. "You were always secretive about your boyfriends and not-boyfriends."

The last thing Stacy had time for was a romantic entanglement, even with Jonathan, who was a low-commitment kind of guy and wouldn't mind only seeing her once a month. She wasn't into that type. Although he'd been one of her best friends in college, and they'd always flirted, she couldn't imagine so much as kissing him again.

"Oh, by the way." Jenna's voice interrupted her thoughts. "Word came today that Lenny has dropped the lawsuit against you."

"What? Did he say why?"

"Nope, but does it matter?"

Stacy figured it didn't. Relief washed through her, but wariness followed soon after. If Lenny had dropped the lawsuit, it was because he had something more sinister in mind and didn't want it tracked to him after it happened. She'd found all the more reason to stay at the Drakethorn estate.

"Good news, huh?" Jenna prodded.

"Sure is." Stacy forced her cheeriest tone.

Jenna snickered. "I'm sure he's scared of you, is all."

Stacy agreed, but not for the reasons Jenna thought. They spoke for a few more minutes about the cases Jenna was working on and her upcoming date with Derek before ending the call with see-you-soons and be-safes.

It was late at night when Stacy got off the call, but she wasn't ready to sleep yet. She headed upstairs to the bedroom she had occupied before leaving for college. She was slow to enter the room. It was the first time since she was a teenager that she'd seen her old space.

Her father hadn't touched a single thing except to have someone dust the space every once in a while. Posters of old bands she'd liked littered the walls. A bed covered in richly colored sheets, blankets, and pillows looked untouched. A wide window with a seat overlooked the back portion of the grounds. A bathroom was connected. She decided she would shower in the morning.

She glanced around as if searching for the ghost of her past self before she placed a stack of her mother's journals on a desk where she used to do homework. She slumped into a chair, wondering what it would have been like decorating a room while growing up with a mother to help.

As she eyed the journals, she remembered what she'd read in one earlier that day. Her mother had spoken of the importance of belonging to a coven, even if it was as small as three people. Larger covens ranged between nine and thirteen members. They came in multiples of three, but if the coven was at full capacity, they had a coven mother to lead them, becoming the thirteenth member.

From her mother's writings, she knew Catherine had been in a coven, but she could not tell how many members it had or what it was called. She opened her laptop and quickly searched for covens in the New York area. If there were any witches she could meet, it might be worth finding them. Her father knew much about magic, but he could only teach her so much about spells and wielding raw energy.

The journals would guide her, too, and the advice from the Shinnecock elder helped. None of these things were the same as having a practicing witch to assist her, though. If she was going to get better, she needed a different kind of help.

She scoured social media groups, websites, and articles regarding covens, but nothing came to light. Most of the websites and groups were ambiguous or led to dead ends. Several groups had not been active in years.

"Of course, the mystical isn't a click away," Stacy murmured, her face aglow in the white light of her laptop screen. If witches were treated like domestic terrorists, no way in hell would they advertise themselves online. She was used to doing the majority of her law research on the internet, but finding a coven wasn't the same thing.

She closed her laptop, mumbling, "This is going to require a more traditional approach." She thought over her plan as she settled into bed. First, sleep. Tomorrow, she could begin the search for New York's hidden witches. She considered asking her father for help, but she wanted to do as much of this on her own as she could. Besides, it would be nice to get out of the house tomorrow and explore.

She drifted off to sleep, glad to be spending the night somewhere without the worry of a stalker in the parking lot.

The following afternoon, Stacy had a list of various bookshops in and around the city she could visit to begin her search, thanks to a tip from her mother's journal. Several of the shops were listed on a page, and after searching their names on the internet, she found many of them were still in business.

Only one had a general area written in her mother's elegant script but no specific address. She searched the area on her maps, but no sign of a bookshop was there. Perhaps it had gone out of business. She decided to leave it for now and go there only if it became her last resort.

She didn't know why her mother had recorded the names and addresses of the shops, but it could mean a chance to find more people like her. The worst-case scenario was she didn't find other witches and spent a day among the literary arcane.

The first shop was nestled between a bakery and a barber shop on a street in a less populated area of the city. Trees lined the street, adding shade and shadow to the vicinity. All the bookshops happened to be on the city's outskirts, so Stacy had no problem driving her car to each location. She parked on the street and paid the meter, hoping she would not need long inside.

Madam Poffery's Bookshop and Perfumery had an air of regal luxury from the second Stacy stepped foot inside. The heavy scents of lavender and other floral perfumes filled the air, along with the familiar smell of old books. Deep purple curtains hung from the long windows. The walls were painted a pleasant shade of lavender.

On one side of the shop, books lined shelves in a disorganized fashion. Instead of standing in neat rows, they were piled precariously on top of one another. If one found a book they wanted on the bottom of a twenty-book pile, it was up to them to dig it out.

Several glass cabinets were pushed against the wall on the other side of the shop with copious perfumes on display, all with price tags marked in elegant script. At the back, more shelves held an array of shimmering crystals, all shades of purples and pinks. A record player in the back played soft jazz music.

"Hello?" she called.

"Hello!" a pleasant voice returned. A woman in a frilly purple dress bustled from the back room. She was short and round, with rosy cheeks and gray curls folding around her beaming face. She looked like she'd stepped out of a storybook. "A visitor! Oh, how glad I am to see someone today!"

"Do you not have many customers?" Stacy ventured.

"Not the pleasant kind," the woman muttered, her face souring.

"Are you Madam Poffery?"

Her grin returned. "Indeed! Who else would I be?"

Stacy couldn't imagine what unpleasant people ventured into this shop. Perhaps nosy teenagers who had a mind to annoy its owner. Even so, the street seemed quiet, so Stacy was not surprised to find herself the only visitor. She wasn't sure how she should approach the subject of witchcraft. Madam Poffery could be a witch, but would she be helpful?

"What are you looking for, dear?"

Stacy was still stuck on what the woman had said earlier. "You said not the pleasant kind. What did you mean?"

Madam Poffery explained. "Businessmen who want me to sell the place and all that. Stuck-up lawyers who think they can scare me into giving the place up!"

"Lawyers, huh?"

"This shop has been in my family for generations, and I'm the last of us. I'll be damned if I give it up."

The woman seemed more than willing to speak freely, so Stacy kept the questions rolling as she scanned the shop's contents. "What was your family like? They seem magical if they are responsible for this shop." She said "magical" in the same way she would use "beautiful" but hoped that if Madam Poffery was a witch, she would take the bait.

The shop owner chuckled. "Not magical in any real sense, but my family always had an affinity for fairytales."

Why had she said, "Not in any real sense?" Stacy had been reaching out with her magic, testing to see if it had a companion in this space. She felt nothing. Madam Poffery wasn't who she was looking for. She dug around in her purse before leaving and handed the woman her business card.

"You're right about lawyers being stuck-up, but I'm not like most of them." She smiled. "If you ever need help defending your property, give me a call."

In the second shop, Stacy roamed seemingly endless aisles of incense and crystal balls. There were more scrolls than books, and Stacy concluded the place was more of a collector's store than one for people with any real magic. She left without speaking to anyone.

At the third shop, she probed her magic around as soon as she stepped inside. So far, she hadn't found anything to tell her she was not alone. This shop was full of brooms from movies where witches flew around suspended from the ceiling. She couldn't tell if they were for decoration or sale.

A wardrobe held an array of silken and velvet cloaks. She tested them with her magic, searching for enchantments in the fabrics. Nothing. Several books, crystals, tarot decks, and objects meant for scrying were available.

At the front counter, a book entitled *Ten Steps to Becoming a Witch* was displayed. She frowned, doubting this place was for real witches if there was a ten-step book for sale. She flipped through it, curious to see what tips it gave.

Step 1: Acquire an Understanding of the Occult

The first chapter gave a rundown of the history of witches and occult magic, but from what Stacy had learned in her mother's journals, she knew it to be a sparse, cherry-picked history rife with misinformation.

Step 2: Acquire all the Necessary Supplies

From there, readers were encouraged what to buy. And who would have guessed, but the author of the book just so happened to sell the things he deemed necessary for an aspiring witch?

Step 3: Find a Space to Practice Your Spells

"Hello, ma'am. Can I assist you?" the store clerk's voice asked, making Stacy glance from the book. She closed it, having no plan to read further.

She grinned, already knowing the answer to the question she was about to ask. "Any chance you've got a witch in the back? Not the broom-flying type, more the spell-casting variety?"

The clerk, a middle-aged man with slicked-back black hair and a curving mustache, answered with an amused expression. "Sorry, our witches are currently on sabbatical."

Stacy decided on lunch first, then the fourth spot. It was on the other side of the city, so she had plenty of time to hope it would yield results. She pulled into the crammed lot and realized the only spot left was for a handicapped driver. Normally, she was not one to break even a small law, but…

I won't be long. It'll be fine.

This was the only shop so far with several people inside. As soon as Stacy was a few feet inside the door, she realized it was a children's bookshop. In the front room, a circle of children and their mothers sat, listening to an author reading a story to them. Stacy smiled. The shelves were full of fairytales and fantastical stories for younger audiences. No sign of real magic was in the air, but she was glad she'd stepped in.

Five minutes later, she was back outside and frowning at the sight of a cop by her car. *Of course! I park in the wrong spot for five minutes, and I get in trouble.* She put on a smile and approached the policeman. "Anything wrong, sir?" She hoped he hadn't noticed the spot she'd parked in, but he had.

"Sorry, ma'am, I'll have to write you a ticket for using this spot."

Stacy was tempted to go full legal mode on him. She had gone to such lengths today to find help, and nothing had turned up so far. She clenched her jaw. She could call her father and ask for help, but she wanted to at least get through the list and exhaust her options there. She decided it was best to be honest with the cop and hope he let her off with a warning.

"I know I shouldn't have parked here. It's not an excuse, but this was the only spot left, and I was only going to be inside for a moment. I wasn't trying to hinder a truly handicapped person from using this space."

The cop lowered the citation pad, and a slow smile lifted his lips. "All right, ma'am. I understand, but don't do it again."

She blew out a breath. His eyes lingered on her. Was he... charmed?

"I won't," she promised.

The cop clicked his pen and put it away. "A nice lady like yourself should know better, so I hope we won't be running into each other again. Not under these circumstances, anyway."

What circumstances, then? She had the sense he liked speaking to her, so she hurried to add, "Well, I should get out of this spot pronto!"

He moved aside to let her pass.

As Stacy pulled out of the lot and headed to the fifth location, she chuckled and shook her head. She wondered if a woman's ability to charm a man was simply pheromones. Did all women have a touch of magic in them?

She'd felt hers rising to assist her in the issue with the cop and couldn't help remembering her other recent interactions with younger men. Ever since her magic had stirred, she'd gained more attention while out and about. She recalled the guy from the gym she'd grappled with, then the pair from the grocery store.

She shook her head as she headed toward the final shop. "Down that path of thought lies madness."

CHAPTER EIGHTEEN

> "She hurried at his words, beset with fears,
> For there were sleeping dragons all around,
> At glaring watch, perhaps, with ready spears—
> Down the wide stairs a darkling way they found."
> —*John Keats*, The Eve of St. Agnes

Stacy found a legal parking spot at the last location as the sun drifted toward the horizon, leaving bright red rays shining across her. She had driven to the area her mother had mentioned and took her time around block after block until her gaze finally settled on the only bookshop in the area.

The Saige Page was a small, nondescript brick building between two others with a green-painted wooden sign bearing gold lettering. Next to the lettering was painted a stack of books. The one on top was open with light pouring from it. Magic, she assumed. Stacy entered, her footfalls the only sound on the creaking floorboards as the door closed behind her. The door moved silently with not even a bell above it to alert the store owner of her entrance.

The space was small and different from the other shops she

had visited that day. Plenty of books lined the shelves, but they were crammed together more than the others. Instead of electric lighting, the glow of several candles and lamps illuminated the space. Ancient tomes and various objects like those at the Drakethorn estate were displayed.

Small knives and vials of liquid cluttered the shelves behind the front counter, along with intricate talismans, jewelry, and music boxes. An armchair sat by one of the windows overlooking the street.

Stacy ventured among the shelves, wondering if the store was closed, but someone had forgotten to lock the door. She felt like the only person here. It was very quiet, and she felt that one wrong move would make too much sound. This place demanded reverence. It felt similar to the first time she'd entered her father's secret study. Magic was all around her, especially in the books.

She trailed a hand along a row of spines, and a warm, tingling sensation filled her fingers. A hint of a smile pulled at her lips. She rounded a corner and halted, realizing with relief and apprehension that she wasn't alone.

A twenty-something man browsed a section of books on the occult, his brows drawn. What caught her attention most was the soft glow outlining his body. She stepped toward him without thinking, the magic inside her drawn to his. Yes, he had magic. What was he?

Stacy cleared her throat. "Excuse me, but do you always have a sort of…glow about you?"

The young man turned his head and surveyed her for a beat before producing a wry smile. "Ah, you noticed. I was wondering when you would the second you stepped in. Yes, the glow is part of the normal witch package." He waved a hand. "Same as you."

She stilled. *I have a glow?* Could anyone else see it?

The young man seemed to read her thoughts. "Only other

witches can see it, don't worry. Just as only witches can see this shop. How'd you find it?"

She wasn't ready to answer that question, but his statement made sense. With no one else in the shop, she could see how non-magic-using people would not notice the building's exterior. She concluded he was the owner or at least the only one working here at the moment.

It also explained why she'd found no address in her mother's notes.

She had many questions. He had sensed her come in but hadn't bothered to greet her despite knowing she was a witch the second the door opened. Why? The next question she asked aloud. "I thought witches were women."

The young man smirked and placed the book he'd been holding back on the shelf. He leaned against the wood, folding his arms. "Are you being sexist?"

Stacy flushed. It didn't help that the young man was conventionally attractive. He was about a foot taller than her, with pleasant hazel eyes and tan skin set off by a navy blue sweater. The sleeves were pushed up to his elbows, revealing muscular forearms. Curls of brown hair were tied back. "Name's Ethan. And yes, male witches exist. Surprised?"

Still blushing, she got out, "A bit, yeah. I'm Stacy, and I'm, well…" She waved a hand at their general surroundings. "I'm sort of new to all this."

That smirk returned. She wasn't sure if she liked it or if it made her want to leave. "I can tell."

She bristled.

He eyed her, taking in her aura. His smile disappeared, and his brows drew together as if realizing something about her. Whatever it was, he didn't deem it important enough to say.

Stacy didn't know what to think about it. His observation felt too close, almost intimate, but it wasn't like he was checking her out. "You're powerful for someone so ignorant," he observed.

How did he know that? She wondered what color she glowed. The light around him was somewhere between white and golden, like soft sun rays.

"Good genes?" Stacy quipped, wishing her cheeks would stop burning so red.

Ethan huffed. "Could be. I don't have magical parents, but I got it anyway. I don't think the passing of magic is always genetic. If it is, it can skip generations." He observed her for another moment, then asked again, "How'd you find this place?"

She decided it wouldn't hurt to tell him. "I found the location written in a journal belonging to a family member. I wanted to know why she had recorded it." She motioned to their surroundings. "How long has this shop been around?"

"A long time."

She glowered. She'd given him a specific answer, yet he couldn't elaborate? "Do you own it?"

"In a way."

She figured it wouldn't matter if he had lawful right over the property if only magic-using people could see it. To anyone else, this was a closed-off portion of the brick buildings on either side or disguised as an alley no one could enter.

She didn't bother hiding her annoyance, but before she could ask another question, he inserted, "This place is private enough as it is. We could continue talking here, but I'm hungry. What do you say to going somewhere else and asking me all your questions?"

"Who says I have more questions?" she challenged, not wanting him to use her curiosity about him as leverage. *You came here for help*, she thought. *Let him help you.*

He grinned. "That glow around you is flaring with power. My guess is because it wants to know more."

Stacy forced a smile. "Fine. Can I buy you coffee?"

Ethan went to the door and grabbed his jacket from a hook. "I have to close up shop first."

A quaint café around the corner stayed open until late at night, or so Ethan told Stacy as he locked up. It wasn't far, so they took off on foot. When she entered, the aroma of coffee and pastries hit her. Not a bad place to ask another witch questions, she decided.

Ethan ordered something to eat, and Stacy offered to pay, but he insisted on buying *her* a pastry. "You've been eyeing that raspberry tart crème since we walked in," he commented as he inserted his card at the counter. He was observant, that was certain. Stacy wasn't sure if it unnerved her or made her feel less alone and more understood. She wondered if his keen observance had to do with his magic and if he'd been a witch for a long time.

The longer she ruminated over it, the more convinced she became that they'd always been witches. Though in her case, her magic had slept for most of her life. Whatever the case, she remained eager to sit and question him.

Halfway through the pastry he bought for her, she asked, "Would you mind signing an NDA for this consultation? You know, so neither of us says something about the other that we don't want getting out."

Ethan raised a brow with a pastry halfway from a napkin to his mouth. "Consultation? I thought this was a *conversation*. Are you a lawyer or something?" He laughed as if he'd made a fine joke, but when she nodded, his smile vanished. "You don't want to make a spellbinding contract instead?"

Was he afraid of entering an NDA because she was a lawyer or because of the supposed magical glow she had? She wondered what that glow looked like now. Did it translate the wariness she felt? Could he read it? His soft outline of pale white light remained the same. He seemed balanced and undeterred despite his words.

"It is a conversation. Sorry for jumping ahead. Sometimes, my lawyer brain gets ahead of me. That and the fact I've had a hectic and partly dangerous past several weeks."

"Sounds like a good story," Ethan remarked.

One she would have to tell at a later time when he was less of a stranger and proved he could be trusted. "Can *I* do a spellbinding contract? I've never heard of one before."

Ethan chuckled. "You said you were new to all this, but I didn't realize you were *that* new."

Her features hardened. It sounded like spellbinding was as rudimentary as shielding spells. She half-wished she had never come. She hadn't felt this stupid and ignorant in a long time. Running away now would only make things worse, though, so she kept her ass in the booth.

He caught her expression. "I don't mean to be condescending. I'm surprised, is all. I'd rather do a spell, if you don't mind. Legal jargon is not my thing. I'd have no idea what I was getting myself into." He added a soft laugh that eased her nerves.

"Nothing too bad," Stacy quipped. "You're right to be careful, though. I should have been clearer before. My...situation, you could say, has to do with what you and I have in common. I have enemies in the legal world who aren't playing nice with me."

"And rather than whip them into shape with a spell or two, you'd rather take a subtler approach?" Ethan guessed.

She nodded, surprised to hear him speaking so blatantly about spells and what they were in public. "Don't worry," he assured her. "I have a muffling spell cast over us. Anyone who walks by will hear us talking, but they'll only be able to make out a jumble of words."

Can I do that, too? she thought. "I need help, and the more I talk to you, the more I think you could do something for me."

"Like what?" he asked.

"I don't have anyone else who can tell me anything about being a witch." It took some effort for her to push the word "witch" out, but she remembered Ethan's spell and managed it.

He leaned forward. "I thought you said a family member told you where to find my bookshop. Can't they help you?"

"That was my mother, and she's dead."

He sobered. "I'm sorry."

"It's all right. She died shortly after I was born, so I don't remember much about her."

"Even so." The condescension in his tone vanished, leaving an undeniable sincerity. He didn't seem like a rude person, merely someone who was out of practice when it came to social interactions.

"I'll do the magic NDA," she decided, changing the subject. "Wait. Unless you're a jerk. You're not, right?"

Ethan chuckled. "No more than the average witch. We're not so different, you know. You might be a lawyer, and I might be a lowly bookshop keeper, but we both have magic, and I'm only twenty-five."

Stacy didn't hide her surprise. "Did I do anything to make you think I find myself better for being a lawyer?"

Ethan shrugged. "It's an air you give off, something in your aura. I'm guessing you've had to be defensive most of your life, or at least in recent years. I'd assume a courtroom could do that to a person."

Right, got to work on that, she thought and was further amazed at his read on her. She wasn't one to hide her feelings or to put forward an unreadable persona, but she'd also never felt so seen in her life. Part of her felt too exposed. *Tread carefully,* she told herself. *Just because he's a witch like you doesn't mean he'll have your back.* She wouldn't blame him if he didn't. He barely knew her. Aloud, she told him, "Well, I don't think I'm better."

Ethan pulled up the sleeve of his blue sweater and laid his arm on the table with the palm of his hand up. "That's good. Show me, then."

She stared at his arm. "What?"

"Put your arm over mine, and I'll conduct the spellbinding."

She hesitated, then did as he told her to. She laid her arm over his, fingers curling around the spot below his elbow. He did the same to her.

"Will anyone see what we're doing?" she asked.

"They won't see the magic, if that's what you're asking," Ethan replied. "They'll see us holding our arms like this, but I doubt anyone will guess or care."

"Right. Go on, then."

He chanted a string of words in a language she didn't know. She gasped as threads of pulsing red emerged from around her hand and white from his. They twined together like strings until the magic wrapped their arms. Ethan's hold on her was firm and warm. The threads tightened, then vanished. He let go. "It's done. We're now magically bound not to repeat whatever we say next in the next hour to anyone else."

"And what happens if either of us does?"

"You'll blow into fucking pieces."

The fear in Stacy's eyes made him laugh. "I'm kidding. I used a spellbinding incantation that will only create mild discomfort and irritation to someone who breaks the contract. It'll also prevent us from using our magic for a short time if we do."

She was satisfied with the terms.

Ethan sat back. "So tell me, Stacy with No Last Name. What is it you want to know?"

"Don't tease me about a last name when you haven't told me yours."

"Woodard. Ethan Woodard."

She perched her elbows on the table and asked, "What can you tell me about your bookshop?"

"It was my grandfather's. My parents died when I was young, so my grandparents raised me. Then they died a few years ago, and it's been me and the shop ever since."

"Sounds lonely," she commented.

"It is, especially when only magical people can see the shop, let alone come inside it. You were my first visitor in months."

"Shit."

"Yeah, but a good one, right? I don't normally make spellbinding contracts with my customers." He smiled, and the sight warmed her. She fought off a flush creeping up her cheeks. "What about you?" he asked. "You said your mom died. Got any other family?"

"My dad. He's the one that exposed me to magic."

"And recently, I can tell. It's interesting."

"Why?"

Ethan's gaze settled on her, and she didn't move her eyes from his. "Because for someone whose magic has awoken so recently, it sure is powerful."

"Maybe I was storing it for too long. I'm like a volcano that was dormant for years and is now active."

Amusement shone in his eyes. "That's one way to put it. I've only seen that kind of magical activity in dragon shifters before, but you're a witch. Not sure what it is about you."

She preferred to keep the part about having dragon-shifting blood inside her to herself for now.

"What exactly is it you want help with?" he asked.

"I want to learn new spells and potentially find a coven, or at least other witches who know what they're doing. By what you've told me, you could use a friend or at least an occasional visitor to your shop."

He grinned. "It's worth a try. Why not? I can give you a tip or two. If you're going to be coming by my shop often, you might as well bring pastries from this place."

Her eyes sparkled. "It's a deal." She paused, then asked, "Are *you* part of a coven?"

Ethan shook his head. "I don't think there are many witches in this area anymore. They tend to choose more rural locations where the magic is more potent, and they're out of sight of...well, those who would wish harm upon them."

"But you chose to stay in the city."

"Leaving my family shop would mean giving up the only thing I have left of them," he confessed. "I was interested earlier in how you'd found my shop because I was under the impression no other witches were left in the city. Then you mentioned your mom had written about this place. She must have come here when my grandparents owned it." He tilted his head. "Have you tried other places around the city?"

"Yes, actually. My mom had a whole list."

"How many places?"

What was he getting at? "Five."

His brows shot up. "Interesting. Mind telling me what they are?"

She hesitated, then remembered their contract. It didn't hurt to tell him. She gave him the addresses.

Ethan's eyes glowed with interest. "Very interesting."

"Mind bringing me into the loop?"

He withdrew his phone and took a screenshot of the city on his map app, then edited it in his camera roll until the five locations had red circles drawn around them. "Look at the shape it makes." He drew from one point to another until all five locations had lines running between them.

It formed a pentagram.

"Holy shit."

"Your mom must have known that. Have any clue why?"

"Other than that she was a witch? No."

Ethan sat back. "I'd like to know what it means and what it has to do with my shop."

"Me too." Stacy wondered if she would tell him if she found out.

He eyed her and returned to a previous subject. "What about you? Why are you still in the city?"

"I only found out about my magic a few weeks ago, and my whole life is here. Job, friends, all that."

"Right, and you're a lawyer," he remembered. He checked his watch. "I have to go, but if you want to stop by the shop tomorrow, we can work on a few basic spells. Ones that will get you started."

"Thank you," she replied, rising. She had not imagined this was how her day would end. "It's not like me to beg for help from perfect strangers. Well, near-perfect strangers."

He smiled. "I'll pretend you put emphasis on 'perfect.'"

Her cheeks tinged red. "All the same, I'm glad I found you."

Ethan inclined his head. "I have a feeling you should be thanking your mother for jotting down the address to my shop. If you ever find out about her connection to it, please tell me."

She promised to do that and walked outside with him. She saw him off and stood by the street as night gathered around her. Pleasant energy hummed in her chest. *Finally, I'm making progress.*

CHAPTER NINETEEN

"Stone, Iron, Bronze. We have been here all along. The Ages of the world pass, and we remain. A veil hides us. They have deemed us monsters. What do we owe humankind anymore?"
 —*Unknown*, The Book of Were Creatures and Shifters

"A shielding spell?" Ethan asked, arms crossed as he observed Stacy's stance. "You don't know how to use one yet?"

Stacy bristled at the incredulity in his tone. From their two interactions, she'd learned Ethan often used a tone that didn't match how he felt. He could come off as condescending when he was merely surprised and incredulous when he was overwhelmed.

"I *can* do it," she clarified. "But it's weak, and I could use some tips on improving."

"Right, okay. Show me what you've got so far."

The Saige Page had a wholly different appearance in the middle of the afternoon. Golden sunlight flooded through the windows, washing the floorboards and shelves in a pleasant, warm glow. Beyond the windows, Stacy glimpsed the city-goers passing by, knowing none of them could see the shop or what she was doing inside.

In the daylight, she realized the shop was a lot less organized than she'd perceived it last night. Books were arrayed on the shelves in neat rows, but they were not separated by topic, except the occult section, which Ethan explained were his grandmother's favorite books. Behind the front counter, he had shelves full of herb jars, crystals, various trinkets, and bits and pieces of broken things that needed repairing.

She'd also realized this wasn't only a bookshop.

"You seem to like fixing things," she had commented after observing the multiple small tools littering the counter.

"My specialty," Ethan had replied. She'd discovered he lived in a small apartment upstairs. The shop was an extension of his home.

"I've never seen someone with so much…stuff," Ethan remarked as she placed the items around her.

Stacy glowered. "I was told by a few magical experts that I could do this until I mastered the incantation." She had brought the talismans, crystals, and herbs from her first shielding spell session with her.

Ethan's brow rose. "Experts, huh? But not witches?"

"Not witches."

"You can do this all you want somewhere else, but in my shop, we do it my way."

Stacy was half inclined to march out of the place, maybe break a window or two on the way out. It was that tone he used. Not that it would do anything. He could probably cast a spell to fix it in seconds. She bit her tongue and waited for his instruction.

"First, put all this shit away. There's enough in this shop to contain your magic if it gets out of control."

"I don't want to damage your books."

"Don't worry about them. I put protective spells over everything before you got here." Ethan situated himself on a stool and unwrapped the pastries she had brought for him.

She stood in the middle of the front half of the room, where there was the most space, and closed her eyes. She tugged at the magic deep inside her, drawing it up until it buzzed around her fingers. She wondered what her aura looked like now. She heard Ethan's munching sounds as she allowed the magic to flow around her body, encasing her in protective energy.

"Good, now open your eyes. Look at yourself," Ethan stated.

She did. Her body glowed a soft red. "Is this the same color as my aura glow?"

He nodded, and before she could ask another question, a bolt of magic shot from his hand. It slammed into her shield and broke it apart.

"What the hell!" she exclaimed.

He smirked. "You have to be prepared for unexpected strikes. Your shield shouldn't fall from the first one. Whoever is attacking you could get in a second strike and fucking kill you before you know what happened. Try again."

She bit back her indignation and formed her shield again. This time, she was ready for Ethan's attack. He sent mild bolts of magic at her shield. She held it firm by pouring more magic and focus into it. She had forgotten her mother's cloak today and had to rely on the magical energies of objects in the shop for balance.

"Good," Ethan praised after hitting her a few times and being unable to penetrate her shield. However, she had a feeling he was going easy on her.

"You'll need to work on finding ways to fortify your magic outside of yourself."

"How?" she asked, dropping the shield to regain her focus and energy.

"Find things to harness magic from." He stated this as if it was obvious, then stuffed a second pastry into his mouth. Gods, he really loved those things. Stacy half wished she knew an enchantment to lace them with to get Ethan to be nicer to her.

The longer she thought about it, the more she realized he was being nice despite his sardonic way of showing it. He was helping her even though he had no real reason to. She also realized the charm she had over other men didn't apply to Ethan. He seemed to like her well enough, but not in the way the cop, the guy at the gym, and the pair at the grocery store had. Was it his magic that made him resistant to her?

"The moon, for one," Ethan spoke up, his voice cutting through her thoughts.

"Huh?"

"Magic is more potent under the light of a full moon," Ethan explained. "You can draw it from water sources with a tide or anything natural around you that is infused with magic."

"How the hell would I know what can be used and what can't?" she asked.

"You feel for it. I know you can do that. You started feeling around my shop with your poky magic the instant you came in the other day."

"My magic isn't *poky*."

The knowing smile on his face told her he was teasing.

Stacy imagined telling Jenna about what was going on here. Jenna had teased her about seeing a guy and using her father and witchcraft as a cover-up. If Stacy told her friend she'd been with Ethan all day, Jenna would tease her about sex. *Not that I'm learning spells from another witch so I don't fucking die the first time someone with magic who hates me comes for me,* she thought.

Ethan rifled behind the counter, then brought a small booklet to Stacy. "I've written down a few basic spells in here. Try them in your free time and let me know what happens."

She opened the book, wondering what sort of spells she would find, but Ethan elaborated. "They're small things for convenience. Fixing things, healing spells, and the like. They won't help in combative situations but might come in handy otherwise."

She placed the book in her purse. "How do you know I need anything for combative situations?"

His lips quirked, and he placed his hands in his pockets. "You told me you'd been in danger. I'm guessing you're trying to make sure you won't be anymore."

She figured that conclusion was the obvious one and nodded. "I hope you can see how grateful I am for your help, then."

He shrugged. "You could become a better listener."

She opened her mouth to retort, but he laughed and added, "How about we have drinks sometime soon and build up this newfound rapport?"

Stacy crossed her arms, grinning. "Is that what we're going to call it?"

"Hey, you need me, and there might come a time when I'll need a favor or two from you."

As long as she didn't need to tell him about her true name or dragon heritage anytime soon. She dug out her calendar. "We can pick a time and date for—"

"Call me when you have a free night," he interrupted. "I'll meet you wherever."

Stacy didn't realize until she was back at her car that she'd never asked for his number. Then, climbing into the driver's seat, she found a small card lying there. Ethan's name glittered in gold lettering with a series of numbers written below. She smiled, shaking her head. It was going to be interesting having a friend so attuned to magic.

Stacy was hardly away from the block where Ethan's shop sat when she received a call from Amy. "Everything okay?" she answered.

"You know, not every call to you is a plea for aid in a dire time of need."

Stacy laughed. "You're right. What's up?"

"I'm feeling restless and could blow off some steam. How about another training session?"

"See you at the gym in an hour?"

Amy agreed, and Stacy decided to head to her apartment to change clothes. It would be good to return to her apartment for a few nights since she had run out of things to wear at the Drakethorn estate. It also put her closer to Ethan's shop, where she planned to go for lessons any time she could.

At home, she shot off a text to the number he'd provided for her.

> Some guy broke into my car and left his number.
>
> Weird.

Ethan's reply came less than a minute later.

> ETHAN
> Good thing you're learning new defensive measures.
>
> Not weird.

Stacy grinned, glad he didn't use a word like "spells" in his texts. A muffling spell could be used when they were out in public, but she didn't know about ones to apply to technology.

Not long after, she dressed in workout clothes and headed to the gym. Amy was there when she arrived, talking to the same guy they'd met before.

Stacy's eyes glittered as she approached them. "Simon, was it?"

"Spencer," he corrected, then realized she'd used the wrong name on purpose.

"And you're Susan."

"Ha-ha, very funny."

"You did it first."

They laughed, but Amy rolled her eyes. "Let's not turn today's training into another tough guy versus tough girl. I want to actually build some muscle today."

Spencer inclined his head to Amy but kept his eyes on Stacy. "I was hoping I could help you train. Not instruct you two, but maybe help with weights and..." He fumbled to find another reason.

"Fetch us water?" Stacy crooned.

Amy swatted her friend. "Don't turn Spencer into a water boy."

Spencer laughed. "Anything to help you ladies."

"You're here a lot, aren't you?" Stacy asked.

"I'm a personal trainer, so yes.'

That much was obvious by his fit and toned body, which he showed off by wearing muscle tanks or no shirt at all. For a fleeting moment, Stacy imagined what working out with Ethan would be like. She couldn't picture what he might look like without a shirt on. She banished the thought, not wanting Amy to read anything on her face. She hadn't told anyone about her new witch friend yet.

Spencer led the training session with Amy, and Stacy stood by to give pointers when she felt like it. The session centered more on building muscle and endurance and less on self-defense technique, so Stacy went along with it and seldom interrupted Spencer's methods. Besides, she didn't want to be the friend who spoiled a perfectly good flirtation session.

Spencer found all sorts of ways to touch Amy when not necessary. To Stacy's relief, he wasn't creepy about it, and it didn't take Amy long to do the same. *Before I know it, I'll be third-wheeling all my workouts,* Stacy thought.

She was glad Amy had called her to blow off steam. With the magic building inside her, she had more than one reason to get a daily workout routine in. She preferred going to the gym to beating some guy's ass and soon found herself on the treadmill. After a solid run, she joined Amy and Spencer by the weights. The pair had finished for the day and were sitting on a bench, enjoying light snacks and water.

"You say you've never gone to the gym consistently, but I swear you act like you've been here every day of your life," Spencer commented to Amy as Stacy approached.

Amy's face was red, but Stacy wasn't sure if it was from exertion or blushing. "That's not true, and you know it," she pushed back.

Spencer grinned and eyed Stacy. "You can't tell me Amy has only started going to the gym recently."

"Well, seeing as how she and I only met a few weeks ago, I can't deny her story."

"Besides, I always tell the truth," Amy chirped.

A customer for Spencer came in not long after that, and he bid the two young women goodbye. He left Amy with a wink. "Better see you in here more. You've made my day."

"Soooo," Stacy drawled after Spencer was out of earshot.

"Don't start," Amy warned, but she couldn't help a smile.

Stacy hooked her arm through Amy's as they headed out of the gym. "I'm glad you're finding new ways to blow off steam."

Stacy could only avoid going back to work for so long.

Her desk was piled high with new legal briefs and case files to work through. One plus to having beaten Lenny again last week was that her boss had given her several options for which case to take next. She would spend all day rifling through them, deciding which person most needed her help.

By the time lunch hit, she was only a third of the way through the pile and the cases she had read blurred together. She needed another cup of coffee and plenty to eat. Ever since her magic awoke, she was eating more than ever. It was like the dragon part of her was a literal dragon inside her, growling until it was fed, never satisfied.

She wished she'd spent her morning at Ethan's shop learning new spells and advancing ones she already knew. Instead, she had no clue when she would see him next. They had a night planned for drinks, but she hoped to see him before that.

"What is everyone talking about?" Stacy asked Jenna at lunch. She had noticed an unusual amount of chatter in the office today. More talking than working seemed to be the course of the day. While Stacy had shut herself in her office to read over cases, everyone in the main room had talked.

"We were contacted by another firm this morning," Jenna replied. "Apparently, Lenny won another case against them and is being as obnoxious as ever. A man who works there and has lost to Lenny several times up and quit this morning. He's buddies with a guy who works here, so it got out."

Stacy wondered if Lenny's obnoxiousness was his way of getting the word out that he'd won so she would hear it. She suddenly hoped to find a case on her desk with Lenny on the other side. The more she could take him down, the more...

The thought trailed off as Jenna quipped, "But hey, at least you don't have that stupid lawsuit to deal with. Lenny must have realized how idiotic it was. I mean, if anyone sticks to the rules, it's you, Stacy Drake. He wouldn't be able to pull one over on you."

Stacy forced a smile. "Thanks, Jenna."

Her friend leaned forward, lowering her voice so no one else could hear. "Are you going to tell me what really happened this weekend and who you were with? I saw Jonathan out the other night, so I know it wasn't him."

"The only bed I was in was my childhood room," Stacy replied, a sparkle of amusement in her eyes. "I was taking… lessons. I told you about my new hobby." She sipped her coffee.

Jenna waggled her eyebrows. "Sure, Stace. I'd love to know who your…instructor is if you ever decide to share."

Stacy thought about Ethan and how his personality would clash with Jenna's. It would be amusing to see the pair square off. Jenna left Stacy to finish her lunch, and with no one else to talk to, she checked her messages.

One was from her father.

> **KHAN**
>
> Have a good day back at work. Feel free to come by whenever you'd like.

A second message from Amy had arrived an hour ago.

> **AMY**
>
> Did I tell you I gave Spencer my number? He wants another session. I want to say yes, but I'm swamped with work. Haven't told him what I do yet.

The final message was from Ethan.

> **ETHAN**
>
> I have a book on selenography (that means the study of lunar silence) for you to borrow if you want to know more about the moon. You know, since you're super fascinated with the moon and all.

Stacy fought a smile. She liked it when Ethan messaged her, especially now since he insisted her magic could do better with the help of something like a full moon. She was further grateful for the way he covered up her real reasons for wanting to study the topic. She typed her response and sent it off as her lunch hour ended.

> Buried in legal briefs right now, but I'll try to pick it up when I can.

Stacy was the last to leave the office that day. As she stepped out onto the darkening street, a prickling sensation at the back of her neck gripped her. She stilled, knowing by now the feeling meant she was being watched. She hastened away from the office. Whatever it was could follow her for all she cared. If she was going to face him head-on, it was better to do it in a more obscure location.

She wove through people lining the streets and past taxis at red lights, blaring their horns as she darted across. It did not take her long to reach her apartment. Inside, she scanned the security feeds. Jonathan had helped her set up cameras the last time he was here. "Nothing new," she muttered as she examined the footage. Nothing showed from the night before or now.

She went to shower and wondered if her senses were heightened from her recent magical endeavors or if something more sinister was waiting for her. She shot off a text to Ethan before jumping in the shower.

> I'll be by to pick up that book tonight.

CHAPTER TWENTY

> *"Who watched us pass; and lower, and where the long*
> *Rich galleries, lady-laden, weighed the necks*
> *Of dragons clinging to the crazy walls,*
> *Thicker than drops from thunder, showers of flowers*
> *Fell as we past; and men and boys astride*
> *On wyvern, lion, dragon, griffin, swan,*
> *At all the corners, named us each by name..."*
> —Alfred Lord Tennyson, The Holy Grail

Stacy had to wait until one in the morning before she slipped into Central Park.

She could have gone to the Drakethorn estate to practice her shielding spell, but she needed to be able to drive from her apartment to work after the sun came up. *I won't be here long*, she told herself as she parked her car and slipped into the park. She wanted to pull the magnetic magical energy from the moon and practice her shielding spell. If Ethan was right about the aid the moon would provide, she'd listen to him more moving forward.

She'd waited until the park was closed. Though she was normally the last person to break the law in this fashion, she felt it was for the greater good. The moon was full tonight, and she needed a place to test her spells.

Earlier that night, she'd picked up the book from Ethan, then come here with takeout food and eaten while reading. Now, she stepped foot into the park, noting its emptiness this late at night. It was much quieter than normal, and she shivered.

It was a good thing she'd brought her mother's cloak. She slipped it on as she headed to the center of the park, where the trees separated to show the fullness of the moon above. Its silvery light cast a pleasant glow over the leaves.

Make it quick, she told herself as she took her stance in the center of the clearing. She hadn't brought the satchel full of items this time, wanting to do things Ethan's way. His recommendation to use the moon's power was the reason she'd come here to begin with. She had tried it in her apartment first, but the walls and windows hadn't allowed her to use the natural magic as well. She hadn't risked going to the roof when it was open to anyone who lived in the complex.

She stood and prodded at her natural surroundings with her magic, testing to see what held raw energy and what didn't. Drawing magic up outside herself had been much easier at the Drakethorn estate or in Ethan's shop, where magical items were abundant.

Here, she felt trickles of it in the trees and ground, but it was nowhere near as potent as what ran beneath her family estate. However, she realized she would not always have the option of having natural magic available to her. It was good to practice in a place where she had to draw most of it from within herself.

She spoke the incantation for the shielding spell, and magic flared around her, encasing her body in protective energy. She huffed a sound of disbelief. *I did it!* She fused more magic into it, creating layers to further protect her. The moon truly did help. The shield materialized further down her body until it covered every part of her.

The trick now was in keeping the shield up. Too bad Ethan wasn't around to zap her with spells so she could practice.

A second after the thought crossed Stacy's mind, something punched the outside of her shield and ricocheted off, hitting a nearby tree. The force of the object hitting the shield sent a bolt of pain through her. *What the hell?*

Was that a…

A second bullet hit her shield with the amount of pain she might have experienced if she'd been wearing a Kevlar vest. The shot from somewhere across the clearing had been quiet, but the bullet against her shield had not. A *zing* and a snapping sound followed.

A sniper was somewhere among the trees. She had not entered the park alone. *Shit.*

The third shot almost got through her shield. The magic around her spasmed, hitting her body with enough force to throw her into the underbrush behind her. Her shield dropped as her focus did the same. She landed in a bed of thorny bushes that scratched and tore at her. She cursed. *Fucking Lenny.*

She was sure she could take out the bastard Lenny had sent after her if she could find him. She reinforced her shield, hoping to combat the bullets better as she emerged from the brush.

She stood, cloak billowing around her as a swift, cold wind picked up. She did not feel its chill, thanks to the enchantments in the cloak and the quick rush of her blood. Her magic joined it. A fresh sense of anger welled up. She was determined not to appear shaken as she sprang back into the clearing, snarling, "Come out and face me, bastard!"

He didn't need further encouragement. A dark-clothed figure bounded out from the trees, shocking Stacy with the fact that he was on all fours, then rose with normal arms and legs. He slashed out, and she couldn't tell if it was a knife in his hands or something else.

No sign of a gun was anywhere. He must have given it up and

left it in the underbrush, which meant he thought he had a chance against her hand-to-hand.

Stacy evaded his first strike by dipping left. However, he was too fast for her to get in a solid strike. This was nothing like grappling with Spencer at the gym.

She focused on pouring magic into her shield. It flared bright and red around her, giving her enough light alongside the moon to see the man. He had a clean-shaven face and eyes like silver that burned with fury. Small scars spattered his skin. She had never seen this fucker before. He wasn't any of the men who had followed her previously. Lenny must have gotten tired of failing and hired someone with a more sinister reputation.

These conclusions flew through Stacy's mind as he advanced on her, alternating between lunging and taking a prowling stance. He had a much larger body and seemed to know her next move before she did. She gritted her teeth, fighting her frustration as much as she fought him.

Finally, she lunged toward his waist and managed a solid punch to his gut, then another to his face when he groaned. She hit him hard, far harder than a woman should have been able to and sent him reeling. Shock washed over his face. Lenny hadn't told him the girl he was after might fight back. She wondered if the attacker had seen her shield or if he didn't have magic and convinced himself it was something different.

A low growl shook from his throat, and Stacy could have sworn the ground trembled in response. She determined not to do the same. Her shield guttered as he raked a hand across it. A hand, or...

What the hell was that?

She poured more magic into her shield. At the same time, she glimpsed the change that came over him. First, it was the way his eyes turned from silver to a blazing red. His face grew longer until, instead of a nose, he had a snout. Hair sprung up over his skin, coarse and dark. His hands were no longer hands but paws, and his fingers…

Stacy's eyes widened at the claws protruding from his flesh. He lurched toward her again, raking those claws over her shield. It might as well have been her back with the way she screamed. Agony tore through her. The shield dropped. She was unable to keep it up as pain lashed through her. No one had taught her that having her magic hit could hurt her. She'd have to learn a way to separate the two.

She didn't have time to fling her shield up again before his claws sunk into her upper thigh and dragged down. She gasped as the pain hit her like a wave. She kicked with her other leg. The claws tore out, and blood poured down her leg. Her shield went up, and the figure crashed against it in an effort to claw her again. The force sent him ricocheting off as his bullets had done. He fell to the ground with a heavy *thud*.

That's a fucking werewolf! Stacy realized.

Now was her chance. While he was down, she could get the fuck away from him. Gods, the pain in her thigh was almost blinding. Her clothes were slick with blood. She hoped her father was right about having innate healing abilities. She ignored the hot, pulsing pain in her leg as she took off toward her car. She scrambled for her keys and found them in a pocket of her cloak. Her phone, however, was missing.

Shit. She couldn't go back for it now. That thing would be on his feet soon and coming after her.

She bolted for the edge of the park. Her car was in sight. A growling behind her said the werewolf had gathered himself. She dared a glance over her shoulder to find him back in human form. Her heart pounded wildly as she reached her car. She jerked the door open and had it started less than a second later.

She didn't care about the screech of her tires as she hurried from the lot. She couldn't go back to her apartment. The werewolf would only follow her, and she doubted he would care about cameras or other people seeing him. She needed a place fortified by magic where she could get some help.

Dad's, she thought.

If Khan found out about this and knew she hadn't gone to him for help, he'd be furious. It wasn't like before when she'd fought off big men. This person had as much magic as she did.

Stacy was hardly out onto the street when she spotted the werewolf coming after her on a motorcycle. So this was how it was going to be. A high-speed chase through the fucking city in the middle of the night.

Not how I planned my evening, Stacy thought, hands tightening on the steering wheel. She wished she could call her dad and tell him she was coming, but her phone was lost somewhere in the park. She wound through city streets, taking a route she knew would be less populated. The faster she could get the hell out of here, the better.

She bolted through red lights, not caring as the beast pursued her. He did the same, never stalling for a second. Lenny must have paid the guy a fuck-ton of money to come after her. Why else was he so relentless?

Lenny wanted her dead this time, or at least beaten enough that she couldn't fight him in court. She wished now she had been more open with her father about what Lenny really wanted to do to her. About how long she had been followed and the thugs involved. Too late now.

The city fell away, and she met the open roads heading north. The motorcycle continued after her. She slammed on the gas harder. Now that no other cars were in the way, she could gun it.

Please go away, she pleaded.

It wasn't long before the werewolf caught up to her. His motorcycle raced alongside her car. She wished she had chosen a better vehicle when she purchased this one, but she hadn't exactly been buying to outrace a fucking werewolf determined to claw her apart.

The blood around her leg was still wet, but the pain had abated. She wasn't sure if it was the adrenaline or if her flesh had stitched itself back together using her magic. She wished she could cloak her car in a shielding spell, especially when the werewolf leaped off his motorcycle and landed on the roof.

"Are you fucking crazy?" Stacy exclaimed. She swerved with the force of him hitting her vehicle. Trees loomed. If she crashed now, she'd be done for. She got back onto the road, still going at top speed. Curves appeared ahead. If she didn't slow down, she'd fucking wreck.

A snarl above her told Stacy the werewolf was transforming back into his beast form, making him twice the size he was as a man.

A fist slammed into her roof. Claws raked across it. He meant to tear her car to pieces, then rip her limb from limb! She had to think of something fast. The Drakethorn estate loomed in the distance. Trees arose. An idea sparked in her mind.

If what her father said about her healing abilities was true, she might be able to pull this off. *This had better work,* she thought. *Or else I'm going to look like the dumbest fuck alive.*

Her magic surged as if assuring her that the plan was the right course of action.

She spun her car and hit the trees at the start of the forest on her father's estate. The car crumpled with the impact. The werewolf went silent. Was he hurt enough? Stacy sure as fuck hoped so.

She scrambled from her car, feeling dazed and more than a little banged up. Her magic worked quickly to heal her. She took off through the trees without glancing back. She had to get to the back of the estate and find her father before that thing managed to chase her down again.

Her senses were on high alert as she took off. The trees closed in around her. It was fucking dark here. She came to a spot where the trees overhead allowed the moonlight to flood in. With the heightened sight, she made out where she was going. A small path she recognized started from a clearing and led into the forest. It would be a long venture back up the hill to the estate, but she saw no other way. Turning back would mean running into the werewolf again.

The woods were quiet enough to make her feel uneasy. Her heart pounded faster than ever. The pain in her body continued. A soft wind brushed through the trees. The sound of her feet trampling leaves as she hurried along the path joined it.

Then, clear and cutting, the howl of a wolf filled the air.

Fuck. Stacy limped along the path, wishing she could run at full speed. The crash meant she couldn't. Not until her magic finished healing her. It didn't help that less than an hour ago, she'd had the werewolf's claws embedded in her thigh. She winced at the memory, hoping not to have that happen again. She needed to find her way to the house where the wards could protect her, where Khan could help drive off this beast.

The path she had taken ended in a clearing. It was wider than the last one and flooded with moonlight. She recognized the spot as the place where she had first had training with Khan. The wolf was close on her heels. She knew this by the rush of his paws on the ground and the low growls that trembled along the trees.

Why hadn't the wards stopped him? It hit her then. He'd gotten some of her blood on him. Stacy remembered what her father said about the wards, that anyone with his blood would be able to get through. Had the werewolf been able to undo a small part of the wards with her blood and slip past? It was the only explanation she could think of.

She wouldn't be able to outrun the wolf. She had to turn and face him.

"Here goes nothing," she muttered as she stood at the clearing's center and drew upon the moonlight. Her shield flared to life around her, and she hoped it would hold better this time. She had more magic around her to keep it intact.

Seconds later, the wolf crashed into the clearing, seemingly unharmed from the crash. He collided with her shield without so much as stopping to appraise her. Stacy reeled, but her shield held fast. Now, if she could get a hit or two in…

The werewolf's guttural voice stalled her, sending her into a whirl of surprise as words spilled forth. He sounded half like a wolf and half like a human. "I'll tear off your head, bitch. I need it as proof of your death."

"That's not very nice," Stacy shot back. "I didn't realize werewolves lacked manners."

The werewolf snarled. They circled one another, and Stacy wondered if her eyes blazed gold the same way the werewolf's shone red. "I'll teach you not to mess with my kind," the werewolf uttered, advancing.

"Stay back," Stacy commanded.

"Or what? You know how to use a shield, and you pack a mean punch, but you're weak with magic. You can't use spells and transform."

He was right. Stacy's heart faltered, and so did her shield. She poured more magic into it, not giving the wolf shifter a millisecond to catch her off guard. *I have to get away from here. I need—*

The wolf's voice cut off her thought. "You were stupid to test your powers tonight. You made my job easier. I thought I would have to break into your home, but you came right to me."

"You will learn that taking the job to get me was a big fucking mistake!" Stacy shot back.

She wasn't sure if the sound that came out of him next was a laugh or a growl. "The man who hired me may not have known what you were, but I can smell it on you."

It gave her all the more reason to send his ass back to wherever he came from.

"You will regret following me here." Her voice was low and dangerous.

"What you did to those men in the alley won't work on me," the wolf replied.

How did he know about that?

"Yes, I was there that night when you did it. I saw how you changed, and—"

"Shut the hell up!" Stacy's mind raced. It *had* been her, and she had somehow managed to collect her own clothes before fleeing the scene. Some small part of her, hidden beneath the monstrous form she had taken and did not know how to go back to, had been vigilant enough not to leave a trace. She'd been too furious to stop herself from shredding the thugs, but the Thorn side of her had been smart enough not to leave evidence behind.

The wolf snarled and leaped. This time, when he hit Stacy's shield, the impact was too strong, and she crashed to the ground.

CHAPTER TWENTY-ONE

"A dragon's will must not be trifled with. He is far more than scaled armor and blazing breath. He is a culmination of history, wars of the ages in his wings."
—*Unknown*, The Dragon Codex History, Vol. II

Stacy's whole body pulsed with pain.

It lanced through her every nerve. She felt as though she'd been set on fire.

She landed on the ground, hitting roots hard. They dug into her back. Her shield vanished as her focus slipped. All the air left her lungs.

Struggling to breathe, she watched in horror as the werewolf stalked toward her. His mouth was open, sharp teeth gleaming with saliva. He intended to tear out her throat and take her head back to prove what he'd done. Even so, her heart did not tremble in fear. Pure rage wrestled there. She didn't know how to let it out.

"Aw, the little witch girl has lost all her magic. Whatever will she do?" The wolf's voice was somewhere between a croon and a growl.

"Fuck. You," Stacy managed. He was two feet away. He'd be hovering over her soon. She would feel his hot breath and the drip of his saliva on her face. She winced at the thought. *There's magic left in you yet,* she told herself. *Fucking use it!*

She felt a dismal trickle of energy in the bottom of her well. She reached for it and yanked, her mind on the moon above. Her shield flickered to life once more around her. The wolf laughed. "That won't do you any good, girl."

She didn't know how to use any other spells. She wished she'd listened better when she was younger, paid attention to her self-defense lessons. Perhaps then her father might have taught her about magic sooner. *But my magic wasn't awake then,* she reminded herself. *So it wouldn't have mattered.*

It was awake now, and it was raging. *Use it!*

Another part of her mind queried, *How?*

She pictured how she might pull her magic from her shield and use it as a weapon. She didn't know the incantations or the words to make that happen, but maybe tonight, with the full moon shining above her, she wouldn't have to.

She struggled to her feet. With her shield shimmering around her, the wolf had not been able to pounce. He'd taken too long sizing up his meal. The wolf laughed at her, calling her a fool for thinking she stood a chance.

She pulled magic from her shield, willing it to take on a new form. Any form. Any fucking thing that could be useful.

An orb of light shone in her palm. She hurled it at the wolf.

His yelp filled the clearing as the light collided with him. The sizzling sound of burning fur followed. Stacy couldn't believe it. She gathered another orb. This time, when she threw it, the wolf evaded her attack. It crashed into a tree behind him.

Now was her chance to fucking *run*.

She took off again, choosing the path that led up and out of the woods. Though her body still simmered with pain, she bolted through the trees. Branches reached out to snag at her cloak, but she moved like the wind. Something in her clothes allowed her to flee this fast. Her mother was here with her, even if she could not see it.

The wind whistled through the trees and her hair. The lunging pursuit of the wolf was enough to keep her going despite the exhaustion sliding through her.

Her father's house would soon come into view, and he would protect her. She hoped against all hope that she'd make it. The cloak around her billowed in the night breeze, keeping her warm. Stacy wondered if the enchantments inside her mother's old clothes had helped her produce more magic.

She glanced over her shoulder as the wolf bounded from the woods behind her. She stretched her shield into shards of bright light. He evaded each strike, eyes blazing redder than ever the closer he came. He was pissed off. Good. Let him be. She was about done.

She reached the back portion of the Drakethorn estate. A clear sky spanned overhead. The wolf caught up and crashed into her shield, bouncing off, but his ability to heal quickly aided him. The moon might have helped her, but it also made his power reach its full potential.

Stacy fell again but managed to keep her shield up. This time, the wolf didn't bother with taunting words. He lunged for her again. She squeezed her eyes shut, pouring as much magic as possible into the shield. She didn't know what else to do.

The wolf never collided with her shield.

A deadly silence filled the space, broken by a ground-rattling roar. It cracked through the night, coming from somewhere overhead.

Stacy dared to open her eyes and gasped.

She believed her father when he said he was a dragon, and she had imagined what he might look like, but she hadn't imagined *this*.

Her father's wings splayed across the sky as he soared over the grounds. He was colored a deep red all the way through, darker near the edges, as if they'd been burned by his own fire. His underbelly was a glistening gold. His four legs extended for a landing, his claws making the werewolf's look like manicured nails. A tail as long as a tree whipped out as Khan braced for a landing.

When he touched the ground with full force, everything under Stacy shook. She remembered the small earthquakes she'd caused in her apartment. This was a lot stronger.

The werewolf might have been too full of fury to back down. He snarled, not seeming to comprehend what he was facing. *He's fucking stupid,* Stacy thought. She had warned him, and he hadn't listened. Her father would make the beast back down and turn to human form. They could question him about who sent him here and why—

Stacy thought that would happen, but she soon discovered how wrong she was.

Draconic instincts overtook her father. A gust of fire swept from his nostrils, engulfing the werewolf.

Fucking hell! Stacy's mind screamed.

The werewolf blackened like charred meat, but Khan wasn't finished. His mouth gaped open, huge and full of teeth she didn't want to be anywhere near. She felt hot all over, sweating from head to toe simply because of the fire he'd blazed seconds ago.

She stood at last, gaping as her father's dragon mouth descended on the werewolf. With one bite, he tore the creature in half. The remainder of the werewolf's body thumped to the ground.

Khan ate that part, too.

Stacy's heart hammered. "Holy shit."

She figured dragons had to eat but hadn't thought much about it. What had her father been eating in this form for all those years he had gone without turning human? She didn't want to know. Those were questions for another day.

Khan did not seem to notice his daughter until he had swallowed. He turned, sniffing the air as if searching for other attackers. When he realized there were none, his golden eyes fell upon her. The gold made sense now. Not a shred of green was visible in those dragon eyes. The gold had taken over, and Stacy imagined the same would happen to her if she ever shifted.

My red aura makes sense, too, she thought. It came from her father's dragon blood. One thing confused her, though. When she had pulled magic into orbs to hurl at the wolf, it had been white, not red. *My mother's magic,* she realized. And her mother's magic had her standing now, calming herself with breathing techniques she'd learned over the years.

She was aware the dragon before her was her father, and he wouldn't dare to hurt her. Still, she couldn't help feeling breathless and terrified. She had never seen a real dragon before, had never seen a creature so *huge* in her entire life.

Khan approached her, the ground shaking as he stomped over. His claws raked stark lines in the ground.

"You're…big," was all she could say at first.

Khan huffed, and she wasn't sure if he was annoyed or amused. A hint of a smile tugged at her lips. "Thanks for that, by the way. Stalker problems, right? I guess I'm popular."

The searing look he gave her with those golden eyes told her he was less than pleased by her deflection. "I tried to do it on my own," she admitted. "I have this pride thing where I don't want to ask for help." Her lips quirked. "Wonder where I got it from?"

Khan huffed again. Then, to Stacy's surprise, he changed. The dragon form fell away like scales shedding from a snake. As soon as the scales hit the ground, they vanished. A sizzling sound followed, and smoke wafted from the earth. In its place stood Khan, dressed in black fighting leathers and looking grimmer than ever. The gold in his eyes abated, leaving a soft tinge of green. "Stacy." His voice sounded broken.

"I'm okay." Her voice was thick with emotion. It wasn't until that moment when she saw the anguish on her father's face that she processed what happened. She'd come close to losing her fucking head more than once tonight. All evidence of the attacker was gone, though. "I felt her," she managed. "I felt Mom when I was out there. I did something with my magic that I didn't know I could do."

At last, the grimness in her father's face faded. His eyes glistened with tears, but he merely nodded, not trusting himself to speak yet.

"And when I ran out of the woods, I knew you'd be here. I just knew. And I knew I wasn't going to die."

He nodded once more. Khan approached her, finally managing a few words. "Stacy, you're still bleeding."

She managed a rough laugh. "Yeah, being attacked by a wolf and crashing my car would do that, wouldn't it?"

Khan led her to a stone bench in the garden at the back of the house. She lowered herself onto it, gingerly pulling her torn pant leg away to examine the wound the wolf had left on her thigh. Most of it was closed, but blood still oozed from it.

"Your healing magic is working, but it is not as fast and efficient as it should be. It will take time for your body to learn how to heal itself quickly," Khan remarked. "Supernatural wounds take longer to heal, you see, since there was magic in what the werewolf did to you." He laid a hand over her thigh. Stacy winced, but the pain did not last long as his warm power surged through her.

Stacy watched in awe as her flesh closed, looking brand-new. Not so much as a scar revealed what had happened to her. She had plenty of scrapes and cuts from tonight's events, but her body could mend itself there.

Khan's quiet voice reached her. "You should have told me what you were doing tonight."

Stacy swallowed. "The pride thing, remember? I'll work on it." She paused, then added, "There is one thing I'll ask for your help with now."

"What might that be?"

Stacy sighed. "I'm pretty sure I totaled my car."

A laugh tumbled from Khan's mouth. "Don't worry. I have people for that."

People? His staff hadn't been around all month. Maybe they had come back. Stacy raised a brow. "Do you mean tow truck people or something else?" She shook her head. "Never mind. That doesn't matter right now."

"I've been thinking about better cars for you anyway," Khan told her. "How does a Corvette sound? I've been working on fixing up an old one for the past few months."

Her brows shot up. "I don't think you should be rewarding me after tonight."

He chuckled. "I was going to wait until Christmas, but you need some way to get back home."

Feeling healed, she stood and locked her arms over her chest. She examined her father as if she was meeting him for the first time. "Yeah, I think I'll take you up on that. What if I wreck it, though? I don't want to be barbecued like the werewolf you ate a minute ago." Gods, she still couldn't believe that happened.

"Would you have made it here if you were driving that instead of your old car?" Khan asked.

Stacy considered the question, then nodded. "Most likely. My other car doesn't handle those curves so well."

Khan's features sobered. His voice was somber. "Then I'd give up all the cars in the world to have you safe."

Stacy hadn't cried until that moment. Now, she couldn't keep the tears in. It wasn't about the car or that he'd saved her. It was everything he'd ever done for her despite the secrets and the pressure to lead a life she didn't want. She could forgive him for those things.

He had changed. *She* had changed. He didn't seem disappointed to have a lawyer for a daughter now and hadn't since she first came back to the estate weeks ago. Stacy hadn't been able to admit it then. She'd been afraid he was only being kind to get her to come back and would revert to his old self. He hadn't, though. *I can trust him. He loves me,* she thought.

They lapsed into silence. The moon still shone above them in its bright, full glory. This was a turning point, Stacy realized. She'd always known parts of the world were shrouded in darkness, that malicious and sinister people lurked out of sight. Hidden dark places would always exist in the world, but she could drag the monsters out of the darkness and expose them to the light.

"You will learn more," Khan told her. "You will learn of the horrors and wars I have faced, of the history we cannot undo. You will see how it is all woven together and how it led to now. To you."

Stacy huffed. "No pressure. I'm not, like, the chosen one or anything, am I?"

Her father laughed.

She paused, realizing something else. "That was you, wasn't it?"

"What was?"

"All those times I felt like someone was watching me in the last few weeks. That was you?"

Khan was silent for a long moment. Finally, he nodded. "Yes. I hope you will not be angry with me."

"I thought it was stalkers the whole time. I think it was sometimes, but there were moments when I felt you but couldn't see. I checked the security feeds and everything."

Khan produced a knowing smile. "We dragons might be large

and mighty, but we have our tricks for keeping out of sight. Even from those with the true sight of magic."

Stacy surprised herself by approaching her father and wrapping her arms around him. "Sometimes, I suppose, a daughter needs to understand how protective a dad can be. I love you."

Khan returned the embrace. Stacy felt warm and secure. She hoped her mother was seeing this, wherever she was.

CHAPTER TWENTY-TWO

"Go couch you childwise in the grass,
Believing it's some jungle strange,
Where mighty monsters peer and pass,
Where beetles roam and spiders range.
'Mid gloom and gleam of leaf and blade,
What dragons rasp their painted wings!
O magic world of shine and shade!
O beauty land of Little Things!"
—*Robert William Service*, The Joy of Little Things

Golden sunlight poured into Stacy's room, waking her gently from her long slumber. She rolled over, squinting, and wondered why her minimalistic apartment bedroom looked so cluttered. Then she realized she was not in her apartment but her childhood bedroom, and everything that occurred the night before came rushing back.

She sat up with a jolt, expecting to feel any number of small wounds on her body. She felt nothing but comfort. Not a single limb was stiff or aching. It seemed her magic had healed her while she slept. A smile crossed her lips. She had missed work, and people there probably wondered where she was, but she was alive.

She imagined Lenny at his office or home, pacing and wondering where the hell the werewolf he'd hired was. She didn't have proof of it, only what the werewolf said. She half wished her father hadn't eaten the creature so she could have questioned him, but in the end, did it matter? She was certain Lenny had sent the creature after her, though they would have no real evidence to take to law enforcers. Not that evidence would help her, anyway.

She had other questions. Did Lenny know the hitman was a werewolf? How aware were Lenny and Victor of the supernatural around them?

Lenny would have a bad day when he found out Stacy Drake was still alive. The thought normally would have made her smile, but it sobered her. Lenny had tried to kill her, and he wouldn't stop anytime soon. She had to come up with a plan.

She rose, stretching her legs and glancing out at the grounds. No signs of what had happened last night remained. The claw marks made by both the werewolf and Khan in his dragon form had disappeared along with the scorched ground where Khan's fire had blazed. The night lived on only in her memory, and she was certain it wasn't the last night like that she would have.

However, today was a new day, and she wouldn't waste it in bed. She had healed and felt energized. She checked the clock on her bedside table and realized it was midafternoon. If she was going to get anything done, she needed to start soon. She dressed, and before leaving her bedroom, she glanced at the pile of her mother's journals sitting on the desk. Later, she would consult them for new spells that might help her against shifting enemies.

Catherine would always be around to lend a helping hand, whether through her old clothes, her written words, or the spirit she'd given her daughter last night.

Stacy was full of gratitude as she went downstairs and found her father in his study, organizing various books and papers. He wasn't alone.

She started. "Mr. Blackguard!"

The estate butler turned, surprised to hear her voice, then beamed. "Anastasia! What a surprise. Your father didn't tell me—"

Khan grinned. "I told you I had a surprise for you this morning."

Mr. Blackguard, who had been like an elderly uncle to Stacy all her life, pulled her into a tight embrace. "I am overjoyed to see you have come for a visit." Mr. Blackguard's face bore confusion. No doubt he was trying to determine what triggered the reconciliation between Stacy and her father.

"Mr. Blackguard has come back to work, as well as the cook and the others," Khan remarked, his eyes meeting his daughter's. The green in them twinkled. "I told them I would need more help when it came to training my only child in the legacy of the Drakethorns, both as a dragon shifter and a witch."

Stacy's eyes widened as they returned to the butler. "You know what we are?"

Mr. Blackguard dipped into a ceremonious bow. "We here at the estate have long been aware of the true Drakethorn lineage and have vowed to serve in whatever way we can."

"Mr. Blackguard has particularly fascinating qualities, Stacy," Khan spoke up from behind his desk. "Though he is quite a few centuries old and prefers his human form."

She gaped.

Mr. Blackguard's eyes shone. "I'm afraid I won't be showing off my magic anytime soon, Miss Anastasia. It takes quite a bit of effort now that I am this old."

Khan's eyes glittered. "Ms. Fynnel, however, still uses her magic. How do you think her cooking is so good?"

"Natural talent?" Stacy quipped.

Khan laughed.

She reeled. These people had magic all the time she lived here, and she'd never guessed it. It made sense, though. Her father would have employed people who wouldn't have questioned it if they found the master of the house flying over the place in dragon form. They had been hired to do the basic work of keeping the estate but also to maintain Khan's secrets. She'd have a lot to learn from the staff, too.

"You also protected me as a child," Stacy realized aloud.

Mr. Blackguard nodded. "Indeed, we did, though we were nothing compared to your father. He protected us all."

It made sense that the staff had magic, given the wards surrounding the place. They could have maintained the protections as well. "I was sad when you left us, Anastasia. It felt like losing a family member," Mr. Blackguard added.

She opened her mouth to reply—to apologize or defend herself, she did not know which—but Khan spoke up first. "Stacy was making a name for herself in the city. She has quite a reputation now. We were all sad when she left, but it's been for the best. She had to find her own identity, and it has made her all the better for carrying on the Drakethorn legacy."

Stacy's heart squeezed at his words.

Mr. Blackguard smiled. "I know it is mid-day, but I can have Ms. Fynnel make something up for you."

"No need," she replied. "I have a lot to do today. I'll be going now, but don't worry, Mr. Blackguard. I'll be back soon."

Khan bid his daughter goodbye, then turned to their butler. "Mr. Blackguard, please have the valet pull Stacy's new car around."

Stacy opened the door to *The Saige Page* at about four-thirty, the book on selenography tucked under her arm.

Ethan glanced up from where he stood behind the counter with a surprised expression. His sweater sleeves were rolled to his elbows as he tinkered with a small metal contraption. He halted when she approached and leaned on the counter.

"Well, well. I wasn't sure if I was going to see the very busy Stacy the Attorney today or not." He nodded at the book tucked under her arm. "Did that help?"

Stacy smiled. "It got me into some unnecessary trouble, but I learned a lot." She set the book on the counter, having learned everything from it she needed.

Ethan raised a brow. "Whatever that means. At least the book is still intact."

She glowered. "I have plenty of respect for the arcane."

He grinned. "Come here for a lesson?"

"I only came to return the book. I can see you are busy."

"Are we still on for drinks tomorrow night?"

"Yes, and I wanted to see if we could make spell lessons more frequent."

Ethan arched a brow. "If I didn't know better, I'd think you weren't getting enough of me."

Stacy rolled her eyes but couldn't keep a smile off her face. "I'm hungry to know more. I feel this burning in me to learn as much as I can. Does that make sense?" She had felt that way before last night, long before her magic awoke. She had always been like that, wanting to know more and carve a way forward in her life. She had all the knowledge of the arcane at her fingertips but didn't know where to start.

He nodded. "I know exactly what you mean." Longing glimmered in his eyes. "I've felt that way my whole life, but no one understood me." He seemed as though he was about to add something but decided not to.

She tapped the book. "Thanks for lending this to me. I'm sure I'll be back for more."

He gave her a slight smile. "Until then, we'll plan for drinks, and we can discuss our mutual hunger for knowledge."

She returned the smile, feeling like she'd stumbled on a true kindred spirit. "See you tomorrow, Ethan."

Ethan wasn't the only friend Stacy wanted to see.

She asked Amy to meet her at Bluestone Lane for coffee as the day wound down. She arrived first and settled in the same booth they had occupied before. She was halfway through a cup of coffee and answering a slew of messages from work when Amy entered.

While driving here in her new car, Stacy had considered what she should do next. Learning more about magic was obvious, but she wouldn't keep all her troubles to herself anymore. Amy had become more than a colleague to her. She was also her friend. After what had happened last night, she needed as much help as she could get, and that included Amy and Ethan.

It was time to fill Amy in on some of what had been going on.

The dragon and witch stuff would be overwhelming, so she decided to hold back on that. It was a revelation for another time when Stacy herself had a better understanding of this new world she was part of.

Amy entered wearing business casual clothing and seemed to have gotten off work shortly before coming here. She slid into the booth with a concerned expression. "Everything okay, Stacy? You sounded urgent on the phone. You look different, too. There's a determination in your face I haven't seen before."

Stacy chuckled. "You're observant."

Amy sat, shrugging. "I'm a journalist."

"Ever thinking about writing a column on your new friend?"

Amy grinned. "Maybe. You've caught some public interest. Might boost my career."

Stacy insisted she was joking and asked Amy to order whatever she wanted. "It's on me."

As soon as a waitress had brought Amy a coffee and muffin, Stacy began. "I haven't been totally open about everything going on with me concerning Lenny and Victor. I figured it was time to bring you into the loop. I've learned I can trust you."

"Thank you, Stacy. That means a lot."

"You see, someone attempted to assassinate me last night."

Amy's eyes bulged, and she nearly spit out her coffee. "That was not what I thought you were going to say."

Despite the topic of conversation, Stacy laughed. "Clearly, it didn't work."

"Did you beat the guy's ass like you did in the shipping yard?"

"Not quite. I wish. My dad took care of it."

Amy's brows furrowed, and Stacy went on. "I'm positive Lenny sent the assassin, and he'll be angry when he finds out I'm still alive. I've decided to spend most of my time at my father's… house." The word "estate" almost escaped her mouth. "I'll be safer there."

"But farther away from work."

"I think I'll be cutting back the number of cases I work on."

Amy gave her a quizzical expression, but Stacy wasn't about to share that she would be taking magic lessons and needed less work on her plate. "Don't worry. We'll still have our gym sessions."

Amy grinned, shaking her head. "I'm not worried about that. I'm still reeling over the word 'assassin.'"

"It wasn't the first time, either," Stacy admitted. She shared with Amy the number of times she'd been followed or seen a suspicious person outside her apartment.

When she finished, Amy asked, "Are you going to the police about this?"

Stacy shook her head. "At this level in the game, there isn't even a body to prove what happened to me."

Amy didn't bother hiding her shock. She lowered her voice. "Your father did away with it?"

"You could say that."

Amy blew out a breath.

If only she knew the full extent of the truth. Stacy wished she could tell her, but she feared Amy's humanness would not allow her to believe the parts about magic.

"I guess it doesn't matter," Amy added. "The police are wrapped around Victor's finger. You go to them with this, and Lenny will find a way to worm out of it. I suppose you're cooking up a different plan to take him down?"

Stacy nodded, unafraid to speak about it in public. Amy didn't know it, but Stacy had learned to cast a muffling spell. Anyone walking by couldn't make out the exact words they used. "I want you to come with me to my father's house and live with us for a while. I know it sounds crazy, but Lenny knows we're connected by now. If I'm in danger, so are you. That was why I was so urgent over the phone. I wanted to make sure nothing bad happens to you."

"But my job…"

"I'm sure you can work remotely, especially when your boss finds out where you're going."

Amy arched a brow. "You speak in riddles, Stacy Drake. I thought you were different from other lawyers."

Stacy laughed. She had a card up her sleeve. She hadn't intended to ever play it, not wanting to use her true name as leverage. At this point, however, using it to keep someone else safe couldn't be a bad thing. It was time to use her name for good.

"And what about money? Won't your dad want me to pay rent? I'm sure if I'm taking up space, that…"

She trailed off as Stacy waved a dismissive hand. "You don't have to worry about money or space. My father has plenty of both. This is about trust, and there's no one I trust more than you on this effort." Stacy paused, smiling. "Except maybe my dad."

"You're close to him, aren't you?"

"Closer than I used to be, anyway, which I'm glad for."

Amy eyed her. "I have a feeling I'm going to learn a lot more about you, Stacy. I'll give your proposal good consideration. I'll give you an answer soon, too." She paused, then asked, "Who exactly are you? I'll admit that when we first met, I wanted to be sure I could trust you. I did as much research as I could. I found a lot about you as an attorney and from your college days, but nothing before that."

Stacy gave her a knowing smile. "Have you ever heard of the Drakethorn family?"

Amy's brows furrowed. "Of course. Constantine Drakethorn is like a billionaire or something. Known for crypto and a whole empire, though no one has seen him in the city for over two decades." She paused, and full realization seemed to come over her. "No. You're not…"

"Anastasia Drakethorn."

Amy gasped. "Your family's wealth has always been elusive, almost rumored! I can't believe I've known you this many weeks, and—" She cut herself off with a shake of her head. "I don't believe it."

"You will learn a lot more about me in the coming days," Stacy assured her. "Get used to the surprises."

Wait until Amy learned about the dragon and witch part.

When Stacy had gone to her father about inviting Amy to stay with them, they'd discussed the possibility of her discovering the full truth one day. Stacy had insisted that she could be trusted, but they would use precautions to ensure Amy didn't find out for a while. After all, Stacy hadn't noticed the magic for her whole childhood.

"I didn't want to wave my last name around and use it to get through school and land a good job," Stacy explained. "I wanted to earn it regardless of a name and money. That's why I became Stacy Drake. I'll stay that way in the public eye for a while, at least while Lenny and Victor are enemies number one and two."

"I admire you for that," Amy replied. "I'm shocked, is all. Is it true the Drakethorn estate is north of the city and spans hundreds of acres? I always thought it was a rumor."

"Not a rumor, and you can see it for yourself if you agree to stay there with us."

Amy laughed. "Holy shit, Stacy. I can still call you Stacy, right?"

"Please do."

They both laughed, and Stacy's heart felt full. She had allies. Friends, even. For a moment, she didn't think about Lenny and Victor or the danger they posed. She didn't think of all the people who were victims of their schemes.

She thought of Amy, Ethan, her father, and all the others who would help her moving forward. She thought of her mother and the magic stirring inside her. She was an attorney and magic user who could one day call herself a dragon and a witch.

"We've got an interesting road ahead, Amy. Are you ready?" It would be dangerous, and she wouldn't be able to promise an easy time.

Amy raised her cup to Stacy, seeming to understand the weight of what she was agreeing to. "Show me what you've got, Anastasia Drakethorn."

"Is Mr. Dolos in today?" Stacy asked the secretary as soon as she stepped off the elevator.

"Yes, but he's b—"

"Thank you, Margaret. That's all I need," she interrupted as she breezed past the desk, taking the woman's name from a placard placed in front of her. The secretary gaped, but Stacy disappeared into Lenny's adjoining office before she could say another word.

She strolled into Lenny's ornate office as if she owned it.

Lenny sat behind a large mahogany desk, talking on the phone. As soon as he saw Stacy, he hung up. The shock in his face was wholly unsurprising. He stammered, his face going purple, and finally managed, "What are you doing here?"

His voice was guttural. There was no mistaking the hatred in it.

She smiled. "Surprised to see me?" Of course he was. He'd ordered her dead less than two days ago.

She glanced around his office, taking in the wood paneling, the windows overlooking the city skyline, the array of books and art, and files upon files. "I know you're busy, Lenny, but I figured it was time we stop playing this stupid game of 'who is the better lawyer.' There's enough room for both of us in this world." She'd chosen her words carefully to veil the true meaning, one she hoped Lenny picked up on.

"For whatever reason, you can't stop coming after me, though I am glad you dropped the lawsuit." She was aware Lenny had done it only so her death couldn't be traced back to him. Now that she was alive and standing in his office, he must have a hundred regrets.

He stood, looking angry enough to overturn his desk.

Stacy maintained a cool exterior and a sweetened tone. "I came to inform you that I am taking a backseat when it comes to cases, so we might not run into one another as much in the courtroom. However, I do want you to know we'll see one another in other arenas. There is more than one way to enact justice, and I fully intend to make sure you see how *just* I can be."

Lenny bristled. He definitely knew what she meant. He cleared his throat, face still flushed with fury. "You're a fucking idiot, you know that?"

"Let me guess. I'm a bitch, too, right?" She leaned on his desk, allowing the gold in her eyes to shine brighter than the green. She doubted he saw the red magic emanating around her. "Call me whatever you want, Lenny, but you can't call me a liar or a

coward, two things *you* are. Don't make me list everything else."
Attempted murderer was the one on the tip of her tongue, and he knew it.

A smile returned to her lips. "Have a good day, Lenny."

She turned to leave his office. The second she'd stepped foot inside, she had used her magic to search the space. She had learned what she needed, and a new plan to strike began to form.

Lenny better watch out, Stacy thought as she waved to the bewildered secretary and took the elevator down. *He doesn't know yet that he has a dragon on his tail.*

THE STORY CONTINUES

The story continues with book two, *Scales of Truth*, coming soon to Amazon and Kindle Unlimited.

Claim Your Copy At

AUTHOR'S NOTES

APRIL 8, 2024

Thank you for reading my new new (old) series!

I wrote a three-book series about a supernatural lawyer while I was on hiatus a year or so ago, and we are entending it to six books. In case you haven't read my other series, *The Magic Academy of Paris and Chronicles of the Witchborn*, I have included a bit about me below. For those who read my previous author notes, you can skip that part.

I was born in York and grew up in England. I lived with my maternal aunt and uncle while I was in uni (that's college to my American readers!). Being with them for more than an odd week here and there in the summer made me connect deeply with my Scottish side, and I realized that Scotland was the home of my heart.

I miss wandering the Yorkshire Moors, but the Highlands more than make up for not getting back to York as much as I should! Currently, I live in a wee Borders town with my schnoodle (schnauzer-poodle) Emma. I write to the music of the seagulls since I live right on the harbour in a homely flat by the sea. I quite love my town. It's peaceful and hectic by turns. I have a quiet life here with Emma unless the American contingent is in town. Renée Jagger, the LMBPN author who brought me on board, often visits, and then we go on adventures. At those times, life is not quiet.

It's a party!

I am in the States! Nat and I arrived in Arizona a week ago today to visit Renée, joined by our Kelly half an hour later (you would think we planned that). As usual, we are enjoying the vibes at Renée's house. This is the first time we have been here in the spring, or what she calls, "This is why we live here Part I," and it's lovely outside! She wasn't lying.

The desert doesn't look like anyone would think it does, or not at her house. It's all roses and wisteria hanging down from the trellises and emerging grape leaves, along with birdsong that is almost deafening at times and a fountain soothing us in the background.

We were so glad to see her and Jo, Renée's amazing dog who runs the world. And for those who wonder, we all work in the living and dining rooms while we're here. We have made our own spaces on previous visits, and it's automatic now. Not to worry. The books will keep coming.

Jo supervises by wandering from room to room and regally accepting pats and offerings of cheese.

A Rocket and Etouffee

As usual, we spent the next morning drinking coffee and catching up. Renée told us that SpaceX was launching a Starlink Satellite train from Vandenburg in California that night, so we all piled out to see the Falcon 9 Heavy fly south to deliver its payload. We didn't see the deployed satellite train, which doesn't happen until the rocket is outside the atmosphere. Renée assures me it looks like the reindeer all pushing Santa's sleigh since she saw it while she was out camping, but I have never seen a rocket before, so I was sufficiently chuffed.

AUTHOR'S NOTES

The next night, Renée produced an amazing feast. Nat and I had never had Cajun food, and Renée made both crawfish etouffee and chicken, sausage, and shrimp gumbo from scratch. The gumbo was amazingly spicy, and the etouffee was rich and buttery. And I learned how to make a red roux!

Shea and her husband Andrew joined us, and we talked long into the night. As usual, a good time was had by all.

This morning, we are having a buttermilk cinnamon swirl coffee cake so Alex, who also works for LMBPN as a proofreader, can join us and eat too much, as we all do when we're here. She lives the the same town as Renée, so they see each other often.

I always have to thank LMBPN's staff for making my journey to publication as painless as they could. From the beta team who suggests improvements to the series to Kelly O, who does *everything*, to the editor who smooths my prose to the just-in-time team who catches last-minute errors, it is a joy working with you!

Thank you for taking a chance on my series! If you enjoy it and you have a moment, leaving a review would be very helpful for me (as it is for any writer).

I look forward to catching up with you in the next book.

Izzie Campbell

BOOKS FROM ISABEL

The Chronicles of the WitchBorn
(with Michael Anderle)
The First Witch-Mage (Book 1)
The Witch-Mage Awakens (Book 2)
The Witch-Mage Liberation (Book 3)
The Witch-Mage Uprising (Book 4)
The Witch-Mage Breaking (Book 5)
The Witch-Mage Ascending (Book 6)

The Magic Academy of Paris
(with Michael Anderle)
The Forbidden Incantations (Book 1)
The Treacherous Alchemy (Book 2)
The Cursed Enchantments (Book 3)
The Perilous Secrets (Book 4)
The Sinister Onslaught (Book 5)
A Resilient Requiem (Book 6)

Drakethorn Legal

BOOKS FROM ISABEL

(With Michael Anderle)
A Witch's Legacy (Book 1)
Scales of Truth (Book 2)

CONNECT WITH THE AUTHORS

Connect with Isabel Campbell

Facebook: https://www.facebook.com/IsabelCampbell.author

Website: http://isabelcampbellauthor.com/

Connect with Michael Anderle

Website: http://lmbpn.com

Email List: https://michael.beehiiv.com/

https://www.facebook.com/LMBPNPublishing

https://twitter.com/MichaelAnderle

https://www.instagram.com/lmbpn_publishing/

https://www.bookbub.com/authors/michael-anderle

OTHER LMBPN PUBLISHING BOOKS

To be notified of new releases and special promotions from LMBPN publishing, please join our email list:

http://lmbpn.com/email/

For a complete list of books published by LMBPN please visit the following pages:

https://lmbpn.com/books-by-lmbpn-publishing/

BOOKS BY MICHAEL ANDERLE

Sign up for the LMBPN email list to be notified of new releases and special deals!

https://lmbpn.com/email/

For a complete list of books by Michael Anderle, please visit:

www.lmbpn.com/ma-books/

www.ingramcontent.com/pod-product-compliance
Lightning Source LLC
LaVergne TN
LVHW041910070526
838199LV00051BA/2574